TANGLED JUNE

Other Walker and Company Mysteries by Neil Albert

The January Corpse
February Trouble
Appointment in May

TANGLED JUNE

A Dave Garrett Mystery

NEIL ALBERT

WALKER AND COMPANY

NEW YORK

First published in the United States of America in 1997 by
Walker Publishing Company, Inc.

Published simultaneously in Canada by Thomas Allen & Son Canada,
Limited, Markham, Ontario

Library of Congress Cataloging-in-Publication Data
Albert, Neil.
Tangled June: a Dave Garrett mystery / Neil Albert.
p.   cm.
ISBN 0-8027-3305-0
1. Garrett, Dave (Fictitious character)—Fiction. I. Title.
PS3551.L2634T36   1997
813'.54—dc21   97-1350
CIP

Printed in the United States of America
2 4 6 8 10 9 7 5 3 1

To Bert Rapp
In Loving Memory

Acknowledgments

I WISH TO thank Richard and Lisa Rapp, for their concern and help throughout. They were there at the start of it all. I also wish to thank Rabbi Shaya Sackett, of Congregation Degel Israel, and Carole Silverstein, for their insights on Judaica. Kate Burke has been a fount of information on locating birth parents, and I deeply appreciate her tireless efforts on my behalf. A special thanks to my agent, Barrie Van Dycke, and to my editor, Michael Seidman, for their encouragement throughout this project.

A tip of the hat to Roger Willard, private detective extraordinaire. And my thanks to my friend Les Roberts for the loan of Saxon.

No acknowledgment would be complete without a special thanks to Maureen Corwin and Cindy Garman, of the Lancaster mystery reader's group, who know their worth far better than I can say.

Author's Note

ALTHOUGH THIS BOOK was inspired by my real-life search for my birth parents, I want to emphasize that it is purely a work of fiction. Although the general problem Dave Garrett faces is my own problem as well, I did not intend to describe any particular member of my own extended family in this book. As much as I enjoy the company of Joel Weissberg and Art Potts, they are completely imaginary, and no resemblance to any person, living or dead, is intended.

1

David

Wednesday, 10:30 A.M.

SOMETIMES I THINK it wasn't inevitable. Lisa says it would have happened anyway—if not then, later; and if not exactly the way it did, then somehow. I tell her she's a fatalist. She tells me I'm nuts. Maybe we're both right.

I was in my office, a second-floor walk-up that smelled of mold and overboiled coffee. Today it smelled a little of paint, too; the accretion of graffiti on the front of the building had finally become too much even for my landlord. If experience was any guide, the graffiti artists would begin again within twenty-four hours.

I put my chin on my fist and scowled at the typewriter. I was preparing a report to a client who owned a small Honda dealership. He'd come to me about an inventory shrinkage problem in the parts department. I'd known him for ten years, and I'd bought my Civic from him, even though I could have done a little better at one of the big, high-volume dealerships out near the airport. He was a gentle man, with large, soft blue eyes. His wife had died a lingering death from MS a few years before; since then he'd lavished his affection on his daughter, a plain, shy girl who worked as his receptionist. I looked at the blank piece of paper in the typewriter. I was trying to explain that the thief was his son-in-law and that he was using the money to support a drug habit and a mistress.

Lisa, my assistant, was at the other desk, which mostly was covered with a map of Philadelphia. Empty coffee mugs held down the corners. She was highlighting areas where we'd already gone door-to-door distributing brochures extolling the virtues of Garrett Investigations. Boxes of brochures, piled three and four high, covered the rest of her desk and huddled around her feet like cardboard puppies. The brochures had brought in a couple of nice cases already, enough to allow me to hire her full-time. I wish I could have the satisfaction of saying they were my idea, but they weren't. It's not easy having an assistant with an excess number of good ideas.

I pulled the paper out of the typewriter and crumpled it. Lisa was right; best to drive out there, look the poor man in the eye, and give him the news. I tossed the ball of paper and scored two points in the wastebasket in the far corner. She didn't look up.

I stretched with my hands behind my head and looked at her. Dark brown hair, pulled over to one side in a thick braid that fell down past her breasts. As she worked, she played with the end of the braid. The sunlight came through the filthy window behind her and cast a dappled pattern on her hair. Today was just a paperwork day, and she'd come dressed for it—sneakers, faded jeans, and an old St. Joseph University T-shirt, at least one size too small, that hugged her agreeably but barely reached her waist.

There are chasms in life; marriage and divorce, the birth of children, the death of parents, the start or end of a career. Passing to the other side changes you forever and fogs the memory of how life was before. So sometimes when I think about it I try to recall the exact moment when it all began to change, the last moment before my life went one way instead of another.

I remember it clearly. I was looking at her, and I'd opened my mouth to say I was going out to see the Honda dealer. And if I'd said it, she would have said she'd watch the phones while I was gone and nothing would have changed . . .

But instead, before the first sound came out of my mouth, she put her highlighter down and looked up. "David?"

"Yeah?"

"I've got an idea." She looked down at her desk and then at me again. "This a good time to talk?"

An unnecessary question. Lisa knew my schedule better than I did. "Sure."

"Have you thought about maybe dividing up responsibilities a little differently?"

"No, but you have."

"A little." She shrugged, not very convincingly.

"So let's hear it."

"Using me just as an office manager isn't the best use of my time. I can be doing other things around here."

"Like?"

She played with her braid and tried to sound casual. "Like investigations."

"You do help. You've helped a lot."

"I don't want to be just an assistant. I want to be an investigator on my own."

"And you want to be a partner." We'd talked about it before. When I made her office manager, I thought she'd be satisfied. She was, for about five days. "Lisa, I don't know what I can say I haven't said already. You know the license statute as well as I do. You need years of hands-on investigative experience before you can be licensed. Even being a beat cop isn't enough."

"The state gave you a license."

"They let me count my years as a trial lawyer as investigation. But that was just because somebody felt sorry for me. They'd just taken away my law license."

"I know I can't get a license now. But the more investigations I do—"

"And you're doing them."

She shook her head. "I help you. What about a case on my own, start to finish?"

"We went over this. Just last week."

"I know."

"I'm not going to try to hold you back. When you have some more time in, and when the right case comes along and the client consents, it's yours."

"What about the Mankovik case?"

"That's one I have to do myself. I promised her mother." Lisa dropped her eyes. "And besides, I've been working it for weeks."

She made a show of inspecting the end of her braid. "Okay."

The phone rang. Lisa told the caller she'd call back in a few minutes. Since she didn't write down a number, I assumed it was her mother.

She put down the phone. "Got a minute for some office things?"

"Sure." I was relieved that she wasn't pressing me any further. Lisa could be very stubborn. And I was glad that she took such an interest in the business side. Paperwork has never been my strong suit. My system for balancing my checkbook involved two accounts; I'd use one till it was hopelessly screwed up, then use the second one for a couple of months until the statements from the first one settled down. Lisa thought she could do better.

"The books and records are a mess."

"Tell me something I don't already know."

"Well, I took a little look over the weekend. You don't have any system of tracking your receivables at all, do you?"

"I'm current on all my bills."

"That's payables."

"Oh."

"And did you know your license is up for renewal?"

"They'll send me a notice."

"They did, a month ago. It's due this week."

"So cut the check."

"Already done. But I ran into something funny in your license file. I read over your original application."

"You're right. I have to give you more to do."

She ignored me. "When you applied, you had to supply them with a birth certificate, and you said you didn't have one."

"That's right. It was destroyed in a fire at the hospital."

"You sent them a document called a delayed registration of birth." She spoke the words slowly, as if she'd only thought about the document for the first time that minute. I didn't believe it.

"I got that when I was fourteen. So?"

"So don't you think that's funny?"

"So hospitals have fires." It was my turn to shrug. Being Jewish, I did it better than Lisa. A good Jewish shrug expresses not only the inability of the shrugger to give a satisfactory answer but the limitation of all human knowledge in the face of a mysterious universe. "Even if the odds are a million to one against a birth registration getting lost or destroyed, if there's ten million babies born a year, ten people . . ."

She opened the top drawer of her desk and took out my license file. She drew out a yellowed sheet of paper. "You mean that this doesn't bother you?"

She handed over my delayed birth registration. I hadn't looked at it in years. An old Thermofax, the print gone brown and blurry with age, but still legible. A copy of the original, which was on file in Sacramento, stating that the fact of my birth in Los Angeles, California, May 12, 1946, was hereby recorded. It was signed by my parents and notarized.

I handed it back. "Well, I'm here, aren't I?"

"It doesn't seem very official."

"There must be thousands of people with these things. Home births, hospitals that screw up or have accidents."

"What was your mother doing in Los Angeles?"

"She and my dad were living in Chicago then. She wanted to be with her mother when I was ready to be born."

"She went two thousand miles to be with her mother?"

"I was her first child. She said she wanted to be close to her family."

"You've never been curious?"

"About what?"

"It just seems the kind of thing you ought to know more about."

"What is there to say?"

Lisa looked at the form again, and at me. It was a long look. "I'm sure you're right."

I should have known. Lisa never told me I was right about anything.

2

Lisa

Wednesday, 11:00 A.M.

DAVID PUT ON his jacket in a series of disconnected motions, pulling it on over one shoulder, stopping, and then shrugging his way into the other sleeve. He tried to even out his jacket, but it stayed lopsided. I didn't mind. I liked watching the play of his chest and shoulder muscles under his thin summer shirt. He was wearing a V-neck T-shirt underneath, and the outline showed, just a little, on either side of his tie. Well, a little more on one side than the other, because his tie was crooked, too. I just watched; I didn't want him to think I was nagging. Besides, no matter what he did, it would be crooked again within a few minutes. Clothes never hung right on him. Even at forty-four, with love handles and the beginnings of a paunch, he still looked better out of his clothes than in them. I thought about that while he loaded his briefcase and gave me some unnecessary instructions. I nodded at the right times. By the time the door shut behind him I was remembering the trail of black hair down his belly that almost hid his old scars from the war. They started off straight in the middle of his chest and gradually became curly . . .

I waited till I saw him on the street, getting into his old Honda Civic, and picked up the phone. It was only eight in the morning in Los Angeles; I didn't want Saxon to think his work was unappreciated.

"Saxon Investigations." He had a wonderful voice, full and measured and deep. I wondered what his voice had been like before the acting lessons.

"This is Lisa Wilson, returning your call."

"Hi, Lisa." He said it slowly, every syllable rounded and buttery. "Thanks for calling back."

"You're up early."

He sighed. "I'm sitting on my desk looking at the ducks in the canal, and I'm having a cup of espresso."

"I'm looking at a brick wall across the alley. I won't even tell you what I'm drinking."

He laughed softly, longer than my remark called for, and I remembered what David had told me about Saxon being an incurable womanizer. "So, Lisa; how's Dave?"

I wondered why he started with that one. "Fine, just fine, thanks."

"He ever learn how to read a balance sheet?"

I relaxed a little. "He says if he'd been good with numbers, he would have been an accountant."

He laughed politely. "That's Dave. He's okay, though?"

Whatever the problem was, my little joke hadn't made it go away. "Sure, no problem."

"I've been an investigator a long time. I've never had anything like this."

"You found something already?"

"A few things. Not a lot, I'm sorry to say."

"You worked fast. You went beyond the call of duty, and I appreciate it."

"Sure. Now, speaking of the call of duty—" He was going to give me trouble about something.

"Yes?"

"Is Dave any more than a boss to you?"

"No." I hoped I said it right. I was afraid to say anything more than the one syllable, that my tone would give something away.

"Then why do you care about this?"

I decided to stick with those trusty single syllables. "Me?"

"Well, you haven't mentioned that this was for a client, and if Dave wanted his own birth checked out, he'd call me himself."

"Can I trust you not to take this back to him?"

"Depends what it is."

"I want to be a partner here, but I get the old runaround; no cases of my own till I'm experienced, and I need my own cases to get the experience."

"So you've decided to do this for practice."

"Birth is usually a good place to start."

"But doing someone you know is cheating. You can talk to him over coffee and get the kind of leads you'd never get in a real case."

"I know. I'm never going to let him know about it. This is just an exercise. When I've got this down I'm going to challenge him to pick a name out of the phone book."

"So why him? Why not a name from the book now?"

Saxon wasn't a person to be lied to. "He interests me." I felt something when I said it; a pleasant, gentle twinge that made the room seem a little too warm.

"A lot?"

"It's not clear yet."

"This a premarital investigation?"

I laughed—I hoped, not nervously. "No, nothing like that. It's just that he's a good boss, and I like him."

"Good enough for me."

I decided to press ahead before he tried any more questions. "So what did you find?"

"He's right; the state registry has no record of a David Garrett being born within five years of May 12, 1946."

"You mean he's five years older or younger?"

"No; I just didn't get a search outside those parameters. And to anticipate your next question, the search covered anyone born 'D. Garrett' regardless of the rest of the first name or middle initial."

"Did the LA newspapers carry notices of birth?"

"Only if the parents were newsworthy."

"Hmm."

"The hospital, Western Community, was a real place. They were in business back in '46—"

"Were?"

"It closed in the early sixties sometime."

"Closed? I've never heard of a hospital closing."

"This one did."

"So there's nobody to ask about the fire."

"I checked the newspapers. Nothing. But if it were a small fire, just destroyed some records or the mail room, it might not get mentioned."

"I wonder if the nearest fire company might have records, or an old-timer who'd remember."

"You're good, Lisa."

"I'm flattered."

"I checked. No local records; the centralized records were purged years ago, and there was nobody at the nearest firehouse who would even have been born then. Fighting fires isn't a job for senior citizens."

"Did you ever hear of a hospital having a fire?" I asked.

"Anyplace can have a fire. Nursing homes have their share."

"But wouldn't a hospital have sprinklers?"

"Probably not a small hospital back then. And even if they did, the water would probably ruin a hell of a lot more records than the fire. I can see it—it's 1946, when everybody smoked, and some nurse or records clerk lets a fire get going in her ashtray or in a trash can and somebody reels out the fire hose and soaks the hell out of the place. A stack of certificates turns into pulp or gets flushed down the hall."

"It could happen," I conceded.

"You don't think so."

"I don't think anything yet. I'm just going to keep an open mind."

"You need me to do anything more out here?"

"Not for now. Thanks, and just send me your bill."

"No charge. I was doing some records checks anyway."

"No, bill me. Please."

"Dave's sent me a couple of good cases. No charge, and I mean it."

I thanked him, and we hung up.

Slowly, I turned my chair from side to side while I tried to think like a detective. It squeaked a little, but I liked the noise; soft and rhythmic and intimate. What next? The first problem was that I didn't even know what I was investigating—if I was really investigating anything at all. Maybe it was all as David said. But if not, then what? I was certain he wasn't adopted; the state of California would have been very, very careful to put a proper birth certificate in his adoptive name on file. I didn't think he could be five years older or younger than he thought he was. So maybe he wasn't born in California? If not, where? And if not, why was he told he was born there?

I stopped my chair. I was getting into ultimate questions instead of getting anything accomplished. Okay, so if he wasn't born in California in 1946 he was sure born *somewhere*.

I wasted an hour and who knew how much of David's money on long distance calls. The Pennsylvania Department of Vital Statistics was no help; records were only available to the person named, or to their legal representative. Illinois was even tighter—records were only available on the same limited basis, and they didn't do searches; you sent in your request for a specific record and they either had it or they didn't. By the end of my call to Springfield my neck was sore from the telephone.

I was starting to wonder if just maybe he hadn't been born at all when he reassured me by showing up.

"How'd it go?" I asked, as if I couldn't read it in his face.

"Not good." He took off his jacket and lowered himself into his chair. He sat with his legs stretched out and his head back and closed his eyes. I think he was trying to suggest he was relaxing, but it looked more like exhaustion. I looked at his legs and waited for him to tell me.

"It started bad and got worse," he said. "He didn't want to believe anything I said, called me a crook and a liar, said I was nothing but trouble, and why should he pay me for lies? I got mad right back at him and we had a shouting match in his office. I'm a true professional; I told him to fuck himself and stamped out. He followed me out to the parking lot and we yelled at each other. Then he started crying, right there in front of all the employees and customers. Bawling like a baby and falling to the ground. I helped him back to his office." He looked at his watch. "We spent the rest of the afternoon discussing what to do."

"You've had a long day."

"He paid. A company check, on the spot."

"That's not what I mean, David."

He shrugged. "Well, that's why they call it work."

There was no point in trying to get him to unburden himself any further, so I looked down at the map on my desk and started a round of the venerable game of getting a man to do something you want by persuading him that it's his idea. "You know," I said, "we've never distributed brochures on South Street."

"Really?" Out of the corner of my eye, when he thought I wasn't looking, I caught him rubbing his bad right shoulder. He sighed. "I thought we'd been everywhere by now."

I looked at the map, partly because it was part of the game and partly because looking at him too long was distracting.

"We've done Passyunk, Society Hill as far south as Pine, but no, not South Street."

"I'm beat," he said. "Some other time."

"Okay," I said. Agreeing was easy, as long as I had an alternate plan. "You know, thinking of South Street, what about having dinner with Ralph?" Ralph Torino lived above his gay card and gift shop on South near Second. We'd met him only a month ago, but we'd seen each other several times a week since. Partly because we enjoyed each other's company, and partly because we knew he might not have much time left. His AIDS was progressing. "I could go in and pick him up, get some take-out, drive him out to your place."

"It'd be good to see him one of these days," David said.

Before he had the chance to tell me he was just thinking out loud, I called Ralph; he was thrilled at the invitation, but he'd only accept if he could pick up the bill and bring the wine. . . . I told him we'd argue that out later and said I'd get him around six. He told me not to bother coming into the city, that he felt fine. We agreed to meet near the Gulph Mills exit of the Schuylkill Expressway, and he could follow me to David's from there.

I hung up and turned to David. "So we'll be by around seven. That enough time for you? It's going to be casual."

"Well—"

"If it doesn't suit, Ralph and I can do dinner by ourselves, no problem."

"Nah, that'll be fine."

"I'm going to go home and change before I get him." I stood to go.

"I think Ralph would get a kick out of seeing you in that T-shirt."

"I don't think so." I pinched the hem. "Look, it's shrunk so far it barely goes to my waist."

"We've all changed since college."

I stuck out my tongue.

3

David

Wednesday, 7:00 P.M.

I LEFT THE kitchen window open so I could listen for the sound of their cars in the parking lot. I live on the Main Line between Wayne and Villanova; if you know just a little about Philadelphia, "the Main Line" conjures up visions of gray stone mansions, manicured lawns, cricket clubs, and golf courses. If you know Philadelphia well, then you know better. The Main Line is beautiful, in sections; but it's a long way from Paoli to the Philadelphia city limits, and if you happen to get off Lancaster Pike in the wrong spot and wander into the side streets, you'll find a down-at-the-heels neighborhood that could use fewer plastic lawn ornaments, more frequent trash collection, and a better class of residents. I'm in the first apartment building on your left, second floor rear.

The apartment itself isn't bad—two bedrooms, two baths, and only about twenty minutes from my office if traffic is light. I sleep there, eat breakfast there, and once a week I brew a big pot of coffee that I reheat, cup by cup, in the microwave as I need to. Other than that I don't think about it much.

I threw a doubled-up sheet over the kitchen table and set three places. The wine glasses matched, but the silverware didn't. I seldom had people over to visit at all, let alone to eat. Even when Lisa and I were together, we'd only spent a couple of nights here. There hadn't been anyone since.

I heard car doors slam in the parking lot. Lisa and Ralph were on their way in, Lisa carrying shopping bags and Styrofoam containers from Ralph's favorite Italian restaurant, over on Fifth Street. They waved up at me.

I opened the door and welcomed them. She was still wearing her T-shirt, but she'd changed into some loose green slacks. It occurred to me that Lisa's outfits drew attention either to her backside or her chest, but never both at the same time. It was something I would have to keep an eye on, as her employer.

Ralph's hair was still black and curly, and his skin was deeply tanned. Hard, defined muscles bulged on his bare forearms. I gave him a firm shake; his grip was as strong as ever. "How you doing, Ralph?"

"Fine, a little tired is all."

"Good to see you," I said.

"Thanks for—Lisa, where you going?" he demanded.

"Just getting things ready for dinner."

"Sit down with us, my love. I implore you." He went down on one knee and delicately kissed her hand, starting at the fingertips and working his way up to the wrist. "Oh, Ralph," she said, blushing. But if he'd wanted to go all the way to her shoulder she would have loved it even more. Italians . . . No one else could get away with it.

"Please, Ralph, I need to make the salad."

He tried to look hurt as he stood up. "So it's come to this? You turn down a man of hot blood for a vegetable?"

"A man is only a man, but a cucumber is a cucumber." She

patted the side of his face and disappeared in the direction of the kitchen. Ralph and I exchanged looks.

I shrugged. "Cucumbers."

"Cucumbers." He shook his head slowly. "Got the good stuff?"

Ralph had taught me to drink single-malt Scotch; specifically, Laiphroag, and in a particular way, no ice and just a splash of water. Lisa, who was no drinker, would nurse one through an entire evening while Ralph and I put away more than was good for us.

I made a short one, well watered, for Lisa and took it into the kitchen where she was making the salad.

"Come on and sit with Ralph and me. You can do that later."

"We'll all have dinner together. You guys talk awhile."

I left her drink on the counter and sat down across from Ralph in the living room. He was staring at a collection of speakers, amplifiers, and related electronic equipment that took up most of the opposite wall.

"Nice stereo."

"I got it from a client instead of a fee when I first started out. Two hundred watts per channel, CD player, cassette with Dolby, Bose speakers."

"Impressive."

"One of these days I'm going to get around to hooking it up."

"Cheers," he said.

"Cheers. Good to see you again."

His smile turned a little sad. "For what there is to see."

"You don't look sick."

"If I lie quiet, I don't feel sick. I get up, move around, I get so goddam tired."

"You've got to take it easy."

"People don't sit around much. I never did, before this."

"It can get on your nerves," I said. "When I used to do personal injury work, the clients would tell me having to sit around was worse than the pain."

He swirled around the liquor in his glass, watching the mixing of the alcohol and water. "It gets me thinking, Dave. Last time I sat around this long, hardly moving, it was back in the war. The ambushes. You'd lie all night behind a dike in a rice paddy up to your waist in water and shit, or behind a tree in the jungle with leeches, pitch-black, six or ten hours at a stretch."

"I never did it that long. Two hours on, four off."

"You were in line units, maneuvering by platoons and companies. Special Forces patrols, you only had ten guys. Keeping up security on a perimeter in close country might take everybody."

"So what did you think about back then?"

"How scared I was, and how important it was for me to do a good job. Show the straights I was as tough as them."

"You showed them. Even if they didn't know."

He smiled at me over his drink. "And now when I look back? I think about how funny it is that I didn't mind the mud and the shit and the leeches. And how I didn't think for a damn minute about the big picture, about anything beyond what I was doing. Christ, I didn't even really think about what I was doing, not really. It was black as hell out there. Most nights Ho Chi Minh himself could have walked five feet from my nose, and unless he made a noise I'd never have known about it."

"We did our job."

He drained his glass. "Absent friends."

"*Dos Vedanya*."

I refilled our glasses. He looked in the direction of the kitchen, and then at me.

He lowered his voice. "So, you and Lisa ever get together?"

"Ralph, she *works* for me."

"You care about her."

"She's a good employee."

"Are your eyes brown? Because you're so full of shit."

"Ralph, Ralph, Ralph . . . Before you got sick, didn't you ever learn not to sleep with the help?"

"No."

"Have you ever had anyone who could run the register right? Most of the time they don't charge sales tax."

"We're working on it."

"I rest my case."

"Another thing that gets me thinking," he said, "you know it's Father's Day this Sunday?"

"I didn't think it would be much noticed in your store."

"Lots of gays have kids. For the same reasons straights do. And everybody's got family. You?"

"My dad's gone. Heart attack last year."

"Sorry to hear that."

"He had a good life; he was healthy almost to the very end. He made it to ninety."

"Wait a minute; how old was he when you were born?"

"I guess around forty-five."

"You the youngest?"

"The only. My mom was, let me think a minute, forty when I was born. That was pretty old to have kids back then, not like now."

"You came along a little late in the game."

"In a way. But they only got married in forty-five."

"They weren't exactly kids."

"My dad was a confirmed bachelor till he met her."

"You grow up around your family? Cousins and stuff?"

"My parents moved a lot. When I was born they were living where my dad grew up, in Chicago. When I was two we started moving. Vermont, Washington, California a little while, then back here. I'd see my cousins and uncles maybe once every couple of years."

"That's too bad. Even if they're a pain in the ass, they're still family."

"How does your family treat you?" I asked.

"Some are okay about everything. Some could accept I'm

gay, but now they're scared of getting sick. Some tell me to my face it's God's punishment." He made a dismissive gesture. "When you lost your license and got divorced, wasn't it the same?"

"What happened to me is nothing compared to you."

"For some people it is. So how come you moved so much?"

"My dad's work. He had trouble finding something that suited. He never had much luck. He bought an Admiral TV distributorship right before the Japanese started blowing us away with cheap transistors and tubes. He got into commercial real estate in the early seventies, right before the market collapsed. Died pretty much broke. I had to help him out the last few years. After I lost my license it wasn't easy."

"Your mom still alive?"

"Still has the old house up in the Northeast."

"Any other family around here?"

"My uncle Seymour, used to be a dentist in Chicago. Moved here about ten years ago when he retired."

"To be near your mother?"

I laughed. "He's my father's brother, not hers. No, he and his wife just like it here. They were tired of the Chicago winters, they didn't like Florida. They tried New York and didn't like it, so they moved to Chestnut Hill. It had nothing to do with my mom. They don't get along."

"Too bad, when everybody's getting older like that. How come?"

"So why do you care so much about my family? You care more than I do."

"Got a bus to catch or something?"

"No, but I'm hungry."

Lisa appeared at that moment and announced that everything was ready. Lisa and I were splitting an order of angel hair pasta with low-fat oil. Ralph, God love him, had spaghetti carbonara. Just looking at it seemed to clog my arteries. But, as he said himself, it certainly wasn't going to kill him . . .

Ralph did justice to his dinner, and all three of us contributed to the demolition of a bottle of good Chianti. Ralph and Lisa bantered about cucumbers. We pushed away from the table, full of food and more than a little drunk, and returned to the living room. The conversation flowed over a dozen subjects, from the Flyers and the mayor's chances for reelection to the beauty of Longwood Gardens and the deterioration of lower Bucks County. Out of the corner of my eye I watched Lisa—or, to be exact, Lisa's ass. She wandered around the room, running her hand over my books. She moved lazily, a little drunk and not paying much attention. Then she came to a stop. "Dave, what's this?"

I was in the middle of an argument with Ralph about the Phillies' chances that year, and it took me a moment to focus on the shelf. She was pointing to a photo album, originally white but now brownish yellow. "Family album."

"Mind if I look?"

I shook my head no, and she brought it back to the sofa. As Ralph and I talked, she slowly paged through it.

After a while, I noticed she was staring at one picture in particular. "What's so interesting?" I asked.

She turned the book toward Ralph and me. It was my parent's wedding picture, a big black-and-white glossy taken at the reception at a Chicago hotel. My father and mother were in the center; on his left were three of his brothers, all in dark business suits. My mother's three sisters were to her right.

"Funny," I said. "The suits look okay except for the pleat in the pants; but those bridesmaid's dresses, boy."

"I think there's a law against having one that doesn't look stupid," said Lisa.

Ralph studied the picture. "For a wedding, doesn't look like anyone's having much fun."

"This is just a formal shot, Ralph," I said, but he was right. My father's three brothers stood at attention, looking glum, as far away from the wedding couple as they could get and still be in the picture. My mother's sisters were standing closer to her, but they didn't look any happier. My father and mother stared at the camera with no expression at all.

"There's something else," Lisa said.

I looked at the picture. "What?"

"Don't you see it?" She spoke slowly. She was trying, unsuccessfully, to keep condescension out of her voice.

Ralph rescued me, in a way. "Christ, even I can see it. Look from one brother to the next. Everybody's solidly built, big across the shoulders, average height or maybe a little on the short side. Blunt, hooked noses. Everybody's got a triangular face, and they're all losing their hair. Hell of a family resemblance."

Lisa looked at me. "When this was taken, your dad was about the age you are now."

"That's right."

"And you're tall and thin, with a straight, narrow nose."

"Sort of narrow, I guess."

She went on, "David, you don't look anything like your father."

"Not everybody does."

"Well, look at your mother and her sisters." Lisa pointed, as if I couldn't see it for myself. Mom was short, with blond hair, though her eyebrows gave it away as a dye job. The wedding gown was a complicated affair, with cascades of lace and satin, but I would have guessed that underneath it all she might have been slim. She had a plain, roundish face that looked a little like everybody. Her sisters varied in hairstyle and hair coloring, but they all shared the same round face.

"I didn't look like her when I was younger," I conceded, "but as I get older I think I'm starting to get that roundness in my face."

Ralph and Lisa looked at each other and then put their eyes down. "Well," I said after a moment, "What can I say? Mom used to tell me I was the spitting image of her grandfather, the head rabbi of Kiev."

"Did you ever see a picture?" Ralph asked.

I shook my head. "He died in the old country. My mother's father came over on the boat just before World War I."

"Dave," Ralph said, "Just curious—what do your male cousins look like?"

I had to think a moment. There weren't many of them, on either side, and some I hadn't seen in years. "On my dad's side they all have the Garrett look. On mom's side, well, there's variations, but in general I'd say, short to average height, roundish bodies, thick at the hips, light skin."

"The ones on your mother's side. Balding?" Lisa asked.

"Yes."

"All of them?"

"Yes." There was an uncomfortable silence. "Look, I know what you're thinking. I thought about it when I was fourteen and I got that story about the fire in the hospital. But it doesn't make sense. If I was adopted, there'd be a birth certificate in my adoptive name, right? That's the whole point of having an adoption—you wipe out the old and replace it with the new."

Lisa said, "So you thought about this when you were fourteen?"

"I guess. Hell, every teenager at some time or other is sure his or her parents can't understand what they're going through because the parents aren't really their parents at all, and that somewhere there's a couple who would understand them perfectly, blah, blah, blah."

Ralph looked at the photo again, and at me. "Dave, how can you be from these people?"

"How can I not be?"

"Do you know their blood types?" he asked.

"Dad was O and Mom is O. I'm O, too, so there you are."

"Doesn't prove they're your parents," Ralph pointed out. "It just means they could be."

I looked from one of them to the other. "This is the kind of thing I was talking about a minute ago. There's enough to fuel a fantasy, sure; but is there any proof that I'm not their son?"

"It seems so unlikely," said Lisa.

"So was the Mets winning a World Series."

"David, this is serious."

"What is, exactly?"

Lisa didn't know me well enough to know that when I'm mad, I sometimes become very quiet. "That there could be something you don't know about your birth."

"You remember being born? Then there's something you don't know, too. Going to go to a hypnotist for regression therapy so you can get back to interuterine memories? Just what—"

"David, you know that's—"

"Just what's the point supposed to be? I've got bills and a shitty little riceburner of a car on its last legs and a hundred problems right now, present day, I need to deal with. What's the point in worrying about something I can't change?"

"I'm sorry, I—"

I found myself pointing a finger at her, and I forced myself to drop it. "It's not your business."

"You're right, it's not."

I looked at Ralph. "And it's not your business, either."

"Hey, Dave, I was—"

"Ralph, now tell me whose eyes are brown from so much shit. You and Lisa set this up. You're here to pump me about my parents."

"Dave, this—"

"Don't say anything, Ralph. I'm not putting you on the spot. You did it because Lisa asked you to." I turned to her. "I just want to know what it is to you, one way or the other."

She lowered her face and brushed back her hair around her ear. "I can't believe you don't think it's important."

"So try again. And answer my question—why do you care?"

"I care what happens to you."

"That's nice. Whatever happened at my birth was forty-four years ago. Why care now?"

"If you don't know, then I can't explain it," she said softly. "I'm sorry."

"I'm not really good about being noodged."

"I am sorry, David."

I let out a breath and tried to relax. "And I'm sorry I blew up at you."

We both apologized some more and the matter was dropped, none too soon for me. It was the closest thing to an argument we'd had since February, when we broke up. We had disagreements, of course, daily if not hourly, about the business; but disagreements are logical, and arguments are emotional. Our downfall as a couple was that we hadn't learned to argue. I wondered if working closely with her wasn't creating the same problems over again. No, I didn't wonder; I worried.

The three of us were good enough friends that the incident didn't affect the rest of the evening, which ran on till nearly eleven. Ralph and I had one for the road, and Lisa had a cup of coffee. But it was still on her mind as we stood at the door.

"It's an interesting story, David."

"Doesn't seem all that interesting to me. It's just what happened."

"You know what self-effacing means?"

"I'm afraid to look it up," I said.

She didn't laugh. "Need me first thing in the morning?"

"No."

"Okay to come in late?"

"No problem."

Right.

that's what I think most of the time. When I'm down, I think it's my background. Then I'll page through a woman's magazine, look at the ads for clothes and perfume and makeup, and I know it's not just me.

At a red light I took the time to look at the scars on the back of my right hand. I had good skin, and they were healing well. In a few months they'd be hard to see at all, even if you knew where to look. The scars were a souvenir of a night back in January when David and I were being chased by professional killers. Later that night, after we'd escaped and he'd tended my wounds, we made love by the fireplace in a mountain cabin. I'd never told him how he'd made me feel that night. . . . A car honked behind me, and I moved on.

Chestnut Hill is Philadelphia's second-best-kept secret, second only to the location of the best place to buy a cheese steak. If you're from out of town, Philadelphians will direct you to South Street, Center City, Society Hill, or the Italian Market, but we keep Chestnut Hill for ourselves. The location helps. Tourists come for the historic district and then branch out to Penn's Landing on the water to the east, or Center City to the west. Chestnut Hill is way too far to walk and is cut off from the main tourist areas by the slums of north Philadelphia and by Germantown, which is euphemistically described as "a racially mixed area in the process of urban renewal." Chestnut Hill is a beautiful place, set on rolling hills, with old shade trees and parks all around. The main street, Germantown Pike, still has trolley service, and I had to be careful to keep my wheels from following the tracks. On either side of the street was a solid line of storefront shops painted in subdued colors and selling tasteful clothes, shoes, or luggage. A few coffee bars, restaurants, and, right in the middle of the neighborhood, a large bookstore.

David liked Chestnut Hill well enough, but he hadn't spent his whole life in Philadelphia as I had; to him it was just another pretty neighborhood. But for those of us who remember Philadelphia in the sixties, before South Street, before Society Hill, before the Center City renovations really took hold, it's a special place; unlike the others, not thrown up in a hurry for the Bicentennial or to meet a deadline for a development project. It grew of itself, and only the oldest residents can remember when it wasn't as it is now. I bought my clothes and shoes there, even though the huge mall at King of Prussia would have been more convenient.

I found the street I was looking for and made a right, heading down a steep cobblestoned hill. I started thinking that Saxon was right; investigating someone you already know is cheating. If David hadn't told Ralph he had an uncle in town, I couldn't imagine how I could have discovered him on my own. Or maybe I was being too hard on myself. If someone had hired me to do a background check on David, the person would probably know a fair amount about him already. I knew that background checks were often a follow-up to some kind of application by the person being investigated—for a loan, for a job, whatever—and the investigator would have the application as a starting point. Maybe it wasn't cheating after all. And even if it was, I didn't care.

I found the house I was looking for, parked, and got out. I'd seen David study the exterior of a subject's home before an interview, so I shaded my eyes against the sun and looked around. The house was Victorian Italianate, three stories, and set well back on a lot that sloped uphill from the street. Photography is my hobby, and I tend to see, especially outdoors, with a camera's eye. With some early morning sun I could have done a great formal photograph of the place. I forced myself to shift from photographer to detective. The grounds were manicured, but there was no lawn or porch furniture in sight. Uncle Seymour didn't seem to get a lot of use out of his grounds. No car, either, and no garage—if he was home, I guess he didn't get out much. Philadelphia isn't Manhattan—a car is just as much of a necessity here as anywhere else in America. A small sign on the front door indicated that oxygen was in use. The porch lights were still burning. I guess he didn't come out often enough to notice.

I'd decided I needed to look professional but not intimidating. A simple silk blouse and a dark skirt, with low heels and only a hint of makeup. I'd combed out my hair so it lay down to my shoulder, but I hadn't taken the time to set it. I ran my hand through it again and decided it was all right. At least I was still dry at the temples. I wondered if I shouldn't add a touch more makeup; I was meeting an older man, and maybe I should try to look a little older, too. I have trouble getting the amount of makeup right, and in the last few years I put on so little I might as well have used nothing at all. But if I could see his house from my car, he might be watching me. It wouldn't do to have him see me putting on makeup as if I was in my bathroom.

The door was varnished oak, with a heavily curtained glass panel. Real beveled glass, I noticed. I also noticed a small wooden box nailed to the side of the door with a Hebrew letter on it. I would have to ask Dave what they were called. He'd been right; I knew a fair amount about Seymour just by seeing what was there to be seen.

I knocked with the massive lion's-head knocker several times and settled down to wait. I ran over my questions, wondering how much he knew, but most of all wondering how I should begin. I'd spent the morning with a pack of three-by-five cards, covering various possibilities and how he might answer different questions. The trouble was that I didn't really know what to ask for.

I didn't expect the door to open immediately, and I wasn't disappointed. Three minutes went by before the knob turned and the door swung open.

I was facing one of the oldest men I'd ever seen on two feet. He had probably been my height once, but his back was so bent and his head so sunken into his chest that he wasn't much more than five-two. His pants were pulled up well above his waist, making him look even shorter. His earlobes hung an inch below where they should have ended, and were covered with coarse gray hairs. He probably had as much hair in his eyebrows as on his head, but it was hard to be sure because his scalp was covered with a black skullcap. His skin was deeply wrinkled but also tanned, and despite everything it gave him a certain vitality. I wondered if he sat out in the backyard.

"Dr. Garrett?"

"That's me." He had a quiet, deep voice, scarred with what might have been years of smoking.

"Hi. My name's Lisa Wilson. I work with your nephew David. We talked this—"

"Sure we did. You think 'cause I'm old, I can't remember?" He smiled. "Good thing I got my memories. Not making too many new ones at my age. Well, come in, come in. Let me offer you a chair."

He moved back from the door, into a dim hallway. I wondered if the summer sun hurt his eyes. He shuffled along, touching the wall for balance. Then we turned into a large sitting room crammed with overstuffed furniture and musty books. He slowly lowered himself onto a sofa. The drapes were closed, and the only light came from a small lamp in the far corner. The furniture had been moved around to make room for a hospital bed.

He saw where I was looking. "When I get my bad days, I can't do the stairs."

I thought about how to respond. "It's good to live in your own house."

"What's your name again? Linda?"

"Lisa."

"You're a smart girl, Lisa." He looked around. "You spend a lifetime getting the things you want, and then when you slow down, you leave 'em behind and wind up in a nursing home. What's the point? So many of my friends . . ." I waited for him to go on, but he just let his voice trail off.

"Some people say it's better to be the first to go."

"You got smart friends, Lisa. My Rose died last year." He put one hand on his chest. "Heart. We always thought I would go first, but here I am."

"I'm sorry to hear about your wife."

He nodded. "So how is David, tell me."

I had a plan worked out, how to gently bring David into the conversation, but he threw me off track. "He works too hard."

"He always did. Always impatient, chasing. Never let anything come to him."

"He hasn't changed. When did you see him last?" The moment I asked it I wondered why—he wasn't a missing person.

"He called—eh, maybe a week, two weeks. It was seder last time he was here. Yeah, seder. My first one without Rose."

Seder? Then I remembered—the Passover dinner, at Easter. I became aware of the tiny gold crucifix hanging between my breasts. I saw he was looking at me, and for a moment I thought he was looking right through me, at the cross. Then I realized he was just staring at my breasts. Good for him. "I didn't know Dave was religious."

"He's not. Seder's not really a service, you know. When Rose was alive, I bet that for most of our seders, we had more non-Jews than Jews." He stopped. "I didn't catch your last name."

"Wilson, Lisa Wilson."

He shifted in his chair before he asked the next question. "Not a Jewish name, is it?"

"It's not even the family name. When my grandparents came over from Poland they changed it from Warniack."

"So, Catholic?" I nodded. "Don't get me wrong, Lisa; my best friend in the whole word, knew him sixty years, was Catholic." He launched into the saga of their friendship, starting in dental school. We were up to their service together in a medical unit in World War II when he caught himself. "But you don't want to hear an *alte cocker* babble." He studied my face. "Polish, huh? I can see it, just a little bit around the eyes, a little Slavic. You're a pretty girl, Lisa."

"Thank you."

"And pretty girls have better things to do on sunny mornings than sit with old men. So what can I do for you?"

It was time to go to work. My heart was beating faster, and my mouth was dry. The room was only a little stuffy, but I could feel the perspiration breaking out. "How much has David told you about me?"

He looked embarrassed. "If I'm wrong about this, Lisa, I apologize in advance. Are you the girl he was taking out back in the winter?"

"That's right."

"You're from Miami?"

"That's someone else he was seeing for a while."

"Oy, I'm sorry. But you two went somewhere, didn't you? Mexico or something? I think he sent me a card."

"That's me. And I work for him now."

"You told me that this morning. I remember him talking about you."

I tensed. He was trained in medicine, at least a little. No doctor had ever noticed anything. But if Ralph could tell . . . "About what?"

He saw something in my face that startled him, and I realized how jumpy I'd sounded. "He liked you, that's all," he said soothingly. "He had a real nice time with you."

I felt foolish, and I resolved to light a candle for the surgeon on Curacao with the unpronounceable name. "Oh. Okay."

"That's all he said. Is there something he should have told me?"

He was genuinely puzzled, and I felt myself relax just a little. "No, nothing." I took a breath and went on. "But anyway, there's something going on with his birth records that I was checking into."

His mood changed. He pulled back slightly in his chair, and he lowered his voice. "His birth records?"

"He was born in Los Angeles, but there's no birth certificate, just an affidavit that was done years later, when he went for a driver's license. The hospital has been closed for years. The photos of his parents at the wedding—" I realized that I was babbling and shut up. Not that I was saying so much, but that he'd stopped being an ordinary listener. His hands gripped the arms of the chair, and he was leaning back, away from me.

He looked uncomfortable. "So he sent you to see me?" His voice was gruff and tight.

"I'm here on my own."

"He doesn't know you're here?"

"I'm here for my own reasons." It came out sounding as if David owed me money, so I decided to soften it. "I'm concerned about him."

"So maybe you should be talking to him and not me."

"He doesn't really believe there's anything to know."

"Really?" he asked.

"Really."

He looked away. "I always thought it was funny, he never asked."

"So?"

"I used to wonder, what I would say. My Rose said, keep it to yourself. Don't meddle."

"Please tell me."

He looked at me as if seeing me for the first time. "How long have you known him?"

"Since January."

"You know, he hasn't mentioned you lately."

"We're not a couple. I just work for him." I knew that was a mistake the moment I said it.

"That's what I was thinking."

I knew I wasn't getting anything out of him without a gun,

but I pressed on anyway. "I'm here because he doesn't believe there's anything to even ask about."

He spread his hands. "Maybe you sell him short."

"I believe in him more than he believes in himself." It came out with more force than I intended.

"I can see that, young lady. Dave hasn't had it easy the last few years."

I didn't know if he was including my interference in the list of David's troubles or not, but I knew enough not to argue. "I'd never do anything to hurt him."

"People's ideas of hurt aren't always the same."

Debating moral philosophy wasn't going to open him up, no matter how cleverly I answered; and philosophy was David's field, not mine. I backed off. "You have a lovely home here."

"We like it." He shrugged. "I like it, I mean."

"I hope you have many years yet to enjoy it."

"Whatever is written, is written."

After that we stayed away from the purpose of my visit. Seymour told me about the last trip he and Rose made to Israel, their fiftieth wedding anniversary, and how he'd served two terms as president of his synagogue. He did some gentle probing and found out I was a native Philadelphian, single, no children. He was puzzled when he found I had moved back home with my mother and made a point of inquiring about her health.

It was well past noon when I said I had to be going.

"Let me show you out." He started to get to his feet, but I stood up and gently placed a hand on his shoulder. "Please, it's fine. I can let myself out."

"Are you sure?"

"Don't wear yourself out for nothing. I'll lock it behind me."

He settled back. "You can come again, if you want."

"I'd like that very much." Which was true; although I had more than one reason.

5

David

Thursday, 2:00 P.M.

LISA AND I were conducting industrial surveillance. It sounds impressive, but it wasn't. We were simply parked in my Honda in a far corner of a warehouse parking lot, watching the loading dock through binoculars. High-quality stereos had been disappearing—just a few, and nothing else, but at five hundred dollars a pop wholesale, the owner decided it was worth the expense to stop it. It was early afternoon, and unseasonably warm. Even though the windows were down, I had my jacket off, my tie loosened, and my collar open. Lisa felt the heat more than I did, and the way she was dressed there was nothing she could do about it and stay decent. I wiped my forehead and decided that my next car was going to have to have air-conditioning. I decided not to mention that to Lisa; it would only start an argument about why we hadn't brought her Legend.

Lisa had the binoculars. "Here comes somebody—short, heavyset, balding, around fifty. He's standing on the end of the dock, looking around."

"That's the transportation manager," I said.

"He's going to the end trailer, number five-two-two. Now he's gone inside." She fiddled with the focus knob. "If this has been going on awhile, somebody in management has to be turning a blind eye."

I made a note of the time and his movements. "You've got good instincts, Lisa."

"Not as good as they should be."

"It's a question of practice. Someday you'll be better at this than I am."

"No, I won't."

"I'm not suspicious enough. I trust people too much. You're better at sizing them up."

"He's gone back inside the building." She put down the binoculars and looked at me. "That doesn't take you very far if you can't interview."

"You were a lawyer. You should know about that."

"Talking to someone who's eager to tell you what they know is one thing. I mean investigations."

"So you want to hear 'Garrett on interviewing?' "

"Very much."

"There's a million techniques, but none of them are worth anything if you forget the basic rule. Keep 'em talking. Once you get a conversation going, even if it's about the weather, that's half the battle."

She wiped her forehead. "So if I talk about the heat long enough, the wife will admit she has a boyfriend?"

"She won't admit to *conduct*. But if you do it right, she'll admit she has marriage troubles."

"Just like that?"

"What does it mean to be a friend?" I asked.

"Did we just change subjects?"

"If you're friends with someone you do things together, you talk, you keep in touch, you have interests in common, you help each other out. A good interview creates the same level of comfort and trust as a friendship. That's why people will confide."

"I'm not a very friendly person."

"Sure you are. You're just shy. And that's good, because you don't overwhelm people. You make them come to you, just a little."

"I don't think people are as eager to talk as you think."

"Most people *are* eager; they just may not want to talk about what you want to talk about. You have to work them around."

"So, it's easier to get them talking about anything at all and then change the subject, than to go right to what you want to know?"

"Yeah, but remember you can't be obvious. When in doubt, take it slow."

"Okay." She picked up the binoculars and swept the loading dock again. "Can I ask you something?"

Lisa only said things like that when she was going to impose on me in some way. "Go ahead."

"The other night, when we were looking at the photos?"

" 'We?' "

She ignored my sarcasm. "The ones of your parents?"

"I remember."

"Have you given any more thought to looking into your birth?"

"No."

"If you—"

I spoke slowly and distinctly. "I answered your question, Lisa."

"But don't—"

"No."

"Aren't you going to let me finish?"

"Not as long as you keep bringing up the same goddam subject. It's my life and not yours."

"But we—"

"Hold it, please. There is no 'we.' There's a boss and someone who works for him. There hasn't been anything else since Mexico, and there isn't going to be."

"I could work for a lot of people. I chose you."

"And I'm glad you did. But for someone who wants to be a detective, you do a lousy job of listening."

"What's gotten into you?"

"You want it both ways. You want to boss my life like you were my girlfriend, and you want me to write you a check every Friday, too."

I thought she would turn angry, but she surprised me. She didn't speak for a moment, and when she did her voice was soft. "What's the matter, David?"

"After you left the other night I did some thinking."

"About your parents?"

"No. About Mexico."

She gave a nervous half smile and brushed her hair back behind her ear. "What made you think of that?"

"The whole dinner was a setup, Lisa. The two of you got together later to compare notes. The family album—did you remember it, or was that luck?"

"Is that what you think?" she asked.

"Don't insult my intelligence, please."

"I remembered the book from when I used to stay over. So what's that got to do with Mexico?"

"Thinking the other night through made me realize something else, too." When she didn't answer, I went on. "The big fight in Mexico? I spent five months trying to figure out what I did wrong, what it was all about. I didn't do anything. You picked it, didn't you? You wanted to break us up."

She folded her arms across her chest. "You think you're that irresistible that no one would ever have a gripe?"

"Whatever is wrong with me, if I snore, or drink too much, or don't wipe my mouth after a meal, I was doing all those things before we ever left the States."

"Since all I do is work for you, I don't think it matters any-more."

"I'd like to know why you wanted out."

She didn't answer for a long time. "It's like you said, David."

"What's that?"

"I'm just an employee. I work the job, and then I get to go home. *You* can't have it both ways, either."

I started the car. "Make a notation, Lisa. Two-twenty in the afternoon. Surveillance terminated."

I wish I could say that the moving air felt good on the drive back to my office, but in truth nothing felt good at all.

6

Lisa

Thursday, 2:20 P.M.

IT WAS A long drive back to my car, and I felt like an idiot every mile of it.

After six months we were still strangers. We both felt we hid things from each other. Well, I *was* secretive; people like me grow up with a poker face, or they don't survive at all. But David was more complicated; he thought he was comfortable with his emotions, and he was kidding himself. He could show irritation easily enough. But when he was really angry, he frightened me. His voice would drop, and he'd speak very slowly, cold as ice. The first couple of times it happened I'd mistaken it for nonchalance. Now I was trying to do better. I looked over at him; sunglasses hid his eyes, and his mouth was set in a thin, straight line. I wasn't doing very well. I bit my lip and tried not to cry.

David dropped me off back at the office and told me to watch the phones for the rest of the afternoon. Just the instructions; nothing more or less, and delivered with so little inflection he might as well have been reading. He also told me he was going to do some interviews. Right.

The office had no air-conditioning, and it had been closed up all morning; going inside was like entering a steam bath, except that steam baths don't smell of fresh paint. By the time I'd taken down the messages from the answering service, my slip was soaked through.

The hell with the office. I called Uncle Seymour and asked if I could come by, and he said sure.

I set the air-conditioning in my car on high, and by the time I reached his house at least I was cool again. I checked my appearance in the rearview mirror; my hair was a mess, and so was my makeup. I tied back my hair and wiped my face with some tissues. I was too upset to care anymore.

When I opened the door, the heat was waiting for me. It was close and sticky, the kind of weather that brings a thunderstorm. By the time I was halfway up the walk I could feel the sweat breaking out, and by the time he answered the door I was wet all over again.

He was wearing a long-sleeved shirt, trousers, and polished dress shoes. "Lisa, it's good to see you."

"I hope I'm not intruding."

"When I'm too busy with company, I'll tell you." He led me back to the front room, which was even hotter than outside.

"You don't mind the heat?" I asked.

"At my age it's a blessing. The hotter the better. But please, open a window if you want."

It was a generous offer, given how much he liked the heat, but I should have passed. None of the windows had been opened since the Carter administration. Five minutes of wrestling produced two very dirty hands, a broken fingernail, and the barest ghost of a warm breeze drifting in through the two-inch gap I'd created. But still, it was worth the trouble. It worked off my agitation.

"So how's David doing?" he asked when I came back from washing my hands.

"Dave's good." I encouraged him to talk about David; not his birth, but what he was like as a child, a teenager, a college student. Uncle Seymour loved to talk, and I was surprised how much he knew about his nephew. It appeared that David was his favorite. I asked him why.

"Well, he didn't have it all that easy."

"How so?"

He raised his hands, palms up, showing me David's troubles. "Kids should be around other kids. And they should be around the rest of the family. David had it lonely. He was the youngest cousin, and he grew up by himself; we didn't see him more than once every couple of years."

"Why was that?"

"Ah, lots of reasons."

I backed off. "So tell me about your kids." In reply I got ten minutes of Manny, the best prostodontist in Saint Louis, prodigious contributor to the United Jewish Appeal, and frequent traveler to Israel. Manny's children hadn't followed in their father's footsteps; Samuel was a rabbi, and Rachel was an organizer for the Socialist Workers' Party. "Sammy's a good boy, got a nice wife," was all he said about him. "My Rachel, Lisa, you should meet her. Fire in the belly, that's her. Five-foot-two and not afraid of anybody. Goes around the country in an old station wagon, everywhere, in terrible neighborhoods, even down in the south. She—" Seymour stopped. "Something the matter, Lisa?"

"Am I that easy to read?"

"You seem confused. Am I rambling too much?"

"It's just . . . you mind if I'm a little blunt?"

"You're always welcome to speak your mind in this house."

"In my family, if one of my cousins was a priest and one was a Communist . . . I don't know, it seems kind of backward."

He smiled like the world's oldest imp and gave a gesture I

can only describe as a one-handed shrug. "As I was talking, I was thinking you might see it that way. But Jews don't revere rabbis the way Christians do priests. A rabbi is a teacher, not your personal connection to God. A rabbi we respect, we don't say he's holy—we say he's learned."

"And Rachel?"

The little grin returned. "Everybody's a little bit of a hypocrite, Lisa."

"You can't stop with just that."

"I must know a dozen guys my age at the synagogue men's club. All our life we've voted Republican, stuck up even for that schmuck Nixon, gave money." he sighed. "And when somebody talks about the Abraham Lincoln Brigade we all get misty-eyed."

"She's doing what you dream of."

"And you know something? You get older, you dream more, not less."

"Was David radical when he was younger?"

"Not like Rachel, but a little. When she was Young Socialists, he was American Civil Liberties Union. She'd go south as a Freedom Rider, he'd organize a car wash for the NAACP."

"Were his parents interested in politics?"

He snorted. "The only Jews I ever knew who belonged to the John Birch Society."

"So where did David get his politics?"

"I don't know where he got his ideas, except not at home. Maybe in reaction to the dreck he heard. But it wasn't from Rachel—they didn't see each other much—"

"You said 'at home' and not 'from his parents.' "

"It wasn't a close family."

"Why was that?"

"David and his parents were very different people."

"Sam and Rachel are pretty different from Manny. And from you."

"Lisa, are you in love with him?"

"I think so."

"Is he in love with you?"

"I wish I knew."

"So, you shy or something?"

"Uncle Seymour, can I confide something?"

"I'd be honored."

"I'm not very good about dealing with men. I . . . lived alone for a long time in a small town. When David came along it was like a bolt from the blue. It happened so fast, I'd barely caught my breath before we were in Mexico together. Things started happening even faster, we were together all the time. I started getting scared that it was out of control."

"So you left him."

"I trumped up a fight."

"Dave's a generous guy, but I didn't figure him for someone who'd hire a girl who dumped him."

"He doesn't know it was deliberate. Not for certain, anyway."

Seymour turned it over in his mind. "Because you were scared of getting more involved?"

"I never said I was smart."

"You're plenty smart, Lisa. So, you think that if you can tell him something he doesn't know about his past, that he doesn't want to know, he'll want to see you again? Is that why you're here?"

"It sounds stupid when you say it out loud," I said. "But yes, in part. And in part because I like talking to you. When he's your age I bet he's going to be just like you are now."

"God forbid. Does he know you're here?"

"I can't make it easy for you. He doesn't, and he'd be mad if he knew."

"I'm not surprised."

"Did you try to ever tell him anything?"

"A couple of times. He wasn't interested. Not angry, just not interested."

I just sat and waited. It was time to let him come to me. The breeze had stopped, and I was sweltering. Sweat was running down my chest and between my breasts. I didn't even want to think about what my hair looked like, or my makeup, or how my ears were sticking out. Somewhere I heard a clock ticking; and far away, a hint of traffic noise.

Seymour leaned back into the sofa, his eyes focused on something long ago. "I've been waiting most of my life for somebody to ask me."

I put the palms of my hands flat in my lap and waited.

"I didn't think it would be someone like you, Lisa. I always figured Dave would ask, or maybe Terri, but they got divorced before it ever came up."

"But now it's time."

Seymour raised a stubby finger and gestured at a glass-fronted cabinet near the bed. "Lisa, there's some good brandy I've been saving, and this is as good a time as any. Pour us a couple of stiff ones."

I unlocked the cabinet. The bottle was dusty, but the snifters were clean. "I don't normally drink during working hours," I said.

"You care about David?"

"Yes, I do."

"Then this isn't normal working hours."

I sat back down. On his cue, we clicked our glasses. I wasn't used to brandy, and I could feel it burning all the way down. The room seemed even warmer, and I regretted wearing a slip.

"You were saying about the hospital where he was born?" Seymour asked.

"Closed."

"And the reason he doesn't have a birth certificate is because there was a fire?"

"That's what he was told," I said.

"By his mother."

"Yes. And I suppose his father too."

"No, his dad wasn't out there. If he told David that, he was just repeating what Barbara told him."

"So you don't believe the fire story?" I asked.

He measured his words. "Fire story. Fairy story."

"I've seen pictures of the family. Wedding pictures."

"So you know what the Garrett look is."

"He says everyone has it but him."

"He's right. 'Garrett.' " He smiled. "Your real name is, what again?"

"Warniack."

" 'Garrett,' my grandfather picked up at Ellis Island. Before that it was Petrokansky."

"David Petrokansky. Doesn't exactly fall off the tongue."

"He's no more Petrokansky than he is Garrett; by blood, anyway." He took a sip of brandy. "I don't mean it to sound harsh. He's a good boy, and I love him dearly. But—" he waved his hands helplessly.

"So what's the story?"

"I don't have all the details. They don't matter much anyway. But I stand by what I said."

"Go on."

He just looked at me and then at his brandy.

"He ought to be here, right?" I asked.

"You care about him. What do you think?"

"I think you want me to prepare him for the news."

"Some things you shouldn't get secondhand."

I drank some more brandy. "Has anyone ever said anything to David about this?"

"He sees his relatives, how they look compared to him. He's got his own two eyes. He's known for years about no birth certificate, right? If he wanted to talk, he could have come to me."

"He thinks it's just a paperwork problem."

"He thinks that because he wants to. Who was I to go and tell him different?"

"So why did you tell me now?"

"Because you asked, and because you had part of the puzzle already, and because I'm old. And because you care about him. It's in good hands with you."

"Do you want me to tell him?"

"Whoever said the truth sets you free was meshuga. The truth is a burden. You carry it. I'm tired."

"I don't know what to do."

"You're going to get him to come back to hear it from me."

I rubbed my temples. The heat and the brandy were a bad combination. "I'm not sure what I ought to do."

He smiled. "How are you *not* going to?"

"You're a smart man, Uncle Seymour."

He shrugged.

7

David

Thursday, 6:00 P.M.

I WAS LATE getting back to the office; partly because of a break in the Mankovik case, but mainly because I was trying to avoid Lisa. She'd given me enough aggravation for one day already.

The overhead light was out, which I expected. There was enough evening and weekend work that I liked to shut the office at five. But when I came in Lisa was lying down on the office sofa with her eyes closed and her hands at her temples.

I shut the door. "What's wrong?"

"Headache," she whispered between clenched teeth.

I dropped my own voice. "Migraine?" She nodded slightly.

I knew what to do; she'd had one before, in Mexico. The landlord was cheap in a hundred ways, but for some reason he'd provided no-nonsense drapes. I pulled the curtains and made the room dark as night. I stole a double handful of paper towels from the rest room and borrowed some ice from the office refrigerator of the accountant on the first floor, who was working late. I turned the towels into a cold compress and put it against her forehead. She held it in place with her hands, and I touched her fingers. Her skin was warm and flushed. "Hot?" I asked.

"Burning," she murmured. Fever, or something like it, was another of her symptoms. The day she had one in Mexico, I'd thought she had an infection.

The room was stuffy, and she was dressed far too warmly for the day even if she'd been well. Everything was soaked, including her skirt. I found a sheet in the closet, part of the bedding I kept on hand in case I needed to spend the night in the office, and covered her as far as her chin. Then it was back to the bathroom for cold water, which I sprinkled over the sheet.

I pulled my desk chair around and sat with her in the dark. There was nothing to do but keep her cool and quiet and let her heal herself.

Sickness reminds you of sickness. I thought about all the times I'd sat at bedsides of the ill, the hurt, the dying. It was a long list, starting with my grandfather nearly thirty years ago. Then, in my twenties, more men in the war than I wanted to remember. Then my wife's mother, my wife after her suicide attempt, my mother, my father's last illness. Lisa's migraine in Mexico. My deathbed watch for Susan in March. I liked to think I'd been a comfort to some of them. I'd had my share of thanks from the ones who recovered. As far as the ones who hadn't, I wondered if I would ever know. As I got older, I thought about that more and more. I thought about my last view of Susan's face, before I shut the door. The life was gone, but so was the anger. I hoped I'd helped her find a quiet death.

Lisa stirred. "More ice?" I asked.

"Yeah. Good idea." The accountant was getting ready to close up, so I took his entire ice tray. He started to ask what kind of a party I was having, but I waved him off.

I made up a fresh compress and drizzled the rest of the ice

water over the sheet. She twitched as the cold water soaked through to her skin.

It wasn't too long before she raised her head. She kept the compress in place, but she opened her eyes. "Jesus," she said softly.

I leaned close to whisper, "How are you feeling?" By way of reply, she put her head down and closed her eyes. By now my vision was adapted to the dark, and I could see her clearly. I watched droplets of water from the compress inch slowly down her temple. Some of them caught in her hair; others ran down the side of her jaw and collected in a little puddle in the hollow of her shoulder. From time to time I blotted it with a paper towel. I gently put my fingertips in the hollow, to see how warm she was. She turned her head and pressed her lips to the back of my hand. I left it where it was.

Her breath was on my hand, warm and regular. I worried. She'd told me her headaches were always associated with stress. I wondered what could be bothering her that badly. A selfish thought intruded; maybe she had a better offer and was working up the nerve to tell me she was quitting. Not having Lisa around . . . I shut down my brain. If that was what was coming, it would have to get here on its own.

She opened her eyes and lifted her lips away from my hand. "How do you feel?" I asked.

"Like the Roto-Rooter man's been inside my head."

"Take it easy."

She paused. "I feel more tired now than anything. Sleepy."

"When you're feeling up to it, I'll take you home."

"I need to sleep afterward."

"Think you can sit up?" She nodded, and I put my arms around her. She let the compress fall away and held onto me. Her front was chilled from the wet sheet, but her back was warm. Slowly I drew her up into a sitting position on the couch and released her.

"Dizzy?" I asked.

She took a breath before she answered. "Like I woke up from a deep sleep."

"You have any medication for this?"

"Don't get them often enough. Maybe one every four or five years."

"This is your second in six months." She didn't answer. "What caused this one?" But she just shook her head weakly.

I found a second, dry sheet in the closet, pulled away the wet one, and gently patted her dry as best I could. It wasn't completely successful. Her clothing was soaked, and it wetted the sheet wherever I touched it. When I was done, she took the sheet and tried to pat the worst of the moisture out of her hair. "How do I look?" she asked.

"It's hard to tell in the dark."

"Liar."

"You look fine to me."

She lowered her head, and her hair fell across her face. She started to tremble, then stopped and was still. "Can you take me home now, David?"

Outside it was dusk; too early for car headlights, and too late for bright sunlight. She shaded her eyes anyway, and I helped her to her car. My Civic could sit all night in the neighborhood unmolested; Lisa's Legend needed to get out of there.

We didn't speak on the drive to her house. The only important question I had was how was she feeling, and I'd already asked it enough for one day.

For the past few months Lisa had been living with her widowed mother in an apartment in the Overbrook section of Philadelphia. Overbrook, as any Philadelphian will tell you, is in the western part of Philadelphia, but it's definitely not part of West Philadelphia. The difference is more than semantic; it has those little touches that West Philadelphia lacks. To name just a few, it's clean, reasonably safe, the buildings aren't surrounded by concertina wire, and your car will probably still be there in the morning.

Lisa's apartment was on the first floor. As I helped her up the walk a pair of elderly ladies walking a poodle gave us the once-over. They only kept moving after they got a good look at Lisa and she waved to them. I could see why Lisa's mom felt safe here.

Taped to the screen door was a note. "Read it for me, will you?" Lisa asked. "My eyes are still dancing around."

"It's from your mom. She and your aunt Elizabeth went to Atlantic City for the weekend. There's a number in case you need to call."

"Great." She opened up the door and went inside without turning on the light. I followed her in. "Can I get you anything?"

She lowered herself onto the living-room sofa in the dark. "A big glass of water would be great. Not too cold."

"You're going to soak your mom's cushions," I said. "Your clothes are still wet." She didn't move, so I pulled her to her feet. She padded off down the hall while I went to the kitchen. I had to put on the light over the sink to find the glassware. Why is it that no one ever lays out their kitchen in a way you can understand?

I stumbled over something in the darkness of the hall and put on the light. Her shoes. Farther down the hall was her skirt; the blouse was just inside the bedroom door. I left her bedroom light off. She was on her side in a fetal position, still wearing her slip. Her breathing was slow and steady. As I listened, she started to snore softly.

I put down the glass and looked around. The light from the hall showed me a bare room, with the bed, a dresser, and an end table as the only furniture. I knew Lisa had been living here several months, but there wasn't much evidence. It didn't look like a place she intended to stay for very long. No pictures on the walls. A single picture on the dresser, facedown. I didn't turn it up; I was curious, but she was entitled to her privacy. I took a comforter from the other bed and covered her.

I gently shut the door behind me and found a beer in the fridge. There was no kitchen table, so I sat at the dining room table and took off my shoes. I looked around in the light thrown by the fixture over the sink in the kitchen. It was an overstuffed room, filled with furniture I assumed was from their house. Not expensive or even terribly tasteful, but solid, cozy, here to stay.

I nursed my beer and thought about Lisa's migraine. She said her headaches came from stress. Maybe the stress of having to tell me she was taking another job. If that was it, I didn't have the right to be upset or surprised. The hours at Garrett Investigations were long, the pay was minimal, and there wasn't much opportunity for her to meet eligible men. Under the licensing statute she was years away from eligibility for her own PI license; all I could offer her was more of the same. She needed my job a lot less than I needed her.

So Lisa was going to get up and tell me thanks, but it was time for her to move on. I was sure she had something lined up, and I wondered what it was. She was qualified for lots of jobs; more than I was, as a matter of fact. I thought about how life was passing me by, how I kept failing at things; my marriage; my career as a lawyer; Kate; and Lisa. The only good employee I'd ever had.

I checked in. She'd rolled onto her back, but she was still snoring. I found myself a second beer and sat on the sofa. The cushion was damp from Lisa, but I sat where I was; my body heat would dry it out soon enough. The living room was dark, and I left it that way. I put my head back and tried to think about something positive. The Mankovik case, for example. The girl was doing a long sentence for drugs in the state penitentiary for women. I'd promised her mother I would see what I could do, just before the woman died protecting me. I'd been lucky; even though the girl's trial had been years ago, it happened in a small town, and all the witnesses and lawyers were still available. I had just located a witness who supported the girl's alibi, whom the public defender had never interviewed. At the very least it was grounds for a new trial. If I was the DA . . .

"David?"

I woke up. The room was dark, but enough light filtered through the drapes from the street for me to see that Lisa was standing over me. One hand was holding her robe together at the throat; the other was touching my shoulder.

"David?" she whispered.

"Good to see you up." For some reason I was whispering, too.

"I've got water going for some herbal tea. Would you like some?"

"Sure."

We padded through the living room to the dining room. It was dark, and so quiet I could hear my stockinged feet on the carpet. The only light was from the kitchen, and neither of us made a move to change anything. I could hear the faint whirr of the refrigerator motor. Lisa was wearing a thin white cotton robe, pulled tightly together. It was hardly thicker than a T-shirt, but it had long, flowing sleeves that ended in embroidered cuffs. I thought I could hear them rubbing softly against the tabletop when she moved.

Both of us were listening to the silence. "What time is it?" I finally asked.

"Nearly four."

"How are you feeling?"

She smiled. "You must be getting tired of asking that by now."

"I'll be tired when the answer is 'fine.' "

"I feel rested now."

"You should. You slept a good eight hours."

She brushed her hair away from one side of her face. "I've been up for a couple of hours."

"What have you been doing?" I asked.

"Watching you sleep."

Before I could respond, the teakettle began whistling.

We sat facing each other with our tea. The light from the kitchen left half of Lisa's face in shadow, and her hair had fallen down around both sides. Only her eyes stood out clearly, strong and dark.

The tea smelled of orange and cinnamon. "This is good," I said softly. "The dark. The quiet. You know, outside are five million people who are all going to get up in two hours and turn on lights and drive cars and make noise, but right now, right here, it's just us."

"It reminds me of that morning in Mexico, waking up before dawn, on the beach."

"Yes."

"David, I can't say enough to thank you for tonight. Helping me, staying over, you're wonderful."

"You'd do the same for me."

She put down her cup and brushed her hair behind her ear. "David?" I didn't answer; I knew that when she played with her hair she was nervous. "David, there's something I have to tell you."

Here it was, the kiss-off. Things slowed down, and we seemed to move farther apart—but somehow the details were clearer than ever. She was about to tell me she was going. Probably by the end of the week. Two weeks at the outside. I'd never sit quietly with her like this again. Just then she didn't look her best; no makeup, her hair tousled, her face puffy from sleep. But because it was the end, she was never dearer. "Sure."

She took a breath. "The migraine—I've been really stressed today. I did something I shouldn't have, and now it's out of control, and I'm really sorry."

It didn't sound good, but it didn't sound like what I was afraid of, either. "Go on."

"If I'd ever thought this would happen, I never would have started."

I waited.

"You know that business with your delayed registration of birth?" she said. "Well, I thought it would impress you if I could get to the bottom of a mystery in your own background, so I started checking." She told me about what she'd learned from Saxon and Uncle Seymour.

When she was done I counted to ten once, and then again. I'd been so ready to deal with her quitting that I didn't have the focus to react to her story about Uncle Seymour. I tried to keep in mind that she was sincerely concerned about me, enough to drive herself to a migraine. "So what does Uncle Seymour want to tell me?"

"I don't know. Are you mad at me?"

Before I answered, I thought about how I'd felt the moment I thought she was about to tell me she was quitting. "For being interested, no. For going to my family . . . yes." I was lying; just then I couldn't be mad at all.

"I didn't think you'd let me if I asked your permission."

"You would have been right."

"You'd rather not know?"

I tried to sound just a little stern. "A private investigator has to have a good reason to poke around, and as far as I'm concerned, the only good reason is that your client has decided for himself that he wants to know."

"I didn't do it for fun."

"Uncle Seymour is a nice man, but I don't count him as being very reliable."

"He seems in pretty good shape to me."

"I don't mean he's senile—he and my mother never got along. I don't think they've spoken in the ten years since

Seymour and Aunt Rose moved here. And my mother hasn't seen him since the funeral. If my mother didn't feel so strongly about being obliged to go to funerals, she would have skipped it."

"You think he'd make something up to get back at your mother?"

"If he had something to tell me, he could have done it pretty much any time in the last thirty years. Why wait till everything is impossible to prove or disprove?"

"He said he's always been there if you wanted to talk."

I curbed my first, angry response and remembered Lisa's migraine. "I suppose that's true," I said softly.

"Are we going to go talk to him?"

"I don't think I have a choice."

"Sure you do."

"He's my only relative, besides my mother, in the state. I see him every month or so. I don't go to see him now, I'll be seeing him for the Fourth of July anyway. The subject will come up then. So either I go see him now or cut him off forever."

"I know all that. I just want to know if you want me along."

I thought about it. Whatever he wanted to tell me was family business, but Lisa had started all this, and in a way she was as much a part of it as I was. "Sure," I said, and shrugged. It was simpler than explaining how I felt.

8

David

Friday, 10:45 A.M.

WE WERE SITTING in Lisa's Legend, parked outside Uncle Seymour's house. I'd told him we'd be by at eleven, and it was quarter till. It was still raining, and the temperature had dropped to the seventies. Lisa was wearing the yellow sundress I liked so much, the one with the square neckline, the tasteful floral pattern, and the hem that showed her legs almost to her hips. I've always liked flowers, and the fewer the better. I looked at her legs and thought about the little black dress she'd worn in Mexico, with no underwear, and how, no matter when I touched her, she was always ready, and what we'd done that night on the beach . . .

"What are you thinking?" she asked.

"That I'm glad you're feeling better."

"You're not thinking about your parents?"

"Not really." I collected my thoughts. "Whatever happened, it was a long time ago, and it doesn't affect who I am."

She shook her head. "I can't understand that."

"Well, does it make a difference?"

"Whatever he has to say, at least he thinks it's important. And I don't think he's wrong."

"I'm curious, sure; but tell me—what could he have to say that's going to change anything?"

"You don't want to be here, do you?"

"I have to be here."

"No, you don't."

"I have to be here because Uncle Seymour asked you to get me to come. I'm here out of respect for that."

She put her hand on my arm. "David, I'm sorry if you feel I've dragged you into something."

"It doesn't have much to do with you, really. He decided he wanted to get something off his chest, and you came along."

She withdrew her hand. "Don't patronize me."

"Huh?"

"If you think I was wrong to stir this up, then tell me so. Don't pretend I'm just somebody who was told to pass along a message."

I counted to ten. "I think . . . that it's eleven o'clock." I got out and didn't slam the door.

When we got to the porch, Uncle Seymour opened the door. He was wearing a dress shirt and what looked like slacks from a suit. He even had on a pair of black dress shoes. Normally he wore a sports shirt or maybe a sweater; only Passover and the High Holidays were cause to wear a suit and tie anymore. He looked ill at ease.

I gave him a hug. "Hi, Uncle Seymour."

"Glad you're here, David." He hugged me, and, to my surprise, Lisa too. "Come in."

The house was musty and airless, but a window was open in the front room where we sat down. I made a point of sitting Lisa closer to the window. She might be well enough to argue with me, but she was' still unsteady, and I wanted her to have some air. Uncle Seymour sat in his usual chair with a snifter of brandy at his elbow. He offered us some, but we declined.

I asked after his health and moved on. "Lisa said you wanted to see me."

"She's a nice girl."

"I hope you don't mind she's along."

"I'm glad both of you are here." He paused. "This isn't easy."

We waited.

"I've been sitting on this so long, it's hard to finally talk about it. But none of us are getting any younger, are we? Maybe, sometimes, I think I should take it to my grave, like Rose did. She always said, leave well enough alone. It's not your business. But I think, if it's not mine, then whose? If not me, who else? No one else has done it." He drank some brandy. Neither Lisa nor I said anything. He'd been waiting for half his life, and he was entitled to some ceremony.

"David, you were a wonderful boy. We were all so proud of you. Never any trouble, did well in school, made us all proud even if we didn't see much of you. I think that's why no one said anything; we loved you too much. If you'd been bad, well, who knows?"

Lisa stirred. "Sometimes keeping things hidden isn't a favor."

"I want you to know one thing, David. This is going to be hard for you to accept, but I've got nothing against your mother. She and I never saw eye to eye, and I don't think she was all that good for my brother. But this has nothing to do with it." He took some more brandy and looked around nervously. His delay was more than ceremony; the secret had been hidden so long it had deep roots holding it to the darkness.

He put down his glass and took a deep breath. "You sure you want to hear this?"

"Go ahead," I said softly.

"The end of '45, November or so, your mother says she has to go out to California. She tells different people different stories. She told Rose she had a cousin who was 'in trouble,' and she had to help straighten things out. She told me her mother was sick, without saying with what, that she needed to help out. She told Nathan's wife that she was sick, that she couldn't stand the cold, and that she needed some sun for the winter. My cousin Lenny said she told him she had a chance to work on a movie as a script girl; that's what she says she did before she married your dad. But the details didn't matter—none of us believed any of it."

"Why not?"

"She and your father didn't seem to get along. We all thought they were separating."

Lisa broke in. "What did David's father say?"

" 'Barbara's gone to be with her family for a while' was all he would say. We didn't press him. We didn't want to interfere. And it would have been—whatever they did was their own business."

"You mean Barbara went off, and everybody forgot about it?" Lisa asked.

"Nobody forgot anything. This was a long time ago, just after the war. People still respected other people's privacy. If there was a family problem, the family's job was to keep it quiet, not let the neighbors know the family business, not go on one of these *verkachta* talk shows coast to coast like they do these days."

"David's father knew how the family felt about her, didn't he?" she asked.

"We didn't want to make a bad situation worse." It wasn't a direct answer, but I wasn't here to rake over old family quarrels. After a moment he went on. "So comes the summer of '46, and she shows up back in town with you."

"She told everybody she found out she was pregnant after she left," I guessed.

"I think she assumed we would think that. She didn't say anything, and we didn't ask."

"What did everybody think?"

"Maybe that's exactly what happened, David." But he gave a disbelieving shrug. "She'd lived on her own in California for years before she got married. She could have seen an old boyfriend when she got back. Or she could have had someone else in Chicago, for all we knew. We didn't see a lot of them."

"Nobody did anything? Or said anything to Dad?"

He put up his hand helplessly. "Do what, David? Say what? We talked, among the brothers and sisters, but—what's to do? Was I supposed to tell your father—" He stopped; there was no need to finish the sentence.

I broke the silence. "Mom never actually told me how long she was in LA. I always assumed it was just the last few weeks of her pregnancy." I shook my head. "It never occurred to me to ask."

Lisa was way ahead of me. "When you saw Barbara, how old was David?"

"He was newborn, less than a month old. Maybe just two weeks."

"Barbara's appearance?"

"No change from when she left, as far as I could see. No weight gain, no change in her complexion, breasts not noticeably engorged. No edema in the extremities."

"And you were looking for changes?" she asked.

"We didn't know what to believe, but we didn't believe a word of what she said."

I looked at the floor. "Is it possible my father never realized?"

"David, your father was a good man, may he rest in peace. I was closer to him than anyone else in the family, at least till he moved away. He loved you very much. He loved your mother, too." He hesitated. "He wasn't a doctor; he was in sales. People weren't so worldly then. He didn't have a lot of experience with women before he met your mother. Did he notice that she didn't seem any different just a couple of weeks after supposedly delivering a baby? Possibly. Maybe she put him off for a long time. Did he decide he'd been had? I like to think he would have told me if he thought that."

"You were so close. You were the only medical person in the family then. He never asked you? Confided anything?"

"David, if he had any doubts he took them to his grave."

Lisa spoke. "It would be nice to be able to ask him."

Seymour shook his head. "He didn't know anything because he didn't want to know. It would have been a waste of time. The only one who can tell David what really happened is his mother."

"What about this cousin of my mother's? The one who was in trouble?"

"She never mentioned a name."

"On my mother's side there's only one female cousin, and she had a baby of her own just a couple of months after I was born."

Seymour looked at me. "Could you be a twin?"

"My cousin was married. That was her second baby, and she had another the next year. Doesn't fit the 'being in trouble' part."

"Second cousins? Nieces?" he prodded. "Anybody at all?"

"No. Everybody would have been way too young or too old."

Lisa spoke. "That's not going to make it any easier."

"What?" I asked.

"Finding your birth mother."

That was the last thing I needed. "Lisa, why don't you mind your own business for five minutes?" I turned back to Uncle Seymour. "So how come now? Why wait so long? Till Dad's dead? Or is that why?"

"You need me to answer that?"

"So Mom's feelings don't matter?"

"No matter what you say to her, it won't be anything new."

"You've given this a lot of thought."

He met my eyes, then looked away. "Since Rose died, it's been on my mind."

"You thought of not ever telling me."

"Rose always said I should keep it to myself, may she rest in peace. But you know something? I feel better that I told you."

"You weren't going to say anything, were you? Not till Lisa came along."

He shrugged. "Sometimes it's good to get a new perspective."

I looked over at Lisa. She was looking out the window with her hands folded in her lap, a million miles away. "Lisa?" She looked at me without speaking. "Anything you want to ask?" She shook her head.

I talked to Uncle Seymour a little longer, and then we said our good-byes.

9

Lisa

Friday, noon

WE WERE SITTING in my car, parked out front of Uncle Seymour's. I was humiliated about how he told me to shut up in front of his uncle, but this was David's moment, not mine. I tried to keep my own anger under control and listen for his at the same time. It wasn't easy. "So what are you going to do now?" I asked.

"Do?"

"Are you going to look for your birth parents?"

"Why?"

"Wouldn't you like to know who your family is?"

"I already know."

"I mean, you could have brothers and sisters."

"If I want to meet total strangers, I can stick my finger in the city phone book."

I hoped that speaking very slowly would keep the anger out of my voice. "But they're not strangers, they're your family."

He looked out the window. "I guess."

"What if your mother, your birth mother, is sick? What if she's going to die soon?"

"People die every day."

"When you were twenty, did you want to have children?"

He was so startled he just answered, "No."

"But you'd changed your mind by the time you were thirty-five, hadn't you?"

"Yeah."

"Well, what if you don't always feel the way you do now? About finding your birth mother? And by then it's too late?"

He hesitated. "I'll think about it." But he sounded like he'd said that only because I'd caught him without a better answer.

As much as I wanted to talk, to draw him out, it wasn't the right time. I decided to quit before I alienated him for good. "Shall we get some lunch and get back to work?" I asked.

"I have some appointments." We both knew he didn't. "You can just drop me back at the office."

I started the car. Work was the last thing on my mind. Getting away from David was the first. I dropped him off and went home. When we parted, he hadn't asked if I was going to be covering the phones, so I didn't have to lie. What I did have to do, on the drive back to my mother's apartment, is face how badly it was going. I went home and took a nap till two. And then I made a call.

South Street, as a street, had existed since Penn's time. As the name suggested, it was the southern boundary of his planned "greene country towne" that the more highbrow tourist brochures talk about in the first five pages. When I was growing up, and even after law school, it was simply an undistinguished residential street with row houses in various stages of disrepair and some down-at-the-heels stores and cafés. But one day around 1980, Philadelphians awoke to find that South Street was suddenly a neighborhood; and one unlike anything else in the city. Within a few months every hawker of records and tapes, flashy clothing, gourmet pizza, and upscale novelties had opened a neon-festooned operation designed to separate yuppies from their money. Over the years it grew in size and intensity. Bars and exotic restaurants flooded in, along with go-go dancing (or whatever they called it these days), jazz clubs, and some slightly more dubious businesses.

Ralph's business was part of the second wave; a card and gift shop up front on the first floor that catered to gays and lesbians, and his own living quarters upstairs. And in the rear of the first floor? I liked Ralph too much to want to know the details, but I knew that the commercial explosion of the South Street area had displaced some of the old-time Italian numbers rooms and gambling operations. I suspected that something was going on in the back that didn't fall within the Philadelphia zoning ordinance.

I got out of my Legend and locked it behind me. The streets were crowded, mostly with people who looked like they should be in offices in Center City. It was hot, with the promise of a thunderstorm later, but not unbearable. And a gentle breeze, drifting off the Delaware, felt good against my skin.

I was a familiar sight in his store, and the man at the counter waved me through to the stairs. Upstairs, when I knocked, Ralph yelled that the door was unlocked.

Ralph was sitting in a recliner, looking down through floor-to-ceiling windows onto South Street. "Good to see you, Lisa."

"Thanks for having me over."

"It's the first time you've been here without David." When I didn't answer, he just turned and looked out the window at the people on the street below. Ralph was nursing a Laiphroag. I shivered a bit at the thought of alcohol and poured myself some water. He watched me and smiled. Ralph had a marvelous sense of mood; from the moment he'd picked up the phone, he'd known not to ask any questions.

I sat next to him, and we looked out the window together.

IT WAS PLEASANT just to sit there and collect my thoughts. Inside the apartment the air conditioner held the summer heat at bay. I kicked off my shoes, and the thick shag carpeting felt like mink under my feet.

It was a friendly silence, the kind that comes only with people who feel no tension in each other's presence. The trouble is, when two people are together who know each other well and they're both avoiding the obvious subject, some odd topics can surface.

"Lisa?" He was looking out the window, but not at anything in particular. And he was blushing. "Can I ask you something personal?"

"Sure."

He turned a little toward me and gestured in the general direction of my stomach. "It's none of my business, but . . ."

"You're curious."

"I've never known anybody like you."

"And I've never talked to anybody about it."

"Never?"

I heard my voice getting tighter. "David and I had already been to bed before he knew. One time, years ago, I tried to tell a guy I was seeing. It got pretty ugly."

"I'm sorry."

"I haven't thought about him in a long time." Which was a lie; on a bad day it was as fresh and painful as the night it happened. His screaming, his face twisted in anger, me and my clothes being thrown out the door. For a moment I thought I was going to cry. I clenched my teeth and forced myself to remember it was old news, that now I was with a friend. "I don't mind talking to you."

"Sure?"

"Sure."

He made his gesture again, this time a little lower. "They give you the works?"

I had to giggle, despite how embarrassed I was; or maybe because I was embarrassed. "The works. I've been with four men since the operation, and none of them noticed anything. There's nothing special."

To my surprise, he reached over and patted my cheek. "You shouldn't talk about yourself that way."

I held his hand against my face for a moment. It smelled of soap and aftershave. "I never wanted to be Elizabeth Taylor. I just want to be an ordinary woman."

"You're not ordinary. You're very pretty."

I rubbed his fingers and then let go. "Do I make you sorry you're gay?"

It was his turn to laugh. "No woman ever did, no offense."

"Not ever?"

"Back when you were a guy, were you interested in girls?"

His question surprised me. "No."

"Guys?"

"No. I wasn't gay."

"So who did you go for?"

"Nobody at all, really. It's hard to explain."

"I don't have a bus to catch."

"You're a man, Ralph. You like your body. It's just that guys turn you on and not girls. It's pretty simple."

"Being gay isn't simple."

"No. But neither is looking at your own body every morning like it doesn't have anything to do with you. Before the operation I didn't feel like a man. I thought about guys, but I was never, ever gay. I thought about men the way women do. It was the woman in me trying to get out. Does that make any sense?"

He rubbed his chin slowly. I could see him trying his best, but he was no better equipped to really understand than David was. I felt very lonely.

He gave up struggling with the psychology. "So everything really works?"

"If you want to know the truth, it works too well."

"No such thing."

"When I'm with someone I care about, not even in bed, I mean just in the same room . . . I'm ready."

"Someone like Dave?"

I found myself brushing my hair back from my ear and I was annoyed with myself for being nervous in front of a friend. "Now you *are* getting too personal."

He gave a self-satisfied smile. "That's exactly what he said once when I asked him a question like that." When I didn't answer, he went on. "You know what his problem is, don't you?"

"He says it's unfair for a boss to have a relationship with an employee. I think it's a lot simpler than that." Now it was my turn to gesture at my body.

Ralph shook his head. "He isn't bothered a bit."

I felt myself flush. "Why shouldn't he be?"

"Lisa, that's a goddam good question. A lot of straight guys would head for the hills. I just think that you're lucky."

"I can't compete for Dave."

"Compete?" he laughed. "You don't have to."

"That 'employer' business is lame, Ralph—"

He shook his head emphatically. "He's sat in that chair enough times, and we've talked about things—" He saw the look on my face and raised his hand. "No, not about this. About lots of things. Lisa, he's not perfect. But he's honest, and he's responsible. Tell him he has to watch out for somebody, and he'll never rest till the job is done. When he was a platoon sergeant one time, he carried his gear and the gear of two new guys in hundred-degree heat. He spent two days in the infirmary with heatstroke."

"I didn't know."

"The other night when we had dinner, you wore your old college T-shirt, from when you were a guy. How come?"

"It was what I was wearing at work."

"What did he think?"

"He teased me a little. He said I had a sense of humor to wear it."

"Why did you wear it?"

"It was a dress-down day, there—"

"Come on, Lisa; you've got twenty T-shirts. Why that one?"

"To see how he handled it."

"Now we're getting somewhere. So he passed?"

"He passed." I looked at my hands; manicured, polished nails, but bigger than a woman my size would have. "I used to think no one would ever want me if they knew. But I think I was wrong. I can't go through life apologizing for what I am."

"That sounds like something David would say."

"He did, actually."

"I got something to say, it isn't very polite, but under the circumstances, huh?"

"Okay," I said.

"Your past, you got a problem—"

"There's so much prejudice—"

"Bullshit!" he said, so loud that I jumped back in my chair. "Sorry." He paused for a moment. "Lisa, the problem with your past is real simple. You just don't know much about attracting men."

"I know, believe me."

He was so ready with his next remark that my surrender took him off balance. He caught himself and smiled. "Well, then; 'nuf said."

"I'd be happy for any advice."

"Then you came to the wrong place. What would I know about attracting straight guys?"

I fixed Ralph another drink and poured myself some more water. "Ralph?"

"Mmm?"

"I'm ready to talk about what happened today, if you're ready to listen."

"I thought you'd never ask."

I went through everything that had happened. There was a lot to tell; my second meeting with Uncle Seymour, my migraine, the meeting this morning, our fights. When I was done, Ralph got up and made himself a tall one. "Shit."

"Shit, what, exactly?" I asked.

"The two of you." He shook his head, exasperated. "I never thought I'd ever meet a person who thought too much. Now I've met two." He waved the hand that held the glass. "You got to realize, this stuff with his parents is important to him, but not the same way it is to you. And you're crowding him; you're not giving him time to let it sink in."

"He says he doesn't want to talk about it."

"Not till he's had a chance to live with it. When he's ready, he'll talk. And he'll talk to you, if you don't keep screwing up."

"Why me? Why not you or his mother or Uncle Seymour?"

"Because there's nothing more to say to Seymour, unless the old guy was holding out. His mom's going to lie like a rug. She hasn't kept a lid on it for forty-four years because she's been too busy. There's no point in talking to her until he has something to confront her with. And why not me? Because you're more important to him, and because what you went through is kind of the same thing. You had to start out from scratch about your present; he has to do it about his past."

"Mmm. That's an interesting thought."

"Jesus fucking Christ," he said, and stood up, both hands balled into fists. "That's what's wrong with the both of you! The two of you just nod and say 'a very useful insight' or some such crap and don't do anything with it."

"So what should I do?"

His face red, pacing back and forth and stopping from time to time to shake a finger in my face, he told me.

10

David

Friday, 5:00 P.M.

WHEN I REACHED my apartment, the blinking light on the answering machine told me I had a message. I put a cup of leftover coffee in the microwave and hit the playback button.

"David, this is your mother. Something has come up. Please give me a call as soon as you get in." The message had been recorded at eleven that morning; I wondered why she hadn't tried my office. And I wondered if somehow she knew about my conversation with Uncle Seymour.

Stewing about it wasn't going to make it any easier. I took a sip of coffee and picked up the phone.

"Hello, Garretts." She hadn't changed her way of answering the phone in the year since Dad had died.

"Hi, Mom; it's Dave." I'd often thought it a stupid thing for an only child to say, but it was our routine.

"David, where have you been? I've been trying to reach you for hours."

"You can get me through the office."

"You weren't in."

"I'm out a lot, Mom, on cases. You could have left a message."

"Can you come over? I need to talk to you."

I wasn't nearly ready to see her face to face. "How about tomorrow, Mom? It'll be Saturday."

"Tonight will be better. I've got a chicken in the oven."

I sighed. Some night at dinner, when I was around ten years old, I must have expressed some kind of approval for roast chicken. In thirty years I hadn't been able to persuade her that any other culinary possibilities existed. "Fine, Mom. See you at seven."

"Good, David. And I'll make you a nice kugel." I managed to get off the phone without letting her know that I liked kugel even less than roast chicken.

My mother lives in the Great Northeast, a vast area that sprang up in the fifties, after the success of Levittown. Politically it is part of the City of Philadelphia, but in every other way it's a suburb, with mile upon mile of identical single-family houses on quarter-acre lots, strip malls that have seen better days, and a surprising number of cemeteries. The Northeast isn't entirely uniform. Down near the Delaware, where the neighborhoods dated from before World War II, are grimy row houses sheathed in gray formstone, old trolley tracks, and innumerable corner bars. The older areas are dirty and even dangerous, but at least they have character and authenticity. But where my mother lives is purest Northeast, which means middle class, white, sterile, and very possibly Jewish. The population of the Northeast came in large part from Jews fleeing North Philadelphia after the war. Lisa wasn't old enough to remember when North Philadelphia had been Jewish, but her mother had told her stories of the little shops and sidewalk markets and pushcarts. The two of them hated the Northeast; partly for draining away the old neighborhoods, but mainly for being so boring. I found it hard to disagree.

My mother's apartment was on the third floor, but the Northeast is so flat that she had a view of Temple University to the south, Chestnut Hill to the west, and New Jersey to the east. Even for someone in the white-bread Northeast, she lived in isolation. She'd never met some of her neighbors, and she seldom went out. Her only companion was a cat named Stan. Everything she needed—food, clothing, dry cleaning—was delivered. I used to wonder why she'd bothered to move from Chicago at all. Partly her isolation was physical. She had advanced emphysema and needed to be near oxygen at all times. But even more, she liked being alone just fine.

She was in the kitchen, standing over the stove, wearing an apron over a housedress. The oxygen bottle was on a little dolly next to her on the floor, but she wasn't using it at the moment. Her hair was that peculiar shade of blue that some women of a certain age adopt. Mom was short, and even when she was younger she tended to plumpness. Widowhood had been her excuse to let herself go. Her hips and stomach strained against the blue cotton print of her dress. She was stirring something in a saucepan when I came in. When she saw me, she stopped and gave me a big hug. "Hello, honey. I'm glad you could come."

I kissed her on the cheek. "Hi, Mom."

"I was worried about you."

"There's nothing to worry about."

"The gravy's a little thick." She took off her apron. "Let's sit down a minute."

I poured myself a Scotch, and we sat in the living room. She towed her oxygen bottle behind her and played with the green plastic nasal tube, but she didn't put it on. I swirled the Scotch around in my glass. Mom gave me a look that told me it was bigger than I needed. If she'd only known how big a drink I needed just then . . .

"So, honey," she said. "Everything okay at work?"

"Fine, Mom. With the new cases, we're pretty busy."

"You hear from Terri?"

"Not since the divorce was final." And you know that, I added silently.

She shrugged, just a little. "I ran into her mother in the market, we were buying for Pesach, she said to say hello."

"I've got nothing against Terri's mother."

She played with the nasal tube some more. "I think that maybe Terri wants to see you again."

"Terri cost me my license to practice law."

"Taking the bar exam for her was your own decision, David. You have to accept that."

"I accept it just fine. And I also accept that after she failed it herself four times she had a year to noodge me to take it for her."

"She feels very bad about that, you know."

I took a gulp. It went down too fast, and I didn't get any pleasure out of it. "Makes two of us."

"David—"

"Mom, she was the one who left me, in case you don't remember. I was prepared to stay and deal with it all, but she cut and ran. She made her choice."

"David, life is short. You had some good years together. You're not getting any younger." She hesitated. "Neither is she."

"So, her biological clock is ticking?"

"David, sometimes you—"

"And this is one of those times, Mom. Give it a rest."

By her sigh, she told me I was ungrateful, stubborn, hard-hearted, and just plain wrong. "David, I didn't ask you over just about that. You're a grown man, and you make your own decisions." At least, "decisions" was the word that came out of her mouth. Somehow, I could have sworn she said "mistakes."

"Okay, Mom; no problem."

"The other business—there's something in California."

"Yes?" It was all I trusted myself to say.

"Auntie Rachel is very ill. I got the news this morning. I tried to call you, but I—"

"Auntie Rachel?"

"After all this time."

The story was part of the family legend. Not long after the war, Aunt Rachel was given penicillin for an infection. It was still a fairly new drug then, and her doctor didn't realize that some people are highly allergic. She went into a coma and never came out. No husband and no children. It was the first time I'd heard her name spoken in many years. Until Mom reminded me, I hadn't known if she was still alive.

"Did I ever meet her?"

"Not that you would remember. She was always in the hospital. From even before you were born."

Her last word made my hand jump. "Is she your aunt?"

"My sister. She was the youngest of all of us. She was the baby."

"And she's taken a turn for the worse?"

"I got a call this morning. It's pneumonia." She said it as if it were a dread killer, and I realized that during most of her adult years, it had been. "And they can't give her antibiotics 'cause her kidneys are so bad."

"She in a hospital?"

"They just moved her. They say there's nothing they can do, that it's a matter of a couple days."

"I'm sorry, Momma."

"It's—hard. It's like she died twice."

"You've never talked about her much."

"It's been so long; you forget, and yet you don't forget." She briskly wiped away a tear. "Remember I took you to see her once?"

"No."

"You were five. I wasn't sure you were old enough, but your father said you might as well come along."

"I can't remember it at all."

"There was nothing to remember. You looked, and then you went out in the hall and read a book."

"So you want me to go?"

"One of us ought to be there."

"I'll start calling for reservations. I'll have to get there quick." Strictly observant Jews hold funerals within twenty-four hours, unless it would involve a burial on the Sabbath.

"No; there's people coming from out of town, so if something happens in the next couple days, they'll set it for the end of the week." We looked at each other. The intermarriage rate among my cousins was around 80 percent, and no one was following the old customs anymore. When my mother's brother died a few years before, they'd even had an open casket. "One of us ought to be there."

"No problem, Mom."

"You're a good boy, David. You're such a help."

"It's family, Mom. I'm just sorry you can't come with me."

"So, you ready for dinner?"

"Sure." My mother was a terrible cook, sparing of spices and overdoing the vegetables to the point of mush. She dished out something that probably started the day as a perfectly decent breast of chicken.

I took a bite. Normally I could get through one of her meals politely, even when I wasn't hungry, but tonight my appetite had deserted me completely. She saw me put down my fork. "Isn't it done enough?" she asked.

It was just this side of cremated already, but that wasn't the problem. "I've been talking to Uncle Seymour, Mom."

"It's good for you to stay in touch, David. He's so lonely. Your father would be proud of you."

"We were talking about you, Mom."

"I haven't seen him lately. Should we have him over for Shabbos?"

"We were talking about my birth, Mom."

"Your birth? He wasn't even there."

I took a breath and just opened my mouth and let it come out. "He told me you didn't go out to California when I was about to be born—you were out there for months and months."

"That's right," she nodded. "I went when I found out I was going to have you."

"I always thought you were only there a few weeks."

She looked genuinely puzzled. "No, I don't think I ever said so. Did I tell you that?"

She was right—it was only my assumption. "Why did you spend all that time away from Dad?"

She shrugged. "We talked about it, and he said it was okay if that's what I wanted."

"I'm having a little trouble understanding this, Mom."

"You were my first baby. My mother, my whole family, was at home. Your father was a good man, but he wasn't any help. I started to get morning sickness, and he'd get sick, too. I'd have to clean up after both of us. I'm not blaming him, David. His sisters always took care of him, not the other way around, and he wasn't prepared for it."

"So how long were you gone?"

She thought a moment. "It's so long, it's hard to remember. When I left I hadn't been sick very long. I probably wasn't even three months along. You were three weeks old when we came back. So, I guess I was gone about seven months."

"What did you do out there all that time?"

She patted her stomach and smiled. "Got fat and let my mother take care of me."

"Didn't Dad ever visit?"

"Travel wasn't so easy back then, David. It wasn't like you could get on a jet in Chicago and be in Los Angeles in three hours. He was supposed to come out a couple of times, but either something would come up or he couldn't get anyone to watch the store long enough. We talked on the phone every week."

"So it was you and Grandpa and Grandma? Was Aunt Rachel with you?"

"Oh, no. She was already in the nursing home. When you were born, she'd been there for years already. We visited her every week. It was hard on Mom and Dad. They still thought there might be a miracle." She paused, remembering. "Dad was still hoping, right up to the time he died."

"She lived a long time."

"Such a waste. She was a beautiful woman."

I sighed. "This business with my birth certificate, Mom."

"They told me there was a fire."

"Did it happen when you were still in the hospital?"

"I don't know. I only found out about it when I was trying to get you a Social Security number, when you got your first savings account. You were fourteen, remember? You had money saved from caddying for your father."

"You didn't know before that?"

She looked embarrassed. "Well, I had the bills from the hospital and the doctor and the insurance papers, and I thought the birth certificate was in with them, but I can't say I actually remember seeing it. I put everything away, and by the time you were fourteen we'd moved about six times. I thought I'd just lost it in the moving, but when I called for a duplicate they told me to call the courthouse, and the lady at the courthouse said that they didn't have a record, and so I called back the hospital and they left me on hold a long time. Then they came back on and said that lots of records and birth certificates had been lost in a fire; but they were very nice, and they told me that the lady in the courthouse could help me, and they were right. She—the courthouse lady, I mean—told me that I could fill out a form to put your birth on record, and she even sent it to me. Your dad and I signed it, we had it all notarized, and then we sent it to be filed. They sent us a copy showing it had been put on record, and that was that."

"Did they ever say anything more about the fire?"

"No, just that there was a fire, and that yours wasn't the only one destroyed." She thought about it. "You know, they didn't even say the fire was at the hospital, not in so many words. It could have been a fire in the mail truck or at the post office, I guess."

"Mom, Uncle Seymour got me thinking."

"What about, honey?"

"He says no one in the family ever saw you pregnant."

"No one on your father's side, that's right. None of them visited. I was only three months along when I left."

I took a breath. "Uncle Seymour doesn't think you and Dad are my birth parents."

"He's getting confused, David. You can see for yourself, he's no spring chicken." She shrugged, "You know, sometimes when you get older, you dwell on the past, your mind gets caught up in funny ideas."

"Is he right, Mom?"

"David, why would you ask me that? Do you think it's true?"

"I don't know. That's why I'm asking."

"Well, it's not true. But . . . I can understand why you would think so—"

"Because—"

"David, you were always a good son. You're a good son to me, and you were a good son to your father. He was very proud of you. He loved you, in his own way, and I know you loved him too. But I'm not blind. I know the two of you weren't close. He was an old father. Sometimes I used to think, when I would see all the men in their twenties with their kids, playing in the park, and then seeing you and your dad, it was a mistake to start so late. Children take a lot of energy, boys especially, and he wasn't really up to it."

"So?"

"So, I know you missed out on a lot as a child. His age, my being sick so much, being an only child, the moving . . . You used to ask me, when you were five or six, if you were adopted. You thought you were really part of one of the other families in the neighborhood."

"Mom, I'm forty-four now, not six."

She looked uncomfortable. "I didn't want to have to say this, so blunt. But watching you grow up, the way you and your dad got along, I don't know that I'm surprised it's come to this."

"What do you mean?"

"To wanting so much to believe you're someone's son besides his."

"Is that what this is all about?"

She shrugged and looked away. "People believe what they want to believe. I don't like to say it, but it's true."

"Who would want to believe something like this?"

"People don't always realize what they want."

She was right about that. I got up and poured myself another drink. When she saw the size of it she looked at me with open disapproval. "Are you going to be okay to drive, honey?"

"You think I want to believe Uncle Seymour?"

"No. But I think there's a part of you that never loved your father, resented him; that part wants to believe you can start over with a new father."

"But why?"

"Feelings don't always make sense." Her tone sharpened, "And you shouldn't pay attention to them unless you're sure you know what you're doing."

"You're telling me not to look?"

"You're a grown man, David; if you think you can find out more about the hospital fire or the birth certificate, well, that's what you do for a living, isn't it? Just make sure you know why you're doing it."

"If I started looking, why would you say I was looking?"

"You want an answer, honey? Really?"

"Yeah."

She closed her eyes. "To punish your father. To show him you're still angry. To show him that you don't care what it makes the rest of the family think of his memory."

"And what about you?"

She opened her eyes and smiled at me, sadly. "I know you love me. I won't be hurt. But if you start looking I'm along for the ride, aren't I?"

"You're not going to try to stop me?"

"Not anymore than what I've said." She gestured, palms upward. "You want to look, so look."

"This hasn't been easy to talk about."

"It's your own birth. You're entitled."

"You've been—really good about this."

"So can you do for me?"

"What?"

"I'm not saying you have to do it tonight, or that you even have to do it at all, but promise me that you'll at least think about calling Terri?"

"Mom . . . I just don't know."

"You two loved each other so much, before all your troubles. You were such a handsome couple."

"It was a pretty messy divorce, Mom. I don't need to remind you."

She made a dismissive gesture. "Life is short, David. You have to forgive and forget to get along. You still think about her, sometimes?"

"We were married a long time," I said. I was going to say, twelve years, but I didn't want to get into an arithmetic contest in case I was wrong.

I wasn't going to get off so easily.

"But you still think about her, don't you?" she repeated.

"Honestly, Mom, not in a while. Not in six months, at least."

"Six months?" My mother missed nothing. She should have been the detective, not me. "So, you seeing somebody else?"

"No."

"So what about you and the shiksa?"

"She has a name, Mom. It's Lisa. And we're not dating; she just works for me." When Lisa and I had been together, I'd made the mistake of letting my mother know she was Catholic. That was the end of any good feelings Mom might have harbored toward her. If Lisa had been from a good Jewish family, I don't think my mother would have cared that she was a transsexual. My mother's priorities were clear.

"Still, she's with you every day, no?"

"Mom, there's nothing going on, okay?"

"Well, I'm glad to hear it. But will you at least think about calling Terri? Her mom says she misses you terribly."

Yasha Heifitz never played a violin half as well as a Jewish mother can push the guilt buttons in her child. "I'll think about it, Mom, I promise."

"So think about next Friday night, maybe you and me and Terri's mom and her, the four of us?"

"Jesus, mother; if I want to talk to her again it's going to be just the two of us."

"That's a good idea, David. You two need a little privacy. There's so much you need to talk about. I'll call her mom and tell her you'll be calling."

Once again, I'd lost control of a conversation. "Mom, just hold up. When I'm ready to make a call, I'll make it myself."

She looked glum. "I'm just trying to do what's best."

"I know, Mom; but everybody has to decide that for themselves."

"You sure you and the shiksa aren't involved?"

"We're not. And anyway, she's not for me."

"You sure about that?"

I opened my mouth to deliver the reason that would end the conversation once and for all, but nothing came. "It's just not there for us, Mom."

"Well, then." She looked at my nearly empty glass. "Are you going to be all right? Driving home?"

"I'll be fine, Mom."

I finished my drink and left, burdened with an armful of Tupperware containers loaded with overcooked vegetables and inedible roast chicken.

I went home and started drinking, but my heart wasn't in it. I nursed a tall one and contemplated my apartment and my life. Today solid ground had moved under my feet. My mother had been lying to me for forty-four years and was lying even now. Or maybe not. Maybe I wanted to believe it so much I wasn't thinking straight. . . .

I thought about my father. Mom was right; we'd never been close, though Lord knows we'd both tried. He was a quiet man who liked his *Sports Illustrated* and his weekend golf; when I was a teenager I wanted to talk about Freud and Marcuse and Sartre and barely cared about sports at all. We had some huge fights, some of them my fault and some his. But after the fights it was always a return to our truce, never a real understanding. At the time, and for years after, I'd assumed it was how young men grew up. Now, I realized, we had more cause for conflict than either of us ever realized. And the poor SOB probably never knew the truth. Was he any better off not knowing? Was I better off? I didn't think so.

My thoughts weren't going anywhere except in circles. Too much emotion too fast, and too much booze. I was ready to call it an early night when I answered a knock at the door and found Lisa. "Hi," I said. "I'm a little surprised to see you." Her hair was exactly as I liked it; pulled back in a heavy braid over one shoulder. She came inside without being invited, and I smelled Laiphroag on her breath.

I sat at the kitchen table with the bottle at my elbow. She stood straight and stiff, her head erect. She seemed to sway from side to side, but then I realized that was me. "David, we need to talk."

"We do?"

"There's something I need to say."

"Let me guess. You found a problem in the books, so you called the IRS."

"I deserved that one," she said, which stopped me cold. Apologizing wasn't Lisa's strong suit. She sat down at the kitchen table. And then she got up again and began to pace with her arms wrapped around herself.

"What's the matter?" I asked.

"You have a personnel problem at Garrett Investigations."

"I've noticed."

"You hired an idiot."

"No, just a busybody."

She sat down again. She looked at the table and clenched and unclenched a fist. "I don't know how to say this."

"Try blurting it out. You can fill in the details later." If she was going to tell me she was quitting, let's get it over with; but I wasn't going to make it easy by mentioning it first.

She spread both hands, fingers all the way apart, on the tabletop. She pressed down so hard the fingernails were white. I remember one nail was shorter. And I saw the crosshatch of scars on the knuckles of her right hand where she'd cut herself so badly back in January. She raised her face.

"David, I—" she said, and then took a breath. "Are you drunk?"

"Yeppers."

"You shouldn't drink alone."

"You shouldn't spend an evening cross-examining your mother on your own legitimacy."

"You saw her?"

"We had dinner. She called and asked me to come over."

Her hand went up to her face. "My God, what happened?"

"She denied everything, except that she was out there a long time."

"And?"

"And what?"

"Do you believe her?"

"I don't know. She was pretty convincing."

"She has a lot riding on this."

"That's just it. She didn't seem anxious about my questions. Very straightforward, matter-of-fact."

"Really?"

"She wasn't even mad at Uncle Seymour. Not much, anyway."

"Wow. Either she's telling the truth or she's really good," Lisa said.

"Or it's been going on so long she's convinced herself."

"This is . . . I wish I'd been there. I can't imagine it happening."

"I don't know what to think," I said.

"How come she called tonight?"

"Pure coincidence. An aunt of mine is dying out in LA, and she wants me to attend the funeral."

"Sure she didn't know about Uncle Seymour?"

"He sure didn't tell her; and neither did either of us."

"Are you going to look while you're there?"

I avoided a direct answer. "I have to be there anyway."

"David—"

"I'm going to ask around a little, yeah."

"I've never heard you approach someone else's case this way."

"What do you mean?" I asked.

"Mmm, it's hard to investigate your own case. Like being your own lawyer."

"Speak your mind, Lisa."

"Okay. The word that comes to mind is 'half-assed.' You say that jobs worth doing are worth doing well."

"This isn't really a job."

"If someone else was doing it, it would be. Or don't you want to find anything? You want to just go through the motions?"

"No."

"Then when do we leave?" she asked.

" 'We'?"

"We've got a city of fifteen million people and a couple of days to get the truth about something that happened almost fifty years ago. Were you figuring on doing it yourself?"

"Did you ever look up 'relentless' in the dictionary?" I asked.

"I've been too busy."

"You want to come along for this?"

"I started it, and I want to help finish it." She swallowed. "If you'll have me. I've screwed up a lot, and I'm sorry about that. I want to make it up to you."

"Someone should watch the office."

"The office will be fine. David, if you don't mind, it's important to me that I help."

"Then you ought to come along."

"I'll make reservations in the morning."

I looked at my watch. "Call me in the morning. We can talk more then."

She stood up and I opened the door for her. "Lisa, I almost forgot; what was it you wanted to talk about?"

She shook her head. "It'll keep. Will you be up by nine?"

"If I'm not, it'll do me good to get up."

"Good night, then."

"Good night, Lisa."

For a moment I wondered what had seemed so important to her. Then I shut the door and went to bed.

11

David

Monday, 6:00 A.M.

WE WERE ON the early flight from Philadelphia to Los Angeles. Lisa slept soundly with her head against my shoulder till breakfast was served, about an hour into the flight. Then she woke up and ate every bit of hers, some of mine, and the one delivered by mistake to a surly vegetarian across the aisle.

No one over five-eight can possibly enjoy airplane travel, unless they're rich enough to afford first class, and this flight was particularly cramped. Fortunately everyone around us had developed that sense of privacy that allows total strangers to literally rub elbows for hours without acknowledging each other's existence.

"Any of your relatives meeting us at the airport?" she asked.

"None of them know we're coming."

"Oh?"

"Remember, this is my mother's side of the family. Whatever they know, they've been covering it up right along with her all these years. The only way I'll get anything out of them is the same way I'll get it from my mom—confronting them with something they can't deny."

"But they're your family."

"Not really; and anyway, they were hers before they were mine."

"They really are your family, David. I'm sure they think of themselves that way, no matter what they know."

"I suppose."

"It must be hard to think about them that way."

"I respect their loyalty."

"But it's hard, isn't it?"

"It just . . . is. My liking it or not doesn't make any difference."

"Well, exactly how much family is there?"

"Not a lot. My mother was the oldest of four—no, five. The next was a boy, my uncle Ike. He died about six years ago. Diabetes. Then there was my uncle Aaron; hell of a great guy, had a small meatpacking plant. He died of a heart attack a long time ago. Must have been when I was in law school. Uncle Ed, he's still alive, living up in Seattle. Still goes to the office every day, last time I heard. And the last one was the one we're here about, Aunt Rachel."

"Cousins?"

"Not many. Aaron and Ed each had two boys, and Ike had a girl. That's it."

"Could your female cousin be your mother?"

"I thought about that myself. She's old enough, but she's got the perfect alibi. She had a baby of her own a few months after I was born."

"Could your birth date be off and you be a twin?"

"Nah. The baby born after me, it was the second of about five kids my cousin had. She was married then, and she's still married now. Nobody just gives their aunt a baby. Besides, she's very petite, and her husband's blond."

"So what's the plan, boss?"

"There have to be people who can tell me what happened back in 1946, I just need to find them. I talked to Jerry; there are no Polk directories for LA, so I'll have to use old phone books."

"What are you looking for?"

"My mother came here knowing a baby was going to be available. How did she know that?"

"Someone in her family told her."

"Right. So that's not going to lead anywhere, but who told my mother's family? Someone who knew somebody pretty well; it's not the kind of thing people talked about a lot back then."

"I don't see how that helps."

"The birth mother either knew my mother's family or knew someone who knew them. There has to be a connection."

"It could be anything."

"You have to think positive. And you have to think lateral; think about all the different ways it could have happened. Of all the possibilities, one of them is right. The neighborhood. The synagogue. The place my grandfather worked. Whether I can find it or not, there is a connection."

"I have an idea of my own," Lisa said.

"I'm all ears."

"Have you thought that there's another way of going at this?"

"You have a way of asking questions that aren't questions."

She looked uncomfortable. "I don't want you to think of me as domineering."

"I promise. I'll tell you."

"You were born in a certain hospital on a certain day. There should be a birth certificate for you; we just don't know the name. If we can find the birth certificate, we'll have the name and address of the birth mother. And maybe even the birth father."

"You've been talking to Saxon, too."

"And to somebody he passed me along to, a woman who specializes in matching up separated parents and children. Did you know there's a state registry of births in California for each year?"

"No. And I bet you didn't, till yesterday," I said.

"The day before yesterday. Anyway, it's on microfilm, all the births in each year, alphabetical."

"Broken down by county?"

"Not so easy."

"So how does that help?"

"If I look at every birth in the state in 1946, there ought to be at least one on May 12 in Western Community Hospital for a boy. If there's more than one, at least we'll have it narrowed down to just a few."

"This registry, it isn't computerized, is it?"

"No."

"So you have to sit and look at every single birth in the state?"

"If your birth mother was named Zywock, yes, and I can't be sure till I finish."

"Sounds exciting."

"It gets worse. Each county has a set, but they're not public records. I already asked Saxon about going to the LA County courthouse—he told me to not even think about it. So I need to sweet-talk a records clerk in one of the outlying counties."

"Hmm."

"It's your case, if you'd rather have me assisting you."

I shook my head. "No, you're right. If we work this from two angles it'll go twice as fast. Maybe."

"What are you smiling at?"

"John Henry versus the steam engine."

"But we're not going to be competing. It'll be like . . . each one of us working toward each other to meet in the middle."

"With our luck, my birth mother's name really was Zywock."

"Could be."

" 'Zywock.'" I said slowly, turning it over on my tongue. "Good Polish Catholic name."

"You're Jewish, David."

"I guess."

She pressed her lips together and looked out the window.

I'd spent a year in Los Angeles once; when I was in the fifth grade, my parents and I lived with my grandmother. I was never quite sure why. My mother needed heart surgery, but Chicago probably had hospitals just as good. Maybe it had to do with my father losing his appliance business. Maybe not. Mostly I remember being unhappy, away from all my friends, all my toys and books in storage. I'd been back every few years, of course; the usual routine of weddings, fiftieth-anniversary parties, and funerals. As the plane landed, I figured that this was my first time in the state in about ten years.

The Los Angeles International Airport was huge, bright, airy, crowded, and noisy—exactly like twenty other major airports. I noticed something as Lisa and I threaded our way through the crowd toward the central terminal. All around me was the usual babble of voices, but damn few of them were speaking English. By the time we reached the terminal I'd heard Spanish, Japanese, French, German, Arabic, and a couple other languages I couldn't identify.

I found a pay phone and called my mother. Aunt Rachel was worse; her kidneys were failing, and her blood pressure was unstable. It was only a matter of time. I reassured Mom that I was all right; she didn't mention Terri, and I didn't mention Lisa.

We stepped out of the terminal. The heat was nothing like the East Coast's—without the humidity, it felt light. I squinted against the brilliant sunshine and decided that my very first California purchase would be a pair of sunglasses. Almost as soon as I was outside, my eyes began to tear. I wasn't prone to allergies; and anyway, I wasn't sneezing. Then I looked up. Directly overhead the sky was blue; but everywhere else was an evil brownish yellow haze. It was so thick close to the horizon that it blocked the view completely. "What's that?" I asked a skycap.

"That's Disneyland, over that way."

"No, I mean that smoke. Is there a fire or something?"

He followed my finger. "Oh, that. That's just smog."

I wiped my eyes. "Is it like this every day?"

"Sometimes better, sometimes worse. Depends on the wind."

Lisa was coughing. "You have a good sense of smell?" she asked.

"Not really," I said.

"You're lucky."

We picked up a rental car, a nondescript General Motors product, and went searching for the hotel Saxon had recommended just outside the airport complex in a neighborhood that was mainly office buildings and parking lots. From a distance, its two stories just peeking out through the foliage, it looked old and charming; up close we could see that the stucco was really painted concrete; that the roof was fiberglass shingles, not tile; and that the palm trees were all freshly planted. But the lobby was nicely done, with dark wooden furniture and red carpeting, and the front desk staff was efficient and cheerful—more cheerful than we were used to back East, I had to admit.

I had to wait for approval of my credit card at the registration desk, and also for an envelope that Saxon had left for me. We had a couple of minutes to look around the lobby. "Not a bad place," I said.

"It'll do fine."

"Saxon says he spends a lot of time here," I said.

Lisa pointed at the bar that ran clear across an entire wall of the main lobby. "Because of that." She looked at her watch. "I bet that by five-thirty this place is full of lonely secretaries."

"I guess people still do that."

Lisa looked at me, startled, and then smiled. She didn't smile often. She looked out the window. "Did you notice the staff? The people behind the desk are all Anglo; all the lower-level people, all the outside people, are Hispanic."

"I feel like I'm in a rich part of the third world."

A Hispanic bellhop took our bags across the courtyard, around the pool area, and showed us our suite. When I gave him a tip, he smiled broadly and let himself out. He left both bags in the main room of the suite; which bedrooms we carried them to was up to us. I opened the door to my bedroom and put the bag and the envelope from the front desk onto my bed. "What's that?" Lisa asked.

"Old records from the assessment office for the neighborhood where my grandparents lived. I had Saxon contact a local title company for me. It tells me the 1946 owner of every house within six blocks of where they used to live."

"How does that help?"

"Maybe it won't. But maybe I can get a lead on someone who might have lived there, back then."

"Forty-four years is a long time."

"If a young couple bought a place as newlyweds, right after the war, they could still be there. And we're more likely to get something out of the neighbors than out of my relatives."

"Tell me if I've got this right," she said. "We're going to look for Jewish-sounding names, people who would have known your mother's family well . . . and you said LA doesn't have Polk directories. If the person has moved, isn't in the current phone book, we'll have to look in old phone books. If J Smith was in the directory till ten years ago, if we find another J Smith with a new address starting then, we might have a lead."

"That's right."

"Want to get started?"

"Sure you're not tired?"

"It's three now," Lisa said. "It's too late for me to search anything in another county, but we can work here till the libraries close. With two of us it'll go fast."

Who was I to stand in the way of enthusiasm? Within an hour we'd found a nearby branch of the Los Angeles Public Library, housed in a rambling stucco building defaced with graffiti. Broken bottles and crack vials crunched under our feet as we crossed the parking lot. A bored black matron in a security uniform admitted us at the door, and an equally bored black teenager at the reception desk told us where to find the phone books. It was easy to see where they got their attitude—we seemed to be the only other people in the building.

When I opened the envelope of real estate information, I saw immediately I'd taken on too much. My grandparents' old neighborhood wasn't the way I thought of modern subdivisions, with half-acre lots, eight houses to a block—the tax map showed that the houses were on lots that looked no more than thirty feet wide. My six-block sample showed more lots than I could check in a month. I told Lisa we would start just with the block my grandparents had lived on, and work our way outward if there was time. Our system was simple. I wrote down all the names that sounded Jewish, and Lisa checked the 1946 directory to see if we could translate the tax lot number into a street address. Then we checked the current book. If the name no longer appeared, we would work our way back till we found the last year the name was listed at that address, and then we would start looking for the same name at a different address. It was boring, and worse, there was no way of knowing if I was even pursuing the right names. I'd been only eleven when I'd lived here. I didn't recognize any of the names at all. Looking for Jewish-sounding names means you check German and Russian names. You can wind up with lots of good Lutherans and Russian Orthodox and miss the Sephardic Jews and the Jews from everywhere else in the world.

As the hours went by, a discouraging pattern emerged. The names stayed the same, year after year, with very little turnover, till around 1965. Then the old names—the Goldsteins, the Rapoports, the Lepanskys—started disappearing. Within five years every one of the old names was gone. At last I stood up and stretched. "What year were the Watts riots?" I asked.

Lisa was so intent on her work she didn't hear me, so I repeated my question. "I think right around the time your neighborhood turned," she said. "Looks like a white flight."

"And they fled a long way. The names drop out of the old books but don't show up at new addresses."

"An older person, moving to the suburbs for fear of crime, probably goes unlisted," she said. "Especially if it's a widow."

"You learn fast."

"What if we got a current tax map?" she suggested. "Maybe there's somebody still there, with an unlisted number."

"It beats going door-to-door."

We packed up and went back to the hotel. The slight breeze had died as the sun set, and the smog seemed worse than ever. The lobby bar was crowded with women in their twenties in office clothes, drinking and laughing among themselves. A sprinkling of men in dress shirts but without jackets were sitting on bar stools, trying to get themselves noticed. A few women in their thirties and forties, better dressed, sat on the edges by themselves and watched for men.

We ate in the hotel restaurant, which was well out of sight and earshot of the bar. I put down my glass and rolled my neck around, trying to stretch out the muscles.

"What's wrong, David?"

"It's been a long day, and my neck is killing me."

"When we get back to the room I'll rub your neck."

"I tore something back in February. It's deep. Don't bother."

"You never let anyone mother you, do you?"

"I didn't like it when my mother did it, and I don't like it any more now."

"You didn't trust her, even before all this, did you?"

"She has her problems." Lisa waited. "You're right," I finally said. "I didn't."

"That bar in the lobby," Lisa said. "Ever hang around a bar like that? A pickup joint, I mean?"

"Not since Saigon."

"It's depressing, so much loneliness in one place."

"They seem to be enjoying themselves."

"I'm the one who's depressed," she said.

"How come?"

"I don't know that I want to talk about it."

"Come on, Lisa; you can't start and not finish."

"Well, because I did this, twice, a long time ago, and I didn't like it then, and I don't like being reminded." Her hands were trembling.

"Everybody has drives, Lisa."

"It's not me, David. I'm a one-man woman, and I can't live any other way."

"Okay," I said, still puzzled. "So why did you let yourself get picked up?"

"It was . . . after. I had to be sure everything was okay."

"So it's something you needed to do, and you did it. So?"

"I feel bad that I did it." She looked at me. "I'm not like that, you know."

"I know," I said, as puzzled as ever. "What's going on here?"

She started chewing on a fingernail. "It's just that—we're not a couple or anything, but we're together, we came together, and we'll leave together and we see each other every day, and all those women out there looking so *hungry* and sad . . . It just bothers me."

"They didn't look hungry or sad to me; most of them seemed to be having a good time."

She took her fingernail out of her mouth. "Okay, then. Let's just drop it. It's too hard to explain." She compressed her lips and tried her best to look cheerful. "So let's get some sleep. We've got a lot of work to do."

12

Lisa

Tuesday, 4:00 A.M.

I'M NOT A good traveler; I was wide awake at four. I didn't mind; there was so much to do and so little time. I wrapped myself in a robe, knocked on his door, and looked in. He was snoring softly, his face turned to the pillow, his chest uncovered. I stood and watched his chest rise and fall. His chest hair was mostly still dark, but a few hairs were white. None in between. I remembered how it felt, soft but just a little prickly when I rested my face on it. My body remembered, too; I felt my face flush and my knees start to tremble. Before I reached the point of seriously considering doing something impulsive and stupid, I retreated into my own room for a few minutes.

Los Angeles started its day early; I heard car doors in the parking lot and the distant rumble of traffic on a freeway somewhere. When I was ready I opened his door and knocked again, louder this time. The rhythm of his snoring changed, and he opened his eyes a little. After a moment he focused on me.

"Good morning," I said.

"Morning."

"It's getting on toward five." Well, in about forty minutes.

"Okay."

"David, we need to get up. I need to get a second rental car and get going."

He considered. "I don't think they're running out."

"But I have a long drive, maybe three hours."

He looked grumpily at the alarm clock, added together the hours, and made a sour face. "Okay," he muttered, and I left him alone to dress.

We called the front desk and had them arrange for delivery of a car. It was a little after nine by the time I drove onto the Los Angeles freeway system. I was scared to death by the time I'd driven five miles. If rush hour was over, no one had told the thousands of cars that jammed every lane and access ramp. The only freeway I knew well was the Schuylkill Expressway between Philadelphia and Valley Forge—two lanes in either direction, and sometimes no shoulder or median. Los Angeles had on-ramps that were bigger than the entire Expressway, and I couldn't even count how wide the freeways themselves were— five lanes each way? Six? I was afraid to look to the side because the local following distance between vehicles seemed to be about one car length, regardless of speed. Cars wove in and out at seventy miles an hour, changing lanes so rapidly that turn signals wouldn't have helped even if anyone used them. The only exception was the far left lane, which evidently was reserved for carpoolers, buses, and complete maniacs. It was generally empty, except that every couple of minutes a car would overhaul the rest of us, flash by, and disappear.

After a few miles I just turned numb. If someone up ahead stopped short or even slowed down I was going to die, and there was absolutely nothing I could do about it. I focused on the bumper of the car ahead and tried to think about what my priest had told me, that with faith and patience, even purgatory is just a state that will pass. After nearly two hours he was proved right. I saw the Interstate 215 cutoff for San Bernardino, and the traffic moderated into something recognizable. I pulled off at the first gas station and bought a canned iced tea. It tasted terrible, and I wasn't even thirsty, but that wasn't the point.

I drank my tea and looked around. The gas station was on a small rise, and the ground was so flat that I could see at least a mile in every direction. Orchards, dairy farms, and a couple of nurseries. Each farm had unfamiliar machines in the fields that looked like gigantic Tinker Toys; after a while I realized they were for irrigation. Anything that wasn't irrigated was dry as dust. I'd never seen irrigation machinery; in Pennsylvania, the biggest problem with water is where to get rid of it.

By the time the iced tea was gone, I felt composed enough to go on. A couple of miles farther I crossed a low ridge and caught my first glimpse of San Bernardino. My photographer's eye came alive at the possibilities—a city of white and yellow cubes, scattered across the valley as far as I could see, backed up against a series of steep ridges covered with fir and pine trees. From a distance it reminded me of Reading, Pennsylvania; except the colors were all wrong, and it was larger. Much larger. I had to laugh at myself. On a small-scale map San Bernardino was just a dot. I'd never heard of the place. How was I to know it was the size of Pittsburgh?

The suburbs were new, monotonous, and ugly, but some of the older parts of the city were still traditionally Spanish, with red clay tile roofs, stucco, and ornamental ironwork. The gardens were full of desert trees and bushes I couldn't recognize. The courthouse and government buildings were low, functional, unpretentious buildings made from what I guessed was local limestone or sandstone.

I'd been hoping for an out-of-the-way county courthouse with a couple of records clerks with not much to do and no reason not to be helpful to strangers. San Bernardino County was cer-

tainly large—I passed a sign somewhere that gave the population at 1.5 million—but it turned out to be what I needed anyway. The courthouse people were friendly; and if whoever I
asked didn't know, they didn't rest until they'd passed me along
to someone who did. Within half an hour I found that the county
copy of the state birth index wasn't kept with the other county
vital statistics records. I was directed to the law library, where
all it took was an earnest look and a polite smile to convince the
reference librarian that I wasn't going to use the list for something improper. By eleven-thirty I was parked in front of a microfilm reader, slowly scrolling my way through the blessed
events of Abbotts and Adamses. The work was tedious, but I
wasn't bored. No matter how big the haystack, the needle
had to be here. Maybe the certificate right in front of me, or
the next, or the next. If I just paid close enough attention, I'd
find it. I still made plenty of mistakes as an investigator; bad
timing in interviews, ignorance of information resources, failing
to see potential leads—but this was something I was confident
I could do.

The first few entries were interesting; I found myself thinking about what the people were doing now, whether they had
kids of their own, what had happened to them since 1946. After
a few dozen it all began to dull. With all the births in the state
in front of me, progress was slow. I felt a sense of achievement
when I finished "Adams" and started on "Adkins."

The record was huge, but every certificate was identical in
form, and by the time I'd done a few dozen I had a system. I'd
first look at the county of birth, and if it wasn't Los Angeles, my
wrist was already cranking to the next. If it was Los Angeles
County, my eyes shifted up to sex of the baby; if male, then down
and across to the hospital. If I found a male baby at Western Community any time in May I made a note. After about five hundred I'd
only seen two births from Western Community; and the next five
hundred didn't add any others. No wonder the place closed.

I kept at it till five, when the library closed. By then I'd made it nearly to the end of the *F*s. No plausible leads, but at least I was nearly a quarter of the way through the job.

I was hoping that the rush hour would be going in the other direction, but both directions of the freeway seemed equally busy. After a couple of miles, instead of doing seventy bumper-to-bumper, traffic slowed and then came to a dead stop. Every few minutes one lane or another would inch ahead and then stop again. I passed and was passed by a white Mercedes in the next lane at least half a dozen times in the next half hour, neither one of us covering more than three hundred yards the whole time. The cloudless sky was a pale blue, tinged with yellow in the direction of Los Angeles. In Pennsylvania the sky was a darker blue, and near the ocean it picked up traces of gray green. I liked the East better, but I didn't miss the humidity. The radio said ninety-three. It wasn't pleasant, but back East a day like this would be incapacitating.

By the time I reached the hotel it was nearly seven. I'd been sitting so long my legs were starting to go numb.

I unlocked the door. "Hello?"

David was resting on the sofa in the central room, his hands behind his head. His shoes and his tie were off, and he looked as if he'd been settled there for some time. "How you doing?" He sounded tired.

"It's been a long day." I looked at my watch. "If you add nearly four hours of commuting. My eyes are killing me."

"Tell me how it went." When I was finished he checked his watch. "Want to have dinner with a cousin of mine?" he asked. "I'm meeting him in half an hour."

"If I have time for a shower first." I slipped off my shoes. "When did this come up?"

"He left a message."

"Who is it?"

"Art Potts."

"Which one is he?"

"One of Uncle Ike's sons."

I stepped through the open door into my own bedroom. As I undressed, I waited for some elaboration, but nothing came. I put on a white terrycloth robe and sat down across from him. "David, do you not like him?"

"No, he's okay."

"You don't seem very enthused."

"I'm just feeling tired."

"What did you do today?"

"Mmm. Walked around, talked to people. Not much."

"David, is something wrong?"

"No, why?"

"You sound so—I don't know—*flat*. Like you don't care."

He looked at the ceiling. "It's hard to keep going, sometimes."

"Did something happen today?"

"No, not really. I just feel tired."

"Overwhelmed?"

His head moved slightly. "That's a good word for it."

"Want to talk about it?"

"There's really nothing to say. It's what it is."

"You don't have to keep it bottled up, you know."

"Talking doesn't help. We just need to get some answers."

"To what question?"

He looked at me, surprised. "Who my parents are."

"It's how you deal with it."

He looked up at the ceiling. "I'll know that when I find out."

He looked so sad I thought my heart was going to break. My right hand found its way to the knot in my belt. I looked down at the scars on the back of my hand. No matter how much they faded, I thought, they would always be there, connecting David and me. Without being asked, my index finger slid inside the knot. As I watched, my finger pulled on the knot, slowly and gently. The robe opened an inch and I felt a breath of cool air on my legs.

I looked at David. His eyes were half closed, focused on something in the air near the ceiling. "David?"

"Uh-huh?" He didn't look.

I made my finger leave the robe alone. "I have to take my shower now."

"Okay."

David's cousin met us at a nearby restaurant that was decorated in various shades of dark brown plastic. If it was intended to look like wood, the illusion was lost on me. I saw him before he saw us; a mild-looking, balding man, a few years older than David, with wire-rimmed glasses. He was very pale for a southern Californian, and he was wearing one of the few ties I'd seen since we landed, other than the one on David. He smiled and waved when he recognized David.

The two men shook hands, a little awkwardly, making me wonder how often they saw each other and how close they really were. "Art, I'd like you to meet Lisa Wilson, my assistant." Art smiled and held my hand a little longer than necessary. "Very pleased to meet you, Lisa. I hope you enjoy your stay."

"Well, there's your aunt, and the rest is business."

Art's eyes made a practiced sweep of my hands and found no rings. "I hope your boss is giving you some time off."

"Actually we're very busy."

He responded with a bland, vaguely cheerful smile that said maybe he'd get into my pants and maybe he wouldn't; but either way, it was okay. "You guys hungry?" he asked.

"Famished," I answered for both of us. We were shown to a table with a view of a broad street with three gas stations and a couple of parking lots. A perky blond waitress in a black mini-skirt took our drink orders; single-malt Scotch for David, Evian for Art, and tap water for me. I couldn't decide how old she was; her face looked thirty to thirty-five and her breasts were high, but her hands were wrinkled and her thighs were cobwebbed with varicose veins. I decided she must be in the middle of a plastic surgery project.

"I called Aunt Rachel's hospital this afternoon," Art said.

"It didn't look too good yesterday," David said.

"Her kidneys have shut down. Looks like tomorrow or the next day."

"Mom will be glad I was here."

"We all are, David."

"Well, thanks."

"So," Art asked. "What will you be doing between now and the funeral? You said you're here on a case?"

"Yeah," David said. "My own."

Art's lips formed into a thin line. "Do tell."

"An uncle on my father's side tells me he doesn't think my parents are really my parents."

He nodded. "Is Aunt Rachel's funeral why you're here, or were you coming anyway?"

I interrupted. "You don't seem surprised, Art."

"I suppose I'm not."

I looked from one of them to the other. "Does this kind of thing happen in your family a lot?"

"Heck, no, but—"

David put down his drink. "Art, is there something you're not telling me?"

"Dave, you know how we all love you, nobody likes to talk about it out loud, but even without anybody saying anything, there's always been . . . a sense in the family that there's something wrong."

"Go on."

"Dave, this isn't meant to hurt. Hell, when you look around it's really a compliment. But . . . you don't look or act like the rest of us. Everybody else is laid-back, and you've always been a pusher. You don't like the same things. Remember you visited here when you were sixteen? We all wanted to go to the beach and see the malls and drive around the hills, and you wanted to spend every night at an Ingrid Bergman film festival."

"Ingmar Bergman."

"What's the difference? Anyway, you know what I mean."

"Yeah," he said. "I do."

"There's been this feeling in the family as long as I can remember that . . . something wasn't right."

"That's why we're here."

Art put up his hands helplessly. "Dave, I wish I could help you, but I was only four when it happened—whatever 'it' was."

"I wouldn't expect you to know anything. What I need is for somebody of our parent's generation to come clean."

"Not much chance of that. There's not many left, and I think the ones that are left are still scared of Grandpa."

"I must have met him," David said, "but I was too little to remember."

"I remember him, a little," Art said. "According to the people older than me, he toned down a lot with age. He was just a little old man, skinny, from what I remember."

"So what was he like before?"

"From what I hear, a real tyrant. You know, he and Grandma came over from Russia in '17, just kids, newly married. Shaved his beard, refused to speak Yiddish, worked like a sonofabitch, learned English from the newspapers, beat the hell out of the kids if they got out of line."

"I never heard that last part," David said.

"Why do you think everybody left home so early? 'Cause they liked being on their own so much?"

"Mom never talked about him that way."

"It was easy for her. She was in Chicago. She learned her lesson the first time around."

"Huh?"

"Her first marriage, how Grandpa helped break it up."

"What marriage?"

Art stopped. "Oh, shit. You didn't know, did you?"

"Mom's been kind of busy the last forty-four years. I'm sure she'll tell me at the proper time."

Art put his hand up to his face and shook his head slowly. "Jesus Christ, Dave; I'm sorry it came out like this."

"It's been my week for surprises."

"I'm really sorry."

"Don't worry about it."

"Don't worry? I feel like an idiot."

"It's okay, Art. Really it is."

"What the hell. I guess the feline's out of the enclosure, huh? Anyway, the story I hear is that your mother left home as soon as she could and married a guy named Joel Weissberg. They were married ten years, maybe longer. No kids. Grandpa and Grandma didn't approve of him—he was German Jewish, and they wanted her to marry a Russian. They made their lives as hard as they could, all the little shit, you know? Leaving them out of family gatherings, making gifts to every kid but her, telling her he wasn't good enough for her. I don't know if any of that made any difference, but I know they got divorced right after he got back from the war."

"Sort of explains how she was past thirty when she married my dad."

"Everybody thought . . . well, that you knew about it."

"You mean, that I would have figured it out for myself?"

"One way or the other. Sorry I had to be the one to tell you."

I spoke up. "Is Weissberg still alive?"

"Oh, yeah. Everybody liked him, except Grandpa and Grandma. My mom still gets a card from him at Rosh Hashanah every year." He looked at Dave. "You want the address?"

"Sure. He's old enough to know what was going on back then, and he might be willing to talk to me."

"Dave, you know . . . uh, this isn't easy to say—"

"That Weissberg might be my father?"

Art shrugged. "From what you tell me, the timing . . . it's not impossible."

"And what if he is?"

"You . . . prepared for that?"

"About as much as for anything else. Ever hear any speculation on who my parents are?"

"No. The Weissberg thing is my own idea, and even I have to admit it doesn't make a lot of sense. Why divorce him in '44, marry somebody else in '45, and then come out here in '46 to have a child with him?"

"It's very simple," I said. "She wanted his child."

That stopped both of them for a minute. It was David who finally spoke. "But why stay away the whole pregnancy?"

"She wanted to be with the father when you were born," I said. "And it would give her husband more time to miss her."

Art looked at me thoughtfully. "Wow. I never thought about it that way."

David stroked his chin. "It looks like I need Mr. Weissberg's address."

"No problem," Art said. "You going to see him tomorrow?"

Dave shook his head. "Before I do an interview like this, I need to prepare. I need to have as much background as possible."

"It's lucky you do what you do. I mean, you know how to go about this."

"Yeah." He said it so flat there was no room for a response. "So," he went on after a while. "Tell me about Aunt Rachel."

"You want the official version or the truth?"

"Tell me what you know, and we can compare stories."

"The official version was that she was in a coma for years after a penicillin reaction. The truth is that she was nuts, was locked up in a mental ward, and they gave her shock treatments that vegged her out."

"Shock treatments? When did that happen?"

"Long ago, before you were born even."

"Not the kind of thing the family wanted to have the neighbors know."

"Not back then, anyway. That's where the BS about the penicillin came from. I only got the real story a couple of years ago."

"Ever see her?" David asked.

"I probably met her when I was a little kid, but I don't remember. Never saw her after she had her coma."

"Guess we'll see her soon," David said. "They going to have an open casket?"

"I suppose."

Our dinners arrived, along with a second round of drinks. The more I looked at the waitress's breasts, the more I was sure my doctor had done a better job.

Art raised his glass. "To families and their secrets."

We clinked glasses. "Speaking of secrets, Art, I can trade you one back. Remember how they always said Uncle Aaron was a war hero?"

"Wasn't he captain of a PT boat? Sank a Japanese destroyer?"

"That's the family story. He never made it overseas. He spent the war in Sen Pedro as a supply clerk, in and out of the brig for drinking and AWOL."

Art grinned. "How did that one slip out?"

"Mom told me, as a warning, after I'd been drinking too much."

"Well, what about Grandpa?" Art asked. "He sat on his local draft board during the war when he was a deserter from the czar's army."

David shrugged. "The old country, ahh. But what about Great-Grandpa? My mother always said he was the chief rabbi in Kiev."

"My mom said that, too. That he was blind, but he had the

Torah memorized, that he would teach kids Torah for their bar mitzvah, and if they made a mistake he could correct them every time."

"It's a great story, isn't it?" David said.

"It's not true?" Art asked.

"It's from a folktale by Sholem Aleichem."

We had a good laugh at the family's expense, and then the conversation moved on to more pleasant topics. Toward the end of the evening Art began asking me about myself and my work. I answered his questions as briefly as I could, not wanting to encourage a flirtation, but he was persistent. About eleven Art made a show of looking at his watch. "Time for me to hit the road. It's a school day for all of us tomorrow." We settled the check and said our good-nights in the lobby. He turned to me. "Can I drop you at your hotel?"

"I'm staying with David." I saw confusion in his eyes. "There's a suite," I added. He liked that much better.

"Well, if your boss doesn't mind, want to stop at the bar for a nightcap?"

I was flattered. He was warm, intelligent, funny, and not at all bad looking. Too bad I wasn't even slightly interested. "Sorry," I said. "But it's past my bedtime already."

"If you're going to be in town for a while," he said, "maybe I can give you a call?"

"We're going to be pretty busy, Art. With both of us here, there's no one making money in the office."

He gave me another of his bland smiles. "But give me a call if you get a chance, okay?" He handed me his business card as we all said good night.

David didn't say anything on the drive back. When we reached the parking lot, he led us directly to the bar. We sat at a tiny table near the register, and he ordered a double Scotch. I stuck with water. I wondered if he didn't want Art to know how much he was drinking. I didn't wonder out loud.

"So your mother was married before," I ventured.

"You know something else? Art said she didn't have any children with this Weissberg guy. Art doesn't know. He only knows what my mother and her brothers told him."

"You might have a half brother or half sister."

"Or half a dozen. Or it could be like you said; they could be full, not half."

If Barbara had children with Weissberg when they were married, going back to him in 1946 when she wanted another child made more sense. But I kept the thought to myself; David was having enough trouble without any more speculating. He needed a respite.

"You must be tired," I said.

"I lie down, but I don't sleep."

"You were asleep when I looked in on you, around four."

"I must have just fallen asleep. I remember seeing the clock at three-thirty."

"Jet lag?" I asked.

"It was the same before I left."

"Since I started stirring everything up."

"Well, it was there to be stirred."

He put down his drink, and our hands were almost touching on the little tabletop. If I moved my hand just an inch . . . It was a dumb idea, but that night I was prone to them. No, that wasn't right. I'd had nothing but dumb ideas for weeks; starting with the idea of finding out about his birth certificate. I hadn't brought him any peace, only trouble. If it wasn't for me, he wouldn't be sleepless and drunk in a hotel bar. What good was I doing him? And how much longer till he noticed?

I decided I had to get out of there. I didn't know exactly why; if it was for David or for me or if I was just scared. But there was no arguing with what I needed to do.

"I've been thinking," I said.

"Go on."

"If I stay over a night or two in San Bernardino, I can do the job twice as fast. Four hours a day round-trip takes a lot of time."

He thought about it. "Makes sense."

"I'll leave in the morning and stay up there till I'm done, if that's okay."

"I hate to see you doing all that driving every day on these freeways. If that's how you want to do it, no problem."

"Okay, then, I'll pack."

I smiled cheerfully, and we finished our drinks. At four I got up and drove off without waking him. All the way to San Bernardino a saying kept circling through my mind. The one about rats deserting sinking ships.

13

David

Wednesday, 9:00 A.M.

I SLEPT BADLY again. For hours I lay in the dark, too agitated to sleep and too tired to concentrate, till I finally dropped off around three. Lisa was gone when I woke up. I looked around for a note and didn't find one.

I laid back on the bed, staring at the ceiling, and made the best of it. After all, Lisa was only used to the Schuylkill Expressway. People hate the Schuylkill, and maybe even die of boredom or starvation in the traffic jams, but only the most timid are afraid of it. California freeways were another matter. I'd been on them before, and I didn't like them, either. Staying where the work was made sense. Now she'd only have to make the one trip back when she was through.

I had it all figured, except why her leaving bothered me in the first place.

When I got back from breakfast, Art had called, leaving me Weissberg's address and phone number. I sat on the bed a long time with the number in my hand, wondering what I was going to say. Finally I tried the number. To my relief, I got his answering machine. "My name is Dave Garrett," I said. "I'm a private investigator from Philadelphia, and I'm here for a few days on a case. I think you may know some things that would help me in my investigation. Please give me a call." I gave the number of the hotel and hung up.

The real estate records told me that the only person from the old days who still owned a house on my grandparents' old street was one Elsa Rabinowitz. The name didn't trigger any childhood memories, but she and her husband had first moved there in '45, so she was there, just across the street, in 1946. Armed with a city map and a heavy breakfast, I headed across town toward Orange Street, just off La Brea.

As much as I disliked the freeways, the surface streets in the city were a pleasure. They were flatter, wider, and in much better condition than anything in Philadelphia. And when you were half a block from the next intersection, they'd posted the name of the upcoming cross street. When you don't have to spend half your street budget on snow removal and pothole repair, there's money left over for some nice frills.

An hour later, when I finally found Orange Street, I knew immediately that my rental car was wrong for the neighborhood. It was too new, it still had its original hubcaps, and the rear deck didn't have green shag carpeting or even a toy animal with turn indicators for eyes. I parked between a chrome-wheeled '57 Chevy that barely cleared the ground and a jacked-up GTO with mismatched doors and no hood.

In my absence the neighborhood had gone a little downhill and more than a little crazy. Strings of colored lights ran around many of the houses, and in a couple places, even overhead, across the street. Mexican music blared from a dozen places— cars, open windows, and speakers set up on front lawns. Everyone I saw—the young men in tank-top shirts working on cars, the women pushing strollers, the old people sunning themselves on the lawns—was Hispanic.

I got out of my car and looked at my grandparents' old house. Like most of its neighbors, it was two stories, stucco, with a red tile roof. Each house had narrow side yards and a postage-stamp-size front lawn. Some lawns were carefully watered and manicured; others were so cluttered with blankets, coolers, beach umbrellas, and barbecues that they looked like campsites.

The presence of the gringo did not pass unnoticed. It was subtle, but as I crossed to the sidewalk and walked toward Mrs. Rabinowitz's house, the young mothers moved along just a little faster, and a pair of old women in black looked at me and whispered to each other.

The Rabinowitz house was typical. A portable TV, a beach chair and blanket on the front lawn, and a rusty but operable motorcycle parked directly out front. The door handle had been broken and patched with duct tape. There was no doorbell, so I knocked. Instead of the usual tiny glass viewport the door had a hinged section, a little less than a foot square, protected by an ornamental iron grill. The hinge squealed, and I found myself looking at a young Mexican woman through the grate. "I'm looking for Elsa Rabinowitz, please."

She responded with polite Spanish that sounded like a question. "No hablo Espanol," I replied, which pretty much exhausted my Spanish.

The little spy door shut, and the woman came out on the porch, holding the hand of a boy who looked to be ten to twelve. The woman's black hair was pulled back from her face and covered with a white scarf. Her reddish brown skin showed some Indian in her background. She was short and tending to plump, but still pretty. No older than late twenties. Her hands were muscular and rough, with short, broken nails from years of hard work. She looked down at the boy and spoke for what seemed to me to be a very long time. He nodded gravely. "You Inez?" he asked me.

I'd never been asked that one before. "No, I'm not Inez. My name is David Garrett."

He waved a thin brown hand, showing I didn't understand. "No, señor, Inez." Then, more slowly, "I-N-Ez."

"INS? Immigration?" He nodded. "No, I'm not from INS. No Immigration man. Not government. Just me."

"She wants to know what you want."

"I'm looking for the owner of the house, a woman named Elsa Rabinowitz."

"What you want her for?"

"I want to talk to her about how the neighborhood was."

"Why?"

"I used to live around here, too. When I was your age."

The concept of a gringo living on this street was outside the scope of his instructions, so he turned back to his mother, if that's what she was, and they conversed at length in rapid Spanish. "What kinda cop are you?" he finally asked.

"No cop. No cop at all. I come from far away, way back East. I'm just visiting out here." I showed him and his mother my driver's license. As they looked at it I realized how much I was asking. I'd been halfway around the world, gone to school for twenty years, and I couldn't think of the name of a single state in Mexico. Why should these people know Pennsylvania?

The boy wasn't impressed with my license. "So you a tax man?"

"All I want to do is find Elsa Rabinowitz. She doesn't live here, does she?"

"I don't know nothing 'bout that, señor."

"Can we go inside and talk?"

The request alarmed him. "Oh, no. My momma can't be alone with no man."

I sighed and thought about what to try next. And I noticed

something. Slowly, more and more of the neighbors were paying attention. Three teenage boys working on a pickup truck across the street had put down their tools and were openly staring. So was a woman with a baby in her arms in the shade of the tree next door. The woman in front of me noticed it, too, and said something to the boy. "You'd better go now, señor," he said.

"You're not going to tell me how to find Mrs. Rabinowitz, are you?"

He shook his head and stepped forward, his hand extended to push me back off the porch. I sidestepped him and cut between him and his mother. I slipped into the house; and as I did, I took the woman by the wrist and pulled her inside with me. She was too surprised to struggle. I locked the door behind us and released her.

We were in a large room with polished dark wood floors, sparsely but neatly furnished. After the bright sunshine, the room was dark and surprisingly cool. The woman's eyes darted from me to the door to the curtained front window. I stood guard at the door and ignored her son's frantic pounding and shouting.

She met my eyes and said a few words slowly, pleading with me. All I caught was *hombre*, *gringo*, and *casa*.

"Rabinowitz," was all I said. Loud and clear.

She disappeared into the kitchen and came back with a large white envelope. Inside was a form lease, two years old, with Affordable City Realty as the rental agent and Elsa Rabinowitz as the landlord. I scanned it quickly and took notes. Any notices regarding the lease went to the offices of an attorney in Century City. Rent checks went directly to the Vista Vu Nursing Home in West Hollywood. It looked like she assigned her rent checks to the home to help cover her expenses. I scribbled down the nursing home address and got out of there as quickly as I could, murmuring "mucho gracias" repeatedly. Outside, the boy and the rest of the neighbors offered me sullen looks. I slunk back to my car and drove away, followed by a dozen silent stares.

I knew I would never, ever see the old neighborhood again; and that I would have made a lousy conquistador.

The Vista Vu Nursing Home was a lie from the start. No vista at all, and not even a view, unless you counted the gas station across the street and the apartment building across the alley. And judging from the squalor inside, not a lot of nursing went on, either.

I found Mrs. Rabinowitz lying on her side, curled up in wrinkled gray sheets. Four other beds were in the room, but the other three were empty at the moment. Her hair was so thin she almost looked bald. A nasal tube was in place, fastened with dirty adhesive tape. Her mouth was hanging open, and a thin line of drool ran from one corner onto the pillow.

I pulled up a chair next to her bed and sat down. "Mrs. Rabinowitz?" Nothing. "Mrs. Rabinowitz?"

She opened her eyes a little; but blindly, not seeing.

"Mrs. Rabinowitz, my name is Dave Garrett." Her lids stayed nearly shut, but through the slits her eyes began to focus. "Can you hear me?" She nodded slightly.

"Do you remember when you used to live on Orange Street?" She hesitated, then gave another tiny nod.

"Do you remember the Potok family? Myron and Sarah? They lived almost across the street?"

Her eyes opened a little wider, and her mouth moved. I leaned closer to hear and caught the smell of urine and feces. "Did something happen to Sarah?"

My grandmother had been dead twenty years. "Did you know her daughter Barbara?"

She nodded. "She used to play with my Leon. On the swings in the backyard. She fell off and cut her knee. She cried and cried. Where's Leon? Is he coming today? He came yesterday."

"Do you remember the war, Mrs. Rabinowitz?"

"We had gas rationing, and sugar, and it was hard to get meat. But my husband's brother Ike was in meat packing. Any time we wanted, we could get hamburger. Where's Leon?"

"Do you remember Barbara after the war?"

She paused, so long that I repeated the question.

"She . . . played with Leon."

"Barbara's grown up now. Do you remember that?"

She was tiring. "Grown."

"Yes, grown up. Do you remember her visiting her parents after she was grown, after the war?"

"Visiting." She said the word slowly, puzzled.

"She got married and moved away, and then she came home awhile." I hesitated. I hated to ask leading questions, but she wasn't coming up with much on her own. "She said she was going to stay with her folks because she was having a baby. You lived across the street then. Do you remember that?"

Her eyelids began to sag. "She never had a baby."

"Because she was too little? Or because she was never pregnant?"

"No . . . baby." She closed her eyes completely.

"Mrs. Rabinowitz?" But she was out. Her mouth sagged open, and the line of drool began to flow again.

I stopped at the reception desk and asked to see her nurse. I was directed to a plump nurses' aide in a too-tight, not very clean white uniform. Short blond hair, badly dyed, and bad skin. It took her some time to realize who Mrs. Rabinowitz was, but finally she nodded.

"Does she ever talk about the old days? Like around 1945?"

The woman shifted her gum around in her mouth and thought about it. "Not much that I noticed. She don't give us no trouble, not like some, you know."

"Can you think of anything she might have said, especially about someone named Barbara? I'm Barbara's son."

"Barbara?" The gum shifted around some more. "Sorry, can't help you on that one. I can't remember ever really talking to her."

"She mentioned her son Leon. Can you tell me how I can get in touch with him?"

"Leon, huh?" She padded over to the central nurses' station and opened her chart. "No Leon listed as a contact person. Let me check the social summary on her admissions sheet." She flipped through the papers all the way to the bottom. The pages back there were creased, and the edges were ragged. "There was a Leon. Only child. Date of death, 1951."

"Korea, maybe."

She looked puzzled again. "Korea?"

"Never mind." I looked around. How long till I wound up in a place like this? Thirty years? Twenty-five? If I had a stroke, it could be next week. How many years could people spend like this? If something happened, the only person who'd have the guts to blow my brains out would be Ralph, and he was sick himself.

"Thanks for your help. By the way, I think she needs changing."

"That's for the second shift."

"I was next to her. I think she needs it now."

The gum rolled around. "That's for second shift."

I nodded and left.

I sat in my car with the window rolled down. A cool breeze from the west came in, tickling my hair and thinning out the smog. It was only early afternoon, but I was tired. I sat on a bench and watched cars trickle by, mostly older ones. With no road salt to rust them out, cars could drag on for years and years. For all the difference it made. They all ended up in the same place anyway, like people.

I could have gone back to the old neighborhood and rung more doorbells; or visited the old synagogue; but taking on any more trouble was beyond me. More questions, more probing, more smiling and acting and wheedling . . . I didn't have any more to give.

I don't know how long I sat that way, at least an hour. I didn't feel any better; I was sitting there doing nothing while Lisa was hard at work in San Bernardino. My guilt gave me enough energy to at least start the car and navigate back to my hotel. I lay on the bed, staring at the ceiling and wondering what she was doing. I tried to energize myself by thinking about how hard she was working for me, how at least I had to hold up my end. But the point of it all eluded me. Even if there was something to find, was it worth it? What could I possibly do, no matter what I found? No matter what happened, I'd be back in Philadelphia in a couple days, and nothing that happened or didn't happen years ago was going to change that.

I dozed; when I woke up it was nearly seven. I washed my face and went down to the hotel bar for a couple before dinner. When I got back to the room, Lisa hadn't called.

14

Lisa

Wednesday, 9:00 A.M.

THE DRIVE WAS easier, partly because I was ahead of the traffic and partly because now I knew the road. The sun was just coming up when I reached Interstate 215. I stopped at the San Bernardino Hilton, an informal, rambling four-story concrete block building that looked like an overgrown motel, and persuaded them to let me check in early. It was a pleasant room with a balcony overlooking what looked like a college campus in the distance.

I put my elbows on the rail and smelled oranges and ripening melons in the early morning air. David was still sleeping, I hoped. Sixty miles. It was the farthest we'd been apart in two months.

I went inside and unpacked, and I was at the courthouse when they opened the doors at five of nine.

Since the courthouse closed at five, I decided to skip lunch and work straight through the day. I tried to keep in mind that if I missed the one important certificate, I might as well not have come. I tried to be methodical. Every half hour I'd rest my eyes for a minute, stretch out in the chair, and then go back to work.

A little before noon I closed my eyes and took another stretch. I leaned back in my chair, put my hands back, fingers stretched out, and arched my body. I rolled my head around slowly, first one way and then the other.

When I opened my eyes a tall, slender man in a white shirt and tie was looking at me. Or rather, at my chest. I leaned forward and pulled the front of my dress away from my breasts.

I put my elbows on the desk and made a point of staring at the microfilm reader. Out of the corner of my eye I saw his shoes, black and well shined, next to me. "Excuse me," he said.

I looked up. He was young, no more than thirty, with short blond hair, pale skin, and a smattering of freckles. He was wearing a short-sleeved shirt, and the freckles dotted his arms, too. He was smiling. "Yes?" I asked.

"My name is Gary. Gary Niebuhr. Pleased to meet you." He stuck out his hand. It was cool and smooth.

My eyes were starting to ache, and I was in no mood to talk to strange men three thousand miles from home. "Lisa Wilson," I said, and turned back to the machine.

"I haven't seen you here before."

I sighed and looked up again. He was handsome, in a boyish way, but I was busy—and a little embarrassed about the show I'd been putting on. "Gary, if you're going to pick up women, you're going to need a better line than that."

He thought it was funny. "No, it's just that I've been watching you—"

"I bet you have."

His smile flickered off. "That's not what I meant."

"Look, Gary, I really don't care what you meant. This is a public building, and these are public records, and I've got a job to do, so could you please just let me alone?"

"They're not public records."

"Just who made you God?"

"No one made me God, but the state of California made me custodian of all state records deposited in this facility."

"The librarian told me I could look at them."

He didn't look so young anymore. "The librarian is a clerk. I'm the designated records custodian."

"Oh," I said. "I didn't know that."

He glanced at the screen. "Statewide birth index?" he asked, as if he didn't know. "What year?"

"Nineteen-forty-six."

He looked at my face carefully, and I found myself blushing. "Not for yourself," he said. "You're way too young."

"I'm older than you."

"I like that."

"I'm working on a case," I said. "For a private investigator."

"Is he licensed in California?"

"No. He's from Pennsylvania."

"Oh. And you?"

"The same."

He looked at the screen, avoiding my eyes. "Too bad you're not licensed here," he said. I didn't answer. "You're a long way from home."

"It's an important case to him."

"You're going to have to go about it some other way, I'm afraid."

"I've come a long way for this. There's—"

He put up his hand. "Look," he said mildly, "Let's not talk here. It's lunchtime. There's a good place right across the street."

I sighed. There wasn't even the usual female option of "Well, I don't know." It was either lunch, or turn off the machine and drive back to Los Angeles.

I didn't like feeling powerless. "You ask everyone who wants to use the records out to lunch?"

"Just the good-looking women."

I smiled, showing a little teeth. "Aren't you afraid of a sexual harassment claim?"

"You're the one who's asking for something, not me."

"You're asking me to go to lunch."

"There's no law against lunches," he said. "Even in California."

As we walked out of the building I had visions of him whisking me to a dimly lit Italian place and plying me with Chianti while he tried to grope me under a tiny table. Instead he took me to a redbrick plaza with concrete benches in sunlight so bright I needed a hat as well as sunglasses. The plaza was filled with dozens of secretaries and office workers. Some were having lunch; others were talking in small groups or reading. Gary collected more than his share of waves and greetings, presumably from courthouse employees. He bought us a half dozen tacos, beers in paper cups, and a fistful of paper napkins that threatened to blow away with every breeze.

I munched on a taco, lettuce falling from the corner of my mouth, and looked around. Without the LA smog, the California sunlight was wonderful. Even distant objects were sharp, except for the ones dancing in heat mirages. The sky was a wonderful pale blue, laced with delicate cloud streamers, and it seemed closer, somehow, than the sky in Pennsylvania. The sunlight brought out the yellows and blues and subdued the reds and greens, the opposite of what I was used to. "What are you thinking?" he asked.

I opened my mouth, and a bit of taco fell out. I saw that I was making quite a mess in the napkin in my lap. "About photographs I could take."

"This is nothing. You ought to see the view from up in the mountains."

I looked up at the rugged brown-and-green mountains to the north. "I can't even imagine."

"There's no need to." He finished his last taco and rolled up his napkin in a tiny ball. "So tell me why you need these records."

I told him everything. He listened without interruption till I was through. "Quite a story," he said.

"And we only have half."

"The birth records are confidential, you know. People are entitled to their privacy." He looked older when he spoke officially. He sounded as if he was searching for a reason to let me have them, so I just waited.

After a while, he went on. "It's not up to me; it's the state legislature. The books are state property, and they can pass any law they want about who can see them." He paused, waiting for me to say something, but I didn't. David had taught me well. "So you see my problem," he continued lamely.

I played lawyer. "The problem seems to be that the legislature didn't foresee our need. I can't believe anyone would want to keep the records closed in a case like this."

"I'm sure you're right." He squinted in the bright light, even through his sunglasses. Now it was his turn to wait me out.

He won. "What do you mean?" I asked at last.

He squinted at the sun. "I shouldn't be doing this, but maybe I should."

"I would really appreciate it."

He waited, letting my words hang in the air. "If you can keep this quiet, I can help you out."

It was hard to think of a way to express appreciation without seeming to promise him something. "My boss will be very pleased."

"And you?"

It was the second time in twelve hours a Californian had tried to pick me up. No wonder the state was overpopulated. "I appreciate it, too."

That seemed to satisfy him. "Ready to get back?"

I looked at my watch. "This is still your lunch hour."

"I said I'd help you out. Come on."

He led me back inside, back to the library. But instead of going back to the microfilm reader he went to the cabinet where the reels were stored and pulled out a microfilm box. He handed them to me. "A little present."

I looked. "State of California—Birth Index—1946— (Alphabetical)—*Los Angeles County*."

"I thought it would save a little time."

"A little time," I said. It cut down the job by half, maybe two-thirds. "Thanks very much, Gary."

"No problem," he said. "I'll check in later, see how you're doing."

"This is—thanks very much."

"It doesn't do you any good unless you read it."

I put the roll into the reader and went to work. Gary came by a couple of times to check how I was doing; once I chatted with him for a minute, but the other time I was in the middle of copying down information on a likely birth. He just nodded and moved off. I wasn't finished by five, but Gary let everyone else go and locked up. I could hear him doing some paperwork as I ran through the *W*s, the *X*s, and finally the *Z*s.

It was a little after six. "I'm finished." My voice echoed in the empty library. Gary appeared and asked me if I'd had any luck.

"I checked the whole list. There's just one baby born in Western Community Hospital that day. And it was a boy."

As I rewound the microfilm reel he looked at the information I'd copied down. "Theodore Hertel. No father listed. Mother is Angela C. Hertel, 41 Patterson Drive, Los Resa. Looks like you're in luck."

"When we find her, we will be."

"That's not going to be hard."

I put the reel back in its box. "Oh?"

"Los Resa is right here in San Bernardino County. Maybe she lived here but went to LA to have the baby."

I handed him the box. "Gary, thanks again. You've been a lot of help."

"So where are you going now?"

"To check out this address. Is it far?"

He chuckled. "You're really not from around here, are you?"

"What do you mean?"

"Los Resa is a bad-news place."

"I go into north Philadelphia by myself, thank you."

"The county social workers won't go in there without an escort."

"That bad?"

"It's the kind of people who prey on the migrant workers. Drugs, girls, loansharking, cockfights, illegal bars, the whole nine yards."

"You seem to be pretty knowledgeable for a librarian."

"I was a deputy sheriff. I worked up there."

"So now you're in the library?"

"Service-connected disability," he said in a way that told me I shouldn't ask anything more. It was my turn to feel awkward and out of my depth.

"Will you take me there?" I asked.

"Nope."

"What if I told you I'd go without you?"

"Then I'd tell you that you were an idiot."

"I've been called worse."

"It's a closed world up there. They don't like Anglos."

"I'm not trying to move in."

"We're not talking about ordinary Mexicans; it's a town that's half criminals."

"So are parts of North Philadelphia."

"I bet you don't go wandering around *there* at night."

He had a point. "I'm on a tight schedule."

"I bet you have a nice-looking liver, but I'd hate to find out."

His comment was condescending, because I was an easterner and a woman, and I didn't like it. I didn't bother to answer.

"You're really going, aren't you?" He looked me up and down, not as a man to a woman, but just as one person sizing up another. "You're a private eye?"

"That's right."

"Ever been in a real scrape?"

"I saved my boss's life once." I found my finger running through my hair; I didn't like talking about it. "A couple of bad-news bikers. I had to shoot one of them."

"Kill him?"

"No."

"The man you shot, were you close enough to see his eyes?"

"As close as me to you."

He considered this for a moment. "Then you'll be okay."

"I know."

He pursed his lips to hide his smile. "Okay," he said. "I'll take you. If we agree on the ground rules."

"Maybe."

He pointed his finger at the paper in my hand. "We're going to drive to this one address, before dark, ask at the door, and if nobody knows anything, we're going to get the hell out of there. No door-to-door. The longer we're there, the more likely it is to cause trouble. In and out, got it?"

"I hear you."

Outside the courthouse the streets were quiet. It was a fine evening, cloudless, with a dry, dusty breeze from the west. Pennsylvania is full of gentle hills; here, the town was flat as a pool table, and in the distance the mountains shot straight up into the sky. Without the LA smog in my eyes and lungs, I could see how beautiful the state really could be.

We walked to his car, a gray Silverado pickup with a bed

liner, freshly waxed and gleaming in the afternoon sun. Pinstriping, extra running lights, and chrome wheels, polished so brightly I could see my ankles. As Gary opened the door for me, I tried to summon up a mental image of Dave waxing, or even washing, his old Honda.

"What are you smiling about?" he asked.

"The idea that my boss would take care of a car the way you do."

"He's not into cars?" Gary sounded surprised.

I stepped up into the cab and found myself about four feet off the ground. I thought about my skirt and wondered how I was going to get out decently. "He drives a 1980 Civic with one door that doesn't match the rest of the exterior."

Gary got in, and we started off. The engine noise made conversation harder. "Not into cars," he said sadly. "And you?"

I answered with one part of my brain; and with another I realized we were having a first-date conversation. Next it would be where we went to school, or our favorite TV shows, or My Most Recent Book. The subject didn't matter, it was the pumping process that counted; and when he thought he'd been Sensitive and shown enough interest in Me As a Person, he'd be entitled to kiss me . . .

I looked at his hands on the wheel—strong hands, broad and muscled, freckled, with fine red hairs on the knuckles—and I wondered if he was going to try to hold my hand or put his hand on my thigh.

"Lisa?"

"Yes?"

"What is it? You stopped in the middle of telling me about your car."

"Oh—uh. It's okay." I brushed the hair out of my face. The wind blew it right back. "I'm from the East. I don't know that we have as much interest in cars." I looked out the side window so he wouldn't see my face. We were nearly clear of town, moving faster as the countryside became more open. I was amazed by how flat it was; even from my vantage point only a couple of feet off the ground, I could see for miles. "Uh—tell me about Los Resa."

"A long time ago, back in the twenties, it was a little farming town, nothing special. Later on, the Okies moved in. In the fifties, when the farmers started using more Mexicans, it started turning into a shantytown. Migrant housing is—pretty basic. It was still an okay place, but it kept growing and growing, and then the bad element started moving in." He shook his head. "Have you always lived in Philadelphia? I've never been there."

"In 1946, was there a hospital in San Bernardino?"

"Sure. Several. So what's Philadelphia like?"

"So there's no reason someone would have to travel to Los Angeles to have a baby."

"I wouldn't think so, unless there were complications, maybe."

"A woman with a high-risk delivery wouldn't go to Western Community Hospital."

"Never heard of it."

"That's what I mean."

In the distance I saw the late-afternoon sun glinting silver. The reflections spread out on both sides of the road; and as we drew closer I could see they were coming from unpainted tin roofs. Then I saw the first buildings, on the very outskirts of town; shacks hammered together with bits of corrugated metal, canvas, even drywall, strung out at irregular intervals on both sides of the road. No doors or windows. "Where are the people?" I asked.

"It's only June; a lot of the town is empty till near harvest time. And it's still early. Most of the people living here now are still in the fields."

"It's a hard life."

"It's better than they had in Mexico."

We overtook a slow-moving pickup truck packed with tired-looking Mexican men. They looked at us without curiosity as they passed around a gallon jug. "I can't tell if those men are twenty or fifty."

"A couple of seasons in the fields, and they can't tell, either. Now we're getting into the better part of town."

The houses were made of concrete block, and they were spaced at regular intervals, with defined front yards. Some were painted, yellow or white mostly, and nearly all had at least a screen door. I saw children playing in the bare earth front yards. "Compared to what we just saw," I said, "This is positively middle class."

"This is the temporary housing put up in the sixties. The outlying crap is just a few years old. This older part, there's running water in every house. No hot, but at least there's water."

"You grew up around here?"

"Other end of the county, near Twentynine Palms. Desert. But all the growing areas, it's the same. What's that address again?"

"Patterson Drive, number 41."

He slowed as the road widened to four lanes and the town changed once again. Now we were in the oldest part of town, wood-frame buildings with deep porches and shade trees. Groups of young Mexican men stood on the corners or leaned against parked cars, watching the passing traffic. I'd seen enough of north Philadelphia to know that they were on the job. They eyed us with unconcealed hostility as they sized us up. I tried to see ourselves as they saw us. Two Anglos; a nice truck, which meant they had some money. With a woman in the car they probably don't want a girl, although you never can tell—maybe they are looking for a third, or a fourth. They look too rich to want to gamble in the small-stakes games the town has to offer. Government, somehow; and government is always trouble.

The houses needed paint, and the porches were dilapidated, but it was enough to give me a sense of what the town must have been like once; a quiet place where people sat out the heat of the day sipping lemonade on the porch, listening to the radio. I looked at the houses and wondered which one had housed David's mother. He'd gone up and down these streets, inside her, long ago. I wished I'd brought my camera.

Patterson Drive was narrower than the main street, but the houses were set well back behind a screen of shade trees. I couldn't identify the type of tree, but they seemed to be doing badly, with dead limbs and big spaces where the bark was missing. Gary came to a stop; 41 Patterson Drive was a frame bungalow with a scraggly lawn and a car on blocks to one side. I tried to imagine what it had been like in 1946.

"Ready?" Gary asked.

"Sure. I was just thinking."

He squinted at the sun. "We're going to make this quick."

"It doesn't look too bad."

He rolled his eyes. "Check out the place next door."

It was a bungalow much like number 41, except a dozen cars and pickup trucks were parked haphazardly on the lawn. "What about it?"

"That's a lot of cars for a little house. Probably something going on."

"Like?"

"If you knew what to look for in this area, you'd find all kinds of shit—cockfighting in barns, numbers games in back rooms, pot, unlicensed bars, girls, whatever. And it's still light; the real action doesn't start till dark."

"I'll be quick as I can."

We walked through the dust to the front door, and I knocked. Gary stayed several feet behind me, and while I waited I saw that he was keeping an eye on both ends of the house. An ex-cop through and through; I was glad he was along.

The door opened, and I was face to face with an old Mexican woman, shapeless under a brightly striped robe. Her gray hair was tightly pulled back, and her skin was the color of mahogany. Small, dark eyes set deep in a wrinkled face. She regarded me for a moment and said something in Spanish.

"Do you speak English?" She shook her head briefly. I turned back to Gary, who nodded and started speaking to the woman. I knew a couple of words, but their exchange was way too fast for me.

"She's asking us to come in," Gary said. We entered a front sitting room with a sofa obviously rescued from a Dumpster and a couple of mismatched chairs of the same pedigree. I realized we were being formally entertained. She said something to Gary and disappeared into the rear of the house. The rug was threadbare, hardly more than a rag. Strips of yellow flypaper hung in all the corners. "Looks like these people don't have much," I said.

"For Mexicans, in this town, this is middle class."

"So this is where my boss is from."

"Forty-five years is a long time."

She reappeared, bearing a chipped plastic tray laden with three tall glasses of lemonade and a dish of something that looked like cookies, or small pastries. They were formed in intricate shapes and tasted like heaven, sweet and spicy at the same time. She politely took a cookie for herself. I said "muchas gracias" and left the rest of the talking to Gary. He went on at length, explaining our business. The woman listened closely and gave some long responses of her own. The word "Hertel" came up, once from Gary and then several times from the old woman. At last Gary turned to me.

"This lady's name is Marta Morales; this is her son's home. He's away for the moment. Around here, that probably means he's in jail or on the run from the INS. Anyway, she's lived around here her entire life. She lived in one of the block houses as a little girl."

"Does she know the Hertels?"

"Yeah."

"Well?"

"She doesn't want to talk about them. What she knows is bad, and she doesn't want to offend us by spreading it around."

"Why should we care?"

"The Hertels are Anglo. We're Anglo. And besides, we're her guests."

"Tell her the information is exactly what we're here for."

They had a long exchange, this time Gary did most of the talking. Whatever was going on, Mrs. Morales wasn't eager to talk. After several more minutes, she left the room and came back with a ten-year-old San Bernardino phone book. I was surprised till I realized that you only get a new phone book each year if you have a telephone. She opened it up to the *H*s and pointed out an address, which Gary copied down.

"The Hertels moved out of here many years ago, she doesn't remember exactly when. Eventually her son bought the place on some kind of land-sale contract. They sent the payments to a Catherine Hertel in San Bernardino."

"Does she know anything about Dave's mother?"

"Just that Catherine and Angela were sisters."

"Anything about the baby in '46?"

"If she does know, she's not saying."

"What do you think?"

"The baby was Anglo business. She'd have no reason to be interested. And even less reason to tell us." He looked at his watch. "Ready to hit the road?"

"It isn't dark yet."

"But it's near dinnertime. Her son might be waiting to come home."

"She said he was away."

"That's what she said. She's not going to give anything away to a couple of Anglos who look like they might be from the government."

"Could you ask her—"

"Look, Lisa, we've got a lead. I told you we were getting in and out, and now it's time for the out part."

I wished I'd brought my own car. "Thank her very much for me, please."

Mrs. Morales nodded slowly as Gary spoke. Her face was impassive, but her eyes flicked from one of us to the other. She gave a slight smile and showed us to the door.

Gary let me into the truck and started around the front. As I fumbled for my seatbelt, I heard him yell, "Shit!" I slid out in a hurry and saw that both headlights were smashed.

Gary looked around. "They're watching us."

"Where?"

"I don't know. I'm just sure they are."

"What's this about?"

"I told you what kind of a place this was. The law isn't welcome. This is just a little bit of a warning. Get out of town before dark."

"Who would do this?"

"Almost anyone who lives on this street. Especially the house next door. But if I had to guess somebody in particular, it would be Mrs. Morales' son."

"Gary, I'm sorry. I had no business mixing you up in all this."

He let out his breath. "It's been an interesting day."

"I'll pay for the lights."

"My comprehensive will take care of it."

"You've got a deductible; fifty, a hundred? Let me take care of that."

He stiffened. "I can take care of my own bills."

"Gary, this is my responsibility."

"It's my truck. I took you out here."

"It bothers you, taking money from a woman?"

He looked uncomfortable. "Well . . ."

"My boss is paying for it, in the end. It's on my expense account." I tried to imagine David's face when I told him he'd given me an expense account.

"Okay, then." I wrote him out a check, right there on the hood, handed it over, and apologized again. It was important to me not to be in his debt. He stuck it in his shirt pocket without looking at it.

We checked around the truck to make sure we hadn't been left any other presents, and then we started back. On the way he told me about his years as a deputy, how he'd totaled a cruiser, and nearly himself, in a high-speed chase; and how the county had made him deputy director of the law library to get him off a lifetime of workers' compensation. He was funny, brave, and intelligent; and the more I listened, the more I missed David.

By the time we got back to the courthouse, it was nearly dark. He said he lived close by, so I followed him to his apartment with my own car to make sure he arrived safely. He lived in a modern part of the city that could have been almost anywhere; three-story stucco garden apartments, convenience markets, gas stations, motels, and restaurants. He stopped in the parking lot of his apartment building and locked up the truck.

"Gary, I can't tell you how much you helped."

"Happy to do it."

"And I'm sorry about the truck."

He squinted at it, even though the sun was nearly down. "It'll be okay." He looked at me. "Can I take you out to dinner?"

I'd been expecting the question. "Nope. But I'd like to take you. I've been a lot of trouble, and I owe you a decent meal."

"I've never been taken to dinner before." He didn't sound too happy at the idea.

"You mean, not by a woman."

"Well . . ."

"Nothing fancy," I said. "Okay?"

He didn't like it, but he nodded. "There's a decent place across the street," he said.

"Okay, then."

We crossed the street, which was nearly deserted. Inside, it was a dimly lit Italian place with tiny cloth-covered tables. I burst out laughing.

"What is it?" he asked.

"How do you feel about irony?"

"What do you mean?"

There was no point in explaining. "Do you like Chianti?"

"Sure."

It looked to be a good place for pasta. We split appetizers and a bottle of Chianti. I held up my end of the eating, but I let him do most of the drinking. I didn't want alcohol to get in the way of my judgment.

It was a good dinner. He talked about his plans to finish college—he only had an associate's degree—and possibly go on to law school. He was optimistic that the FBI might take him on for a specialized position not involving fieldwork. Or if not, the CIA, or the state auditor general's office, or . . .

He interrupted himself. "What are you thinking?" he asked.

"How interesting it is to be with someone who's so optimistic about the future."

He drained the last of his Chianti. "You're not?"

"A lot has happened to me."

"Divorce?"

"Never married," I said. "I admire you, that you haven't let your accident stop you."

"I'd rather talk about you." He reached across the table and took my hand. He did it just right, better than David, putting his thumb on my palm and stroking the tops of my fingers.

"You've been a great help, Gary, and I appreciate it."

"The day isn't over yet."

"It's getting late," I said.

"You want to come back to my place with me?" he asked.

"I'm very attracted to you. But there's something I have to tell you."

He looked puzzled. "You said you weren't married."

"I'm not. But there's somebody."

"Your boss?"

"Very good," I said.

"He's back in LA, right? You're your own person. He doesn't need to know. I mean, what's the problem?"

"The way I feel about him, I can only feel for one man at a time."

He hesitated and then let go of my hand. "He's a lucky guy."

"Only he doesn't know it."

I settled the bill and we stepped outside. It was fully dark now, but still warm.

"I guess you can find your way back to your hotel," he said.

"Yes, but thank you for asking." I held out my hand to shake. "Good night. And thanks for all your help."

"You're welcome." He put his hands lightly on my shoulders and kissed me. He kissed well. Then he kissed me again. He kissed very well. And before I could even give him that bit of pressure that would tell him to stop, he released me and backed away on his own.

"Interesting," he said. "Good night, Lisa."

Before I could answer, he turned and walked away.

15

Lisa

Wednesday, 9:00 P.M.

SAN BERNARDINO WASN'T a night town. As I drove across the city, my only company was a thin sprinkling of headlights and taillights, and the occasional neon sign. And my thoughts about Gary. My fingertips kept wandering back to my lips.

Catherine Hertel's neighborhood spelled money, but the writing was shaky and faded. The houses were large, with generous front yards, but even in the dark I could see neglect; broken fences, neglected yards, and jalopies left to die at the curb under No Parking signs.

I did what David had taught me; I sat in my car at the curb and just watched. Her house wasn't set back quite as far as the others, and a street light overhead gave me a good view. A big place, frame, two and a half stories, with a wraparound porch. But the steps had rotted out, replaced with an irregular layer of concrete blocks; and the shutters framing the windows were beyond the help of a simple coat of paint. A TV antenna was blown down on one side of the house, one end buried in over-grown bushes. White furniture on the porch, but it was the cheap plastic kind that sells for $4 apiece in discount stores. A single dim light upstairs.

I got out and negotiated the yard and the concrete block stairs; the yard, choked with knee-high weeds, gave me more trouble. At least the blocks had been in place long enough to settle into a firm footing. The porch creaked under my weight, and once I changed my mind about whether a particular spot could hold me.

I rang the bell and then knocked; and as I waited, I was reminded of Uncle Seymour's house, because it was so different. And there was time to reflect on how much of being a detective seemed to involve standing around on people's porches waiting.

No light came on, but the door opened a crack till it was stopped by a brass chain. "What's your business here?" said a sharp female voice.

"I'm looking for Catherine Hertel."

"Who are you?"

I wasn't sure how to answer, and I was annoyed with myself for not being ready. "My name is Lisa Wilson," I said, to give myself some time to think. "Mrs. Morales gave me your name."

"The Mex? What for?"

"I'm trying to—could I please come inside?"

"You got a man out there?"

"A man? No, I'm alone."

She grunted, shut the door to release the chain, and opened it. The hallway was dark, but the smell of mold and must and old cooking drifted out. I wondered when the place had last been aired out.

I stepped inside. She shut the door behind me and turned on an unshaded hundred-watt bulb overhead that cast harsh shadows. She was old, older than Mrs. Morales, but her back was rigidly straight. Gray hair pulled back tightly into a bun, and a long-sleeved housedress that went all the way to her ankles. No rings. Her lips were drawn tight over ill-fitting dentures.

"Thanks," I said.

"So, what does 'Lisa Wilson' want here?"

"You *are* Catherine Hertel, aren't you?"

"This is my house."

"And you have a sister, Angela?"

If possible, her spine got even stiffer. "What do you want to know that for?"

"I'm looking for her—there's—"

"You tell me your business, right now, hear?" An Oklahoma twang came through. I remembered what Gary had said about the Okies in the twenties.

"I'm a private investigator, and I need to ask Angela some questions. About the child she had in 1946."

She formed her hands into fists and put them on her hips. "Well, you can just take your questions and put 'em in a sack and go down to the river with 'em."

"I'm not looking for any trouble; I just want to talk to her."

"Well, she ain't here, ain't been here for years."

"Do you know where she can be reached?" I sounded like a bad receptionist. She just looked at me and folded her arms.

"Ma'am, is there some reason—"

"Don't you 'ma'am' me!"

"I don't want to be a bother, I'd just like to—"

"If you don't want to be a bother, then git!" She opened the door wide and stood to one side, her eyes hard.

"I'd really—"

"Git! Now!"

I git.

It was a depressing drive back to my hotel, and I only felt worse when I was alone back in my room. No David, no results, no Gary; nothing to show except a lead to a hostile sister. I undressed down to my underwear and lay on my bed in the dark, feeling the air-conditioning move over my body. My finger kept moving back to my lips. I'd made a mistake with Catherine; I'd been too eager. David had told me, learn as much as you can *before* you ever interview a key witness; and I'd forgotten. So what might there be to learn? At some point there'd been money for a decent house in Los Resa, and they hadn't needed to sell it right away to buy the San Bernardino house. Now the Hertels were a family on the way down. How did Angela's child figure in? How could I have done the interview better? David had already told me how; get the person talking, and just listen. But how?

The questions came slower and slower, and finally I slept.

At nine the next morning I was back at the San Bernardino County courthouse; but in the office of the county clerk, not the law library. I asked for any criminal records on Angela Hertel and gave them her birth date. When I said I needed to go back fifty years, they said it would take at least an hour, so I used the time to check the civil docket and the register of wills. By eleven, after a few words of explanation from a clerk, I was prepared to talk to Catherine Hertel the way I should have been the first time.

I was ready to leave, a sheaf of photocopies in my hand, when I thought about saying good-bye to Gary. I stood by the elevator, wondering what I would say. I owed him, but I'd already thanked him. What would I say?

I got on the elevator.

THE SUNLIGHT WAS cruel to Catherine's house, revealing the blight in the plantings and the shabby patch jobs in the structure. I marched up the porch and knocked hard.

The door opened, as far as the chain would allow, right away; I wondered if she'd been watching the street. "It's you again." She tried to sound surprised, but it wasn't genuine.

"I'd like to talk some more." I handed my card through the crack.

"Got nothin' to say to you."

"I've been to the courthouse, Miss Hertel."

"That's nothin' to me."

"There's files there, on Angela."

"You read 'em?"

"What I could, yes."

"What you want with me?"

"I'd like to talk, please. This won't take more than a few minutes."

"I don't know what you'd want here."

"I'm a private investigator."

"Are you a Christian?"

"Yes, ma'am, I am."

"Where's your church?"

"Philadelphia. A long way from here."

"I know where Philadelphia is," she snapped, but the way her tongue stumbled over the syllables made me doubt her.

"Mrs. Hertel, can we sit down and talk?"

"About Angela?"

"I have some questions I need answered."

"I don't know what I can tell you."

"Let's sit down and find out."

"I don't think I should be talkin' to you."

I held up my sheaf of papers, not in front of her face, but high enough so she couldn't ignore them. "I know a lot of it already. I'd like to hear the rest."

Seeing the papers seemed to take some of the fight out of her. "What's the difference, anyway?" she muttered.

"I've come a long way to talk to you. It won't take long."

By way of an answer, the door shut and then opened wide.

Mrs. Hertel walked stiffly, the way she did everything else. She took me through several rooms, each one packed so tightly with mountains of old newspapers, magazines, snow tires, old clothes, and boxes that we could barely thread between them. I couldn't tell whether there was furniture underneath the junk or not. At last she showed me into a kitchen straight out of the thirties, and we sat down at a small Formica table. An old-fashioned percolator was perking on the stove, but she didn't offer me anything.

"Can we pray before you start with your questions?" she asked.

"Pray?"

"I always pray for guidance at difficult times." She closed her eyes, clasped her hands, and whispered to herself for several minutes. I lowered my head and waited. Eventually she lifted her eyes. "I can speak to you now."

Now that I've had time to think, I added to myself.

I decided to start out slow. "I've found that belief can be quite a comfort."

Her eyes narrowed. "What church 'xactly you with now?"

"Catholic."

"Catholic, huh? Well, now. I don't know no Catholics; 'cept the Mexes."

"I'm Polish."

"Huh. Never met one of them, neither."

I thought about tossing in another bit of personal information, but I didn't think it would help me gain her confidence. "Mrs. Hertel, I'm investigating a birth in 1946, and your sister's name has come up."

The rock landed in the pond without a ripple. She just looked at me with a dreamy, put-upon expression she probably thought was evocative of Christ at Gethsemane. I went on. "As a matter of fact, your sister is listed as the mother."

"That was so long ago."

"Was she living with you then?"

She shook her head. "I lived in Los Resa then."

"At 41 Patterson Drive?" She nodded. "Well, that's the address Angela gave at the hospital."

"Oh, well that can't be—well, wait a minute, maybe that could be."

"It's important that your answers be correct as best you can remember, ma'am. Take your time. I was taught that a lie is a stain on the face of Christ."

"Oh, I wouldn't lie. I hate liars."

"I'm sure," I said sympathetically. "But if you tell me something that's false, even if you do it without bad intent, it's still false." She looked at me glumly as I went on. "Now, I know it's been a long time, but do you remember Angela having the baby?"

"They took her to the hospital for that."

"The pregnancy, I mean." She gave a vague nod. "And in the summer of 1946 she went off to have the baby?"

"I s'pose so."

"Did she say who the father was?"

"I dunno," she said sullenly.

I was getting nowhere. What had David said? Keep them talking. Talking about anything at all.

"You said you'd been to Philadelphia?"

"Never said that," she said, as if she'd scored a point.

"Well, that you knew where it was."

"I was in New York City once, on a church tour. Horrible place. Don't know for the life of me what made the church decide to meet there."

"When was that?"

She thought about the question so long I thought she hadn't heard me. "Must have been—we was there for the World's Fair; when was that?"

It was my turn to stop and think. "There's been two I know of. One was in the sixties. There was one back in the late thirties."

"That was the one," she said decisively. "Before the war. I

was just out of high school then. Me and my sister both got to go, even though she hadn't graduated yet. Never did, you know."

"That was Angela?"

"Yes, God rest her soul."

I decided to let that pass, for now. "How much younger was she?"

"Six years."

"Was it just the two of you girls?"

"Yes."

"I was out to Los Resa; I bet it was a fun place, growing up, back then."

"Fun?"

"I mean, lots of space to run around, lots to do."

She looked at me scornfully. "You was raised in a city."

"That's right."

"Let me tell you 'bout farm life, honey. You don't know what hard work is. Daddy just had the two of us girls, no boys, and Momma died having Angela. That's how she got her name, you know. Daddy thought she was . . . Momma come back to him. But that's the talk of the devil."

I had an awful thought. "So it was just the three of you?"

"The town wasn't growed up then. We had ten acres of fruit trees, melons, beans, right near the house. Truck farming." I saw a glimmer of animation in her weathered face. "Worked like a dog every day, plowing to harvest, just the three of us, and a Mex or two sometimes, with the pickin'."

"Not much time off, I bet."

"It was hard times, but the winters were slow. And we got by good, for a while anyways."

"What happened?"

"Daddy got took away, and we sold off the acres and kept the house for ourselves. Then Angie had the baby, and I moved to town." She looked around. "It's a lot for a woman on her own to keep up, you know."

"Your dad had to go away because of the trouble with Angie?"

"They should have taken *her* away, not him. She never was anything but trouble."

"She was your cross."

"I bore it as well as I could. I let her come with me, made a home for her, tried to be a good Christian example to her."

"But it didn't do any good."

"It wasn't in the Lord's plan for me. I tried. He knows I tried."

"Whose idea was it to go to Los Angeles to have the baby?"

"Mine. Los Resa was too full of wagging tongues. Even the city—" she looked out the window—"was too close."

"But didn't everyone know . . . from your father's case?"

"They heard about the trouble. Not 'bout any baby. I sent her away before she started to show."

"She had the child at Western Community Hospital."

"I guess that was the name. I was never there. They took the charity cases."

"But you had the land, back then—"

"My daddy didn't work his whole life so his money could be squandered on her sin!" I wondered if she was jealous of her father's attentions to Angela. Especially after all the years, when Angela was still too young, and it was just the two of them. That was the pattern, the father working his way down through the daughters, oldest first. . . . Suddenly I wanted to get out of there.

"What happened when your father got out?"

"He was a broken man. The devil in drink took him. He was here, for a while. Angela had already gone."

"The records show you and Angela both inherited from him, around 1970."

"That was when he died. Old before his time."

"Where's Angela now?"

"I told you, she's dead."

"What happened?"

"She was never anything but trouble to me. She ruined our family's name in this town." She looked away. "She died in Los Angeles."

"What happened?"

"I dunno."

The same dumb, sullen look. Time to try another route. "What was the boy like?"

"I never laid eyes on him."

"What did she do with him?"

"Left him in Los Angeles. Doctor said he'd see the boy got a good home."

"There was no adoption."

She didn't seem surprised, or even interested. "She came back here and acted wild as you please."

"I've seen the records."

"The criminal records, you mean."

"She was arrested twice for prostitution here in the fifties. Did she have a drinking problem? A drug problem?"

"She had an evil heart, that's what she had."

"So, where is she now?"

"Dead, I told you."

"I'm sure she's dead to you. That's your business. I need to find the child, and to do that I need her."

"What makes you think she ain't dead?"

"Angela has a birth certificate and no death certificate."

"They make mistakes."

"Not here." She was silent. "Jesus hates lies, Mrs. Hertel."

"I knew that woman would never stop making trouble."

"The address, ma'am."

"If she gave up the boy, why should she know where he is?"

"I don't know. But it's worth a try."

She tore a scrap of paper off an old calendar and printed an address in a childish scrawl. "That's where she was ten years ago. Wrote and asked for money." I didn't need to be told how Catherine had responded.

I stood to leave. "Any message for your sister, if I find her?"

"Tell her that God's message to sinners is Revelations."

"Revelations."

I went back to the courthouse and photocopied the records on Angela's father. It was exactly as Catherine had said.

I took a long shower and changed my clothes before I started back for Los Angeles.

16

David

Thursday, 7:00 A.M.

I WOKE UP with a hangover, the sheets soaked in sweat, and a vague memory of dreaming about my father. He was standing in a dark suit, just looking at me. I tried to ask him what he wanted, but he didn't answer. He didn't even give a sign he'd heard me. He faded back into the darkness without moving.

I'd slept a full eight hours, but I was tired as ever. I forced myself to my feet, found some aspirin, took a hot shower, and lay down on the bed again. Why hadn't Lisa called? I missed her. She infuriated me sometimes, but she had a way of keeping me going when I wanted to quit. . . . She wouldn't have let me lie in bed like this first thing in the morning. Okay, I thought; I dressed and went down to breakfast. The coffee helped, and so did getting out of the room. If I could just keep putting one foot in front of the other, I could keep going.

I drove back to the old neighborhood. Everything was the same as the day before; the same weather, same people working on the same cars and listening to the same music. I didn't stop on Orange Street. I was looking for the synagogue of my grand-parents. They were Orthodox, which meant they had to live within walking distance of their synagogue. No driving on the Sabbath. I'd gone there a few times; a brick building with worn red carpeting and stained glass windows. Inside it was dark, and it smelled of the furniture polish they used on the pews.

I crisscrossed the area I remembered, but all I found was a down-at-the-heels commercial strip of cheap restaurants, appliance repair stores, and pawnshops. I parked and walked around. This had to be the right place. I remembered being able to see the big department store in the distance; that the street was busy; that it was about this far from their old house. So where was it?

I walked along the commercial strip till I found a shabby delicatessen with a pink neon "Kosher Meat" sign in the window. Half a dozen white plastic tables inside, all empty at this hour. The green-and-white linoleum floor was cracked, but clean. The place smelled of hot grease and baking; and, faintly, the sweetish smell of halvah. Behind the counter was an elderly black man with white hair and thick glasses. He seemed surprised to have a customer so early. "Yes, sir? Can I help you?"

"Smells good in here."

"Wait till closer to noon. We's just gettin' started."

"This your place?"

"Mine and the bank's. Sometimes the city thinks they own it, but they don' help with the bills."

"You know the area?"

He nodded. "Been workin' or livin' 'round here my whole life, and that's some time, let me tell you."

"I lived here for a while, a long time ago. A year, back in the late fifties." Before the riots. I waited for his response.

"It was real nice 'round here then, not like now." He sighed. "Jewish folks all left, Mexicans moved in. That's when I got this place; the owner, he didn't want to come down here no more."

I looked around. Pastrami, brisket, roast chicken, matzo ball soup in jars. "The old-timers still come down to shop?"

"Not hardly. Some of the Mexicans, they like the stuff. I sell a lot of kosher chicken. They know it's fresh." Catholics keeping kosher. He smiled and shook his head.

"I'll take a pastrami on rye, mustard," I said.

"Comes with chips and a pickle."

"Fine. And some coffee, too."

He set to work, carving down the meat into thin slices. His hands were gnarled with age, but he worked quickly, and the slices were even and regular. "You from New York?" he asked.

"Philadelphia. Does it show?"

"You dress a little sharp, and you got a little accent." He hesitated. "And you got some push. People around here take things slower."

"I've noticed." I shrugged. "It's not my town."

"When I was younger I used to take the bus out here from Watts every day. Hour and a half, three transfers. Now I get to live right 'round the corner."

He handed me my sandwich, and I paid. "Got a minute to have coffee with me?" I asked. "I'd like to ask you a couple questions."

"You police?"

"No. I just want to find out about the old neighborhood."

"Okay. I don't get busy till lunchtime."

"My name's Dave Garrett."

"Archie. Archie Williams." We shook hands.

He took off his apron, poured himself some coffee, and we sat at a table near the window. My coffee tasted awful, but the sandwich was good, as good as most of the ones I'd eaten in Philadelphia. I told him so, and he nodded in satisfaction.

"Were you up here back in the fifties?" I asked.

"I've worked up here, doin' one thing or 'nother, since I got outta the Navy, and that was '45. Early discharge, 'cause of VE Day. I was jus' nineteen. That's where I learned to cook. Back then, everything was still segregated. Cook, messboy, all they'd let us do."

"You cook well."

"The Jewish people 'round here, they were all big fans of President Roosevelt; me, it was Harry Truman. You know why?"

"He desegregated the armed forces."

He nodded and pointed a twisted finger. "My oldest boy, he joined the air force. Regular, no Reserve. Vietnam came along, he got to be an officer. Went all the way to full colonel. When he retired they made him a *general*."

"It wasn't all that long ago, the military was the only place you could get a fair shake."

He looked out the window. "Still is."

"I talked to somebody, a few months ago, who joined up after desegregation," I said. "He wanted to make a career of it, too. He joined the army. Enlisted in '50, soon as he was old enough, got shipped to Korea. Lost an eye at the Pusan perimeter, was home again by Christmas. Still eighteen, one eye."

"My boy never had a scratch." He looked at me. "You?"

"Marines. Vietnam. A couple of minor things, then a land mine. Medical discharge." I shrugged. "I get a check every month."

"You're a long way from either Vietnam or Philadelphia, mister."

"My mother's family lived around here, and I lived here a little while, around 1960. I'm looking for anyone who might remember them."

"You writing a book or something?"

"Family history."

"I got a sister who does that. Always on the phone with

people, askin' if they know so-and-so, writing letters. Runs a lot of money. She says she's traced us back to a ship that brought us to New Orleans in 1770."

I was willing to settle for knowing who the hell my mother and father were. "Maybe I've come to the right place. Did you know the old Jewish synagogue around here? Beth Shalom?"

"Did I?" He smiled and stuck out his chest with pride. "Heck, for years I made that place run every weekend, all by myself. I was the shabbos goy."

He said it without a trace of irony. Orthodox Jews refuse to work on Sabbath, which includes turning lights on and off, driving, starting or stopping stoves or furnaces, and even tearing toilet paper. Most congregations hire a non-Jew to handle essential functions in the synagogue on the Sabbath. It was a disparaging term, one of the not-so-lovable Yiddish expressions Jews would prefer to forget. The connotation was "lackey"; but that wasn't how this man saw it. He found dignity in his work, no matter what his employers said behind his back. Good for him.

"My grandfather was Myron Potok."

"I knew him. He was, like, 'sistant president of the synagogue for years."

"What can you tell me about him?"

He hesitated a long time before he answered. "Your grandaddy, he didn't take no shit from nobody."

"How do you mean?"

Again a long pause. "One time there was a bad storm, half the roof blew off, and they needed four thousand dollars to fix it, right away. He just went to the eight guys who were best off and said, give me a check for five hundred dollars, right now. And he wouldn't leave. Took him till after midnight, and I 'spect he pissed a lot of people off, but he got the money."

"You and he get along okay?"

"Mostly. I was a young kid back then; I didn't deal with him much."

Something was being censored, and I didn't know what. I decided to back off and try again later. "Just where is the synagogue?"

"You go out the door and make a right, you'd be standing on it. When everybody moved out after the riots, they built a fancy new building out in Brentwood and tore the old one down." He eyed me carefully. "They didn't even have me out for the dedication."

"They owed you that."

"I thought so."

"My grandfather would have been dead by then. He'd already died when I was here in 1960."

"I remember your grandmother. She was a nice lady. I cut her lawn in the summer."

"You remember their kids, Ike, Aaron, Ed?"

"Just a little. They were older than me, they'd been officers, not just enlisted men; they stopped in once in a while, but they didn't have much to do with me." His voice ended on an inflection that made me wonder how much he resented that.

"What about the girls, Barbara and Rachel?"

"Oh, I remember Barbara. She was older too, but she came back home a lot. My own kids now are just the same. Once the boys grow up, you never see them again; but the girls, they stay close, even when they have kids of their own."

"Do you remember a time, it would have been 1945 and 1946, when she was living with her parents for months and months, not just a visit?"

He thought about it, hard. "Let me think; she was married to somebody named Joel, right?"

"Back during the war, yes."

"I used to hear Joel and her daddy didn't get along. If I'm rememberin' right, he wasn't a believing man, was he?"

"I don't know, but they didn't see eye to eye on a lot of things."

"I remember when Barbara and Joel got divorced, she came

home a few months, then she moved away. . . . And then, must have been a couple of years later, she came back. Must have been here a good six months. I used to see her when I was mowing the lawn."

"Do you know why she was here?"

"Nobody said a thing. She was just there. I'd see her at the window, but we didn't talk much." He smiled. "It's funny; I'm sittin' here thinkin' how I didn't have much to say to Barbara, 'cause she was such an old lady, and I got kids older than she was then. But when you're twenty, twenty-one, somebody in their thirties seems like a million years old."

"Was she married then?"

Again his face showed the effort of concentration. "You know, I think she was; I sort of remember thinking, what's this lady doing here, why isn't she with her husband? But nobody ever said nothin'."

"No rumors?"

"Nope."

"When she left, do you know why she left again?"

"No. I didn't know she was leaving. Just one day I showed up to mow, and she was gone."

"You saw her every couple of weeks?"

"Well, I guess."

"Was she pregnant?"

"Pregnant?" His face creased with the effort. "Jeez, I can't say, one way or t'other. I was outside and I'd just see her, oncst in a while, at the window."

"She was never outside, like sunning herself or anything, when you were doing the lawn?"

"Nope, I'd remember that." Back in the forties, a white woman choosing to be alone with a young black man—he'd remember, all right.

"Is it possible she was, and you didn't notice?"

He thought hard. "How pregnant?"

"All the way to delivery, is what . . . some people say."

"Jeez—I don't ever 'member thinkin', Hey, that lady's pregnant. I would 'member if she was, her bein' alone at home like that. But I didn't spend my time staring at white ladies, neither, you know what I mean."

"If I've got the time frame right, nobody else was living at home then; just Barbara and her parents?"

"That's right."

"What about Rachel?"

At the mention of her name, his face closed up. "She was away."

I tried to smile reassuringly. "Hey, it's not a big secret; she had mental problems."

He studied my face, trying to decide if he could trust me. "Shee-it," he said at last.

"What?"

"She didn't have no 'mental problems.' She had a daddy who couldn't understand a child having a mind of their own. Child, hell; she was a grown woman."

"What went on, Archie?"

"There was nothin' ever between us, but her daddy watched us, like—I don't know. Gave me the creeps." He lowered his eyes. "You didn't have to be in Mississippi for shit to happen."

"Did anything happen? Between the two of you, I mean?"

"Hell, no. She said she liked me and stuff, but I knew she liked lots of guys; and she was going to go to college, into all the books and stuff. There was nothin' in it for me 'cept trouble."

"Were you in trouble with her dad?"

He held up a thumb and forefinger, almost touching. "This close; but he never had a reason. He just kept a real close eye on me, and after she went away for good, it didn't matter none anymore."

"And she'd already gone away for good when Barbara was here?"

"Oh, yeah; I'm sure of that."

"How can you be so sure, forty-four years later?"

" 'Cause I wouldn't have talked to a white lady on her daddy's land unless I was goddam sure her daddy wouldn't mind."

"I hear you."

Some customers appeared at the counter, a young Mexican couple pushing two strollers. "Gotta get back to work."

I stood and extended my hand. "Thanks, Archie. I appreciate your time."

"Hope I made things easier."

"You gave me a lot of new information."

"Not easier, huh?"

"No, not easier. But thanks anyway."

I sat on a bench at a bus stop in front of the deli. Archie had no reason to lie, no reason to even understand the importance of the information. I turned it over in my mind, looking for some way to reject it. Could he have been confused about the time period? Could he be confusing Barbara with someone else? Could someone have bribed or intimidated him to give me a false story?

Not likely.

I sat there a long time, watching the traffic and thinking about how much in life had been taken away; the men in my unit; my career; Terri, Kate; having children; and now, even my parents. I was forty-four. What else was going to go wrong, and how soon?

No answers came. They never do, to questions like that. I forced myself to my feet and went back to work.

My next stop was the new synagogue in Brentwood. I was halfway there when I realized I hadn't asked Archie for the address. For once I was lucky; I stopped at a convenience store half the size of a supermarket, and one of the counter clerks gave me directions.

Brentwood, at least the part I saw, wasn't a town at all but a series of one-lot fortresses, each one secure beyond thick hedges, iron gates, or stone walls. Wide, even sidewalks with no one on them, and wide streets, yellow lines neatly painted, with no traffic. The few vehicles parked at the curb belonged to lawn care operations. I couldn't see many of the front lawns, but the ones that were visible through iron fences were immaculate; no weeds, no bare spots, no ragged edges. No sign of life, either. I wondered exactly who enjoyed them.

I found the synagogue and parked at the side entrance. Apparently the architectural principle behind the new synagogue was to create a building big enough to attract the attention of God. It looked to me like they'd succeeded. The facade was a white marble pair of Moses' tablets, about five stories high, with ten-foot-high Hebrew letters in bronze. The sanctuary itself was an immense space of chrome and glass, with broad aisles and oversize pews of white birch.

The offices were sleek and bright, but on a human scale. I asked to see the rabbi and was told that Rabbi Lasher would be available to see me. I gathered that he was one of several assistant rabbis.

I barely had time to sit down before he appeared, a short, dark man, stooped and very tanned. Glasses and a small beard, too thin to hide his acne scars. He wore a white dress shirt and what looked like the pants from a suit, but no jacket or tie. "I'm Rabbi Lasher. *Shalom.*"

We shook hands. "Dave Garrett, Rabbi. Pleased to meet you."

"Are you . . . a member of the congregation? I'm sorry, I've only been here a few months, and there are so many faces. You don't look familiar."

"I'm from Philadelphia. My mother's family, the Potoks—now the name is Potts—I believe they're members."

"Are you thinking of relocating?" He sounded a little like a real estate agent.

"No. Can we talk somewhere, privately?"

"I don't have an office of my own, but we can use the library." He led me down a long corridor with empty Sunday school classrooms on either side. A left and then a right, and we entered a cozy room with floor-to-ceiling bookshelves on all the walls and a small table, big enough for four, in the middle. The bookshelves and the table were old, and a little familiar. We sat down. "Did this come out of the old shul?" I asked.

"As a matter of fact, it did. At least that's what they tell me. Were you there?"

"As a child. I checked out some books, spent some time in detention for acting up in Sunday school."

He put his hands on the table and interlaced his fingers. "So what can we do for you?"

I told him my story.

"Not adopted," he asked. "You're sure?"

"If I was, there'd be a birth certificate."

He nodded. "Yes, I'm sorry. I'm being stupid." He pursed his lips. "Were you bar mitzvahed?"

"Yes. Why?"

"It's something we should talk about before you go. It's not necessary right now."

"I'd like to know if anyone here at shul knows anything about my background. Specifically, my birth."

"Rabbi Mandelbaum was in charge then. We've had four chief rabbis since."

"Would there be any old-timers you could think of?"

His brow creased. "You see, I spend most of my time with the younger people, the children. . . . So many of the older people have moved away. But there's one—I visit her once a month. Elsa Rabinowitz."

He looked so pleased with himself it was a shame to disappoint him. "I've already seen her. She's stuck in 1950."

"I just stop in and try to give her some comfort. I've never tried to question her."

"That's okay, Rabbi. You may be able to help me, anyway."

"If I can."

"You said Rabbi Mandelbaum was in charge then?"

"He was a refugee from Germany, got out in the late thirties and came here. He served a long time, I don't know exactly how long, but he was very active in raising money for this building. It was very controversial—the scale, the expense." He shrugged. "I think that had something to do with his retirement. We moved here in 1971, and he left not long after."

"When a rabbi counsels a member of the congregation, does he generally take notes?"

"If he thinks there's going to be a continuing . . . need, yes."

"And he'd retain those notes?"

"That would be up to him; but with families, you never know when you might need to refresh your recollection."

I smiled. "Rabbi, did you go to law school, by any chance?"

"USC. How did you guess?"

"Nobody who didn't take Evidence would ever say 'refresh your recollection.' "

He laughed gently. "I didn't care for the law. This is where I always should have been, anyway, helping people."

"I'm hoping you can help me."

He didn't need to ask me how. "The people who spoke to Rabbi Mandelbaum, whether it was . . . Barbara or her parents or whoever, they spoke with confidentiality."

"Her parents are dead."

"Barbara isn't."

"Rabbi, I've been the victim of a fraud my whole life." I spread my hands in a gesture of helplessness. He hesitated, then nodded his understanding.

"Will you help me?" I asked.

He rubbed his chin, trying to look reflective, but just looked nervous. "This is confidential."

"This affects me, not them."

He sighed. "I'll tell you what I can do. I can't just tell you everything that's there, or let you read them yourself. Let me look at them and see if there's anything relevant to you."

"Fine." It was a sensible suggestion, and I kicked myself for not thinking of it first. My concentration wasn't what it used to be.

The rabbi left the room for a few minutes and came back with a sheaf of yellowed typewritten pages in a manila folder. "These are all the records of counseling sessions with the Potok family that Rabbi Mandelbaum kept. They go from 1940 through 1957."

"That was fast," I said.

"Rabbi Mandelbaum was an organized man. Let's see what we've got."

He started to read. His eyes moved quickly, but there must have been fifteen to twenty pages of notes, and there was lots of time to look around the room and think. The room was familiar and strange, at the same time. It reminded me of the library in the synagogue in Chicago where I'd taken Hebrew lessons, and later prepared for my bar mitzvah.

Rabbi Lasher put down the last sheet and looked up. "I'm sorry, Mr. Garrett."

"Oh?"

"Barbara didn't counsel with the rabbi; or if she did, he didn't take notes. Most of this is her father or your Aunt Rachel." He hesitated. "Nothing about you."

I sighed. Another wasted errand in a wasted case in a wasted life. "Rabbi, thank you very much. I appreciate your efforts."

I stood to go, but he motioned me to sit down again. "There's something we should discuss, David."

"All right."

"At this point you have no idea who your mother was, do you?"

"No."

"Is there any reason to think she was Jewish?"

"Not that I can think of."

"David, you can answer me straight out; I won't be offended; but are you observant?"

"Rabbi, I have to say that I'm not. I was raised Conservative. When I was married, my wife and I did the holidays, the High Holy days, but since then—"

"But you had all the training. Can you still speak Hebrew?"

"Rabbi, where is this going?"

"David, this is so hard, I barely know you. But . . . in Judaism, Orthodox or Conservative . . . it's matrilineal descent."

"Someone has to be born of a Jewish woman to be Jewish?"

"Even a legal civil adoption doesn't do it. For the child to be Jewish there would have to be a conversion."

"Starting from scratch, you mean."

"No, no; you have the training; but to be Jewish you would have to convert, David."

"Convert from what?"

"That's an interesting question, but I'm afraid the answer wouldn't be helpful, anyway."

"The bar mitzvah doesn't cut it?"

He shook his head sadly.

I remembered the bar mitzvah, carrying the Torah, chanting my reading to the congregation, sitting on the pulpit with the rabbi. That day I became a man as far as Judaism was concerned, a full-fledged member of the congregation; and it was all a fraud. So here I was, after a lifetime of breaking my back, no religion, no family, no home, nothing to show but a belly crisscrossed with scars earned in a pointless war.

I let out my breath. "Well, I think I've had enough for one day, Rabbi."

"You don't need to run. If you'd—" I stood up and thanked him politely for his time.

We shook hands, and he held on a little longer. "Mr. Garrett, you know that conversion is an option? Would you like to take a minute to—"

I held up my free hand, just a little, but enough for him to see. "Rabbi—" He nodded and released me. I walked out of the synagogue quite alone.

17

Lisa

Thursday, noon

I BARELY REMEMBER the drive back to Los Angeles. I think I cried most of the way. What was I going to say? I was mad at the world, but mostly I was mad at myself. David was the only person who mattered to me, except for my mother, and every time I opened my mouth I was hurting him. In a week I'd stripped him of his parents, and now I was getting ready to do him worse. "Dave, good news; I got to the bottom of it. Your parents are a couple of incestuous Okies." He deserved better. Anybody did. I tried to imagine how I would feel if it happened to me, and nothing came. When I thought of my parents, I could think that I was their son, or that I was their daughter; but the idea that they weren't my parents at all, that someone else was, people I didn't know—it was like trying to imagine I was from Mars.

I tried to anticipate how he'd react, but I couldn't. If he were angry, at least we could have a conversation. I could show him the courthouse records—the birth certificate, the records on

Angela and her father, the estate records. He might be mad, but not so mad we couldn't discuss it. Or maybe he wouldn't want to hear it. He was the client, after all; it was his decision to know or not to know. Maybe it was time for me to take some responsibility for all the damage I was causing and keep it to myself. But did I have the right to decide?

I wasn't crying because I couldn't decide what to do. I cried because I was afraid, no matter what happened, I would lose him.

When I pulled into the hotel parking lot at two, I was surprised to see David's rental. He was so certain that the key to the case was on the streets, not in documents—what was he doing at the motel? Maybe he'd gone somewhere with someone else? But his clothes were in his room, along with his wallet and car keys. The only things missing were his swimming suit and one of the room towels. I washed my face and combed my hair, put on some fresh lipstick, and headed for the pool.

David was stretched out on a lounger, a closed paperback book on one side with an empty glass on top. He was staring up at the sky.

"Hi, David; I'm back."

He turned his head and took off his sunglasses. "Hi."

I sat on the edge of the next lounger. "What are you doing?" I asked.

"Just thinking."

"About the case?"

"Just . . . thinking."

His towel was beside him, still folded. "Been swimming?" I asked.

"I thought I might, but I haven't got around to it yet." He paused. "I'm tired."

"Me, too."

"Take a swim," he said. "If you want."

"Maybe later." I couldn't keep it in any longer. "David, I have a lead."

His head moved in a way that was part shrug, part nod. "Go on."

"I checked the birth index for all babies born in Los Angeles County, May 12, 1946. There was one male baby born that day in Western Community Hospital. It turns out that the mother was from San Bernardino County." I stopped, unsure of how much more to say.

"She came over to LA because she was young and unmarried?"

"That's right. She was just eighteen."

He turned his face up toward the sun but didn't put his glasses back on. "It figures."

"How do you mean?"

"Well, that's where adopted babies come from, isn't it? Young, unwed mothers?"

"Do you want to know more?"

"You've done a lot of work. You did a good job."

"You only need to know if you want to."

"Okay."

"David, I'm serious. Just say the word, and we can just go home."

"We have a funeral to go to. Aunt Rachel died this morning."

"After the funeral, I mean." I held his hand. "David, you're down, aren't you?"

"I'm tired, that's all."

"What did you do all day?"

"I worked hard yesterday."

"I've never known you to take a day off. Not ever."

"So, now you know something new."

"David, we can drop this, if you want."

"No, go ahead."

"The family name is Hertel. They were truck farmers in a little town named Los Resa in the southwestern part of San Bernardino County. I was there—I even was in the house." I hesitated. "Your birth name was Theodore. Your mother's name is Angela. I met your aunt; her name is Catherine. She lives in the city of San Bernardino in an old house. You were an only child. Your father died in 1971."

"The mother?"

"Your mother, I think, is here in Los Angeles."

"You got a lot more accomplished the last two days than I did. And you had to do all the driving."

"I had some help. One of the librarians in the law library showed me some shortcuts." I let go of his hand. "I thought you'd be more . . . excited."

"I wonder why there wasn't a formal adoption."

"Maybe we can ask her."

"You did a good job, Lisa."

"That's not what I want to hear. Don't you want to meet her?"

"I don't know. What would be the point? We know who she is and who he was."

"You're an hour away from the woman who gave birth to you, and you don't want to meet her?"

"Sounds like you're the one who wants to meet her, not me."

"What was the point of doing this, except to meet her?"

"That's a good question. Myself, I never thought there was a fucking point."

I looked down at the concrete. "I'm doing it again, aren't I? Trying to run your life?"

"Uh-huh."

"Please, David, tell me when I do it. I'm sorry." I picked up his hand in both of mine. "I never want to hurt you."

"Okay," he said. "Now tell me the rest."

"I have her address, in the car."

"I mean about my background."

"Like, what?"

"Like, you told me everything except the important stuff. You didn't say a single thing that told me what they're like. I assume it's bad."

"They're the kind of family you don't meet in Philadelphia. Hardscrabble dirt farmers, not educated. Your aunt is a screaming fundamentalist. Baptist is my guess. She insisted on a prayer before she'd answer any questions."

David thought this was funny. "I guess being around her even in the womb turned me into an agnostic."

It was my chance to tell him more, and I let it pass. "Want to meet your mother? You don't have to, you know."

He sighed. "No, you're right; I should. We've come this far." He collected his book and his towel and stood up. "How far away is she?"

"Not far, maybe an hour." He started walking, but I stopped him. "David, this doesn't have to happen so fast. We could have Saxon check her out, make contact by letter, then come see her another time."

"Let's just do it."

"She's going to be surprised."

"We'll tell her we're looking for—what's the name?"

"Theodore Hertel."

"We'll just say we're looking for him; that's all."

"She may recognize you. There could be a family resemblance." He didn't look much like Catherine, except that they were both thin; but I hadn't seen pictures of either Angela or her father. I realized, six hours too late, I should have asked Catherine.

He squinted at the sun. "It's a chance we'll have to take."

An hour and a half later we were parked in a residential area on the fringes of South Central Los Angeles. Even in the sunshine, the neighborhood gave off an air of neglect, of must and dirt and uneaten food dumped into corners and alleys. Hardly anyone was on the streets, even though it was near five. I wondered where everyone was.

We studied the shabby garden apartment building across the street. The concrete walls of the building were deeply cracked; from an earthquake, I supposed. A few broken toys in the front yard were the only decorative elements. I counted half a dozen broken windowpanes, two of which hadn't even been boarded over. The end apartment on the second floor had no door, and there were soot stains around the windows.

"This is the address she gave me," I said.

He studied the apartment building and the street. "Looks like shit," he pronounced.

"Want to go back to the hotel?"

He sighed. "Let's get it over with."

"Are you sure?"

By way of an answer he got out of the car and started across the street. There was nothing I could do but lock up and follow him.

The apartment we wanted was on the first floor. He looked at the ground while we waited for someone to answer his knock; I looked straight ahead and hoped with all my might that nobody was home.

The door was opened by a stringy youth with long, dirty hair and a black T-shirt. With an effort he focused his eyes, first on David and then on me. When he opened his mouth I saw that half his teeth were missing and that the rest were crooked. The smell of marijuana and body odor wafted out of the apartment. "Yeah?"

David just looked at him, so I spoke up. "We're looking for Angela Hertel."

"Shit."

I couldn't tell if he was trying to express concern or defiance, or if that was his standard greeting. "Does she live here?" I asked.

His vacant look became a smirk. "Depends."

I was about to respond when David stepped forward, shoving him out of the way, and stepped inside. "Hey, man," he complained. "I don't need no shit from you. I—" David took a quick look around the living room and turned to him. "Where is she?"

"I don't tell—" Dave shoved him against the wall, hard. When he rebounded, David grabbed him by the chest. "Where is she?"

"In the back, man; in the back. Lemme go!"

David let him go. "So go get her."

He backed away, straightening out the wrinkles in his shirt. "Asshole!"

"And make it fast."

Everything in the living room was devoted to cigarettes, beer, or television. The floor was littered with candy bar wrappers and less identifiable rubbish. Marijuana, tobacco, and sweat filled the air. We looked around and then at each other. Neither one of us was in a hurry to talk.

An interior door opened, and a fat woman in a striped blouse waddled in. Short gray hair, badly cut, heavy-framed glasses, and too much lipstick. She stood behind the sofa and regarded us with a mixture of curiosity and distrust. "Who are you, and what you doing to my Johnny?"

"Angela Hertel?" David asked.

"Who wants to know? And what are you doing here? My—"

"My name is Dave Garrett, and this is Lisa Wilson, my assistant." He produced a business card and handed it over. "I want to ask you some questions." The words came out like clockwork, perfectly timed and dead flat.

"You harassed my Johnny. You ain't got no right—"

"Johnny was being a pain in the ass."

"This is my—"

"Sit down!"

She sat, and we sat down across from her. Johnny watched sullenly from the doorway.

"I understand you're from Los Resa originally," David said.

"Who wants to know?"

He ignored her answer. "Who's Johnny?"

He piped up from behind her. "You don't have to tell—" David stood up and pointed his finger at Johnny's chest. "One more word out of you," he said quietly, "and you won't have any teeth at all." Johnny glared at him for a moment, then retreated into the rear of the apartment. David sat down again. "Who's Johnny?" he repeated.

"My daughter's boy. He stays here sometimes. You the law?"

"Do you have a son?" David asked.

The question startled her, but she shook her head. "Just Becky, that's all."

"What year was Becky born?"

"What's it—"

"What year?"

"She was born . . . 1955."

"Why did you leave Los Resa?"

"I'm not answering no more of these questions. You can—"

David brought his fist down on the coffee table, so hard that every dish and ashtray launched its contents high into the air and landed on the carpet in a clatter. The tabletop cracked from one end to the other. Angela saw it and licked her lips. "The—"

The bedroom door opened and Johnny came out, holding a shotgun pointed at the ceiling. "You get the fuck outta here, asshole!"

David stood up, slowly. "Put it down." He didn't seem frightened, or even surprised.

Johnny took a step closer, clearing the doorway. He was about ten feet away. "I told you, get out!"

Dave stepped away from the sofa and stood facing him, his hands at his sides. I stayed in my chair. "Put it away before someone gets hurt."

Johnny took another step. "You can't talk to me and my grandma like that, you piece of shit. Get out!"

David took a step toward him, and Johnny leveled the gun at David's chest. Johnny's eyes were wide, and his hands were white on the blue gunmetal. The hand on the stock held a couple of red shotgun shells.

David took another step, and Johnny closed the action, ramming a shell into the chamber with a loud metallic *clack*. David's chest was five feet from the muzzle. Neither one of them spoke. No one breathed. My heart stopped beating.

David stepped closer, till his chest was almost touching the muzzle. "Either shoot or put it down. I'm not going to play games with you, kid."

Johnny swallowed, and the muzzle began to tremble. David shoved the barrel out of the way, stepped inside, and tore Johnny's hand away from the trigger guard. I heard a click as he put on the safety; then he wrenched the shotgun out of Johnny's hands and drove the butt into his stomach. Johnny gasped, bent over, and sat down heavily on the floor.

David worked the action, and a shell leaped out and fell on the floor. He looked at it for a moment and sat down again with the shotgun across his knees. "I asked you a question, Mrs. Hertel."

Angela looked ready to faint. Her breathing was shallow and rapid, and her skin was pale. Her fat lips hung apart wetly, her lipstick smeared. "What?"

"You had a baby in Western Community Hospital in 1946; a baby boy. His name was Theodore."

"Yessir."

"He wasn't adopted away. What happened to him?"

She looked at David, and then at the shotgun, and then at me. In the background, Johnny was gasping and trying to get his breath. "It's been—"

David leaned forward till their faces were only a few inches apart. "What happened?"

She broke down then, weeping so hard she pulled up her

feet and rolled herself into a ball on the sofa. A word came out here and there, but mostly it was just crying. David waited about thirty seconds. "What happened?" he repeated.

"You can't blame me; I was just a kid. I never had no chance, I—"

"Shut up and tell me what happened."

She mumbled a couple of words and started a new round of crying; softer this time. David didn't wait for her. "Tell me right now," he said quietly. He lifted the shotgun so that the butt pointed at her belly.

She looked up at the shotgun and froze in the middle of a sob. She swallowed hard and sat up. "I was only eighteen," she whined.

"What happened?"

"I tried to take care of him, but I couldn't. He was never right. Then my milk dried up; I guess I wasn't eatin' right. I tried to feed him grown-up food but he wouldn't eat it."

"How old was he then?"

" 'Bout ten days. I didn't know nothin' 'bout babies back then. I had no money, I was sick myself; I did the best I could for him. I really tried; honest, mister, I did. It's just that we never had a fair shake, neither of us. I was gonna take him to the county; but I couldn't make up my mind. I prayed to the Lord, but He didn't answer." She started sobbing again, and this time he let her.

"Go on," he said after a while.

"You can't blame me, I did my best. I prayed and went to bed, hoping that the Lord would guide me in His ways when I woke up. And when I woke up, He had taken him."

"Theodore was dead?"

"I don't know of what, 'xactly. I think the Lord just wanted him home. Being blind and all, he never would of had it fair. I think—the Lord answered my prayer, you know?"

"So why is there no death certificate?" When she didn't

reply, he supplied the answer on his own. "You disposed of the body. In the trash?"

"The Los Angeles River. There was a big rainstorm, flash floods. I thought it was a sign." She looked at Dave hopefully, and then looked away.

David put down the shotgun, and I followed him out the door. Behind us Angela was saying something.

We got back in the car, and I started driving. I was afraid to meet his eyes.

"There was no way you could have known," he said after a while.

"I should have come here first. Checked it out somehow. I'm sorry I put you through this."

"Lots of cases have false leads."

"I could have avoided this."

"Maybe there was no other way to get the story out of her. The way it happened might be all for the best."

"I should have tried, David; and I'm sorry. You were right. There's a lot to know in this business."

"So you'll learn."

"I'm glad she's not your mother." And I was glad I never told him about Theodore's father.

"My real one could be worse."

"No, she couldn't."

"How about . . . a syphilitic Mexican street whore?"

"Why do you say things like that?"

"You don't think it might not be true? You don't know. Neither do I."

"Want to know what I'm thinking about?" I asked.

"I guess I'm going to know," he said.

"What you did back there."

"Afraid the Hertels are going to take us off their Christmas list?"

"David, you scared me to death."

"I wanted to get to the bottom of it. I didn't want to spend any more time there than I had to."

"You almost didn't spend any more time anywhere."

"It was a calculated risk, and it worked."

"So's Russian roulette. What made you take a chance like that?" He laughed; I was glad to hear it, but the sound startled me. "What are you laughing for?"

"Because when you ask a question in that tone of voice, it's not really a question. You think I was trying to kill myself."

"The thought crossed my mind."

"I was bluffing."

"I think it's now that you're bluffing."

"All's well that ends well."

"David, I don't know how I could live if something happened to you because of all this."

We rode in silence for a while. For no reason, he said, "There's something else."

"Go ahead."

"I talked to a rabbi."

"Oh?"

"If my birth mother isn't some relative, the odds are high she's not Jewish. So that means I'm not Jewish. If I wasn't baptized or confirmed, that means I'm not anything at all."

"Of course you're Jewish; you were raised that way, and you had a bar mitzvah; you told me."

"If I wasn't born Jewish, I shouldn't have been bar mitzvahed. You either have to be born of a Jewish mother or adopted officially."

"You've always told me being Jewish isn't a race, it's a religion."

"It's how it's done. I didn't set the rules."

"David, you scare me when you sound so uninvolved."

"It's just one more of the practical jokes that's been played on me. My sense of humor is getting thin."

He didn't say anything for several blocks. "You know what I was thinking about this afternoon?" he asked. "Joining the marines again."

I thought about my answer. "Because when you were in, you felt like you belonged."

"It sounds stupid when you say it out loud."

"It's the deepest feelings that sound stupidest of all."

"I'm glad she's not my mother, even if my real mother is worse."

I had to giggle despite myself. "And I'm glad he's not your nephew."

" 'A Visit from My Uncle Dave.' A short story complete on this page."

" 'How to Win Friends and Influence People with a Shotgun.' "

It was several blocks before David broke the silence. "That was the only lead, huh?"

"That was the only baby born in that hospital that day."

"So I was born in another hospital. Or on another day. Or at home. Or they destroyed the original birth certificate before it could be filed."

"You know, May 12 in 1946 fell on Mother's Day. Barbara could have picked it because of that."

"It crossed my mind, but it sounded too crazy."

We rode in companionable silence back to the hotel. With every block I allowed myself to feel a little better. By the time we were home I began to entertain the idea that my mistakes hadn't caused any permanent damage. I was afraid to really believe it, but even being able to think about the possibility was a comfort.

We locked up the car and went into the lobby. "Did you have any lunch, David?"

He thought about it. "A pastrami sandwich. And a pickle."

"Pastrami? It's a heart attack on a plate."

"It's not just for breakfast anymore."

I led him to the hotel restaurant. "It's been a long day. We're going to have a drink and a good, solid dinner."

"Maybe a sandwich. I don't know if I'm that hungry."

"Humor me."

David didn't do justice to his dinner, though he more than held up his share of the drinking. I didn't care; I'd pushed enough for one day. He was alive, and he didn't hold the Hertel disaster against me. Nothing else was important.

"It looks like your birth records search is at a dead end," he said. "What's your plan?"

"I don't have one. Without some kind of a lead—a date, a hospital—there's no way to know what to look for."

"When I struck out on my end, I started hoping that the records might help. At least give us a start."

"We're stuck."

He sighed. "You asked me once how it felt to be a blank slate," he said. "I'm feeling blank as blank can be right now. It feels like . . . outside. Of everything, I don't belong to anyone. No religion, no family, not even a name. Just me, alone, no trimmings."

"David, listen to me. It doesn't matter who your parents are. It doesn't matter. It doesn't matter if we ever find out anything or not. Who your parents are is like how much money they left you. It doesn't matter how much you get—it's what you do with it, because that shows what kind of a person you are."

"I feel like my life's been . . . a joke. I spent it thinking I was a good Jewish boy, trying to please my parents, being part of something—that I wasn't. I didn't belong with them. Like one of those experiments where they get newly hatched geese to follow a dog or a vacuum cleaner. It's just that stupid."

"David, remember the day you told me I wasn't different, I was special? Well, so are you. I've never met anyone who was more their own person."

I watched him study his face in his water glass.

"Lisa?"

"Yes?"

"What if . . . I'm Hispanic?"

"So?"

"So what do you mean, 'So?' "

"As in, 'So what?' As long as I've known you I've been hearing about toleration and equality and not being prejudiced. Did you mean all that?"

"It's one thing to say that you don't judge people because they're Hispanic; it's another to think you're one of them."

"Is it?" I brushed the hair away from my face.

He studied his face some more. "I don't see any Indian, but that doesn't mean anything, does it? I could be all Spanish Mexican."

"You could apply for a loan for a minority-owned business. Heck, think of all the affirmative action programs you missed out on."

"Lisa, this is important."

"You could put in for the Taco Bell franchise for West Philadelphia."

"Lisa!"

"I'm giving it every bit of importance it should have."

"You're being goddam stupid."

I waited, quietly, and watched.

"You're doing this deliberately," he said at last. "You want me to see"—he struggled for the words—"to see that what I'm going through—playing with my reflection, it's— it's a waste of time. It doesn't matter. I can't change my genes." He paused. "It's what you did for years, looking at a man in the mirror and trying to see a woman."

"And for a long time after, I'd look at the woman and try to see the man."

"You don't anymore."

"There's nothing to see. The mirror has nothing to tell me. Or you."

"When did you stop looking in the mirror?"

"A while ago." When I met you, I thought to myself.

"Lisa, I'm sorry I said you were stupid. I couldn't have been more wrong."

"It's okay."

"You wanted me to figure it out on my own."

"And you did."

For the first time since I'd known him, David was feeling his liquor. I didn't have to help him back to his room; but I was careful to walk slowly and keep an eye on him. He mumbled good night and closed his bedroom door.

There was no sleep for me.

18

David

Friday, 1:00 A.M.

I WOKE UP, and for a moment I was disoriented. My bedroom was completely dark, and the central room insulated it from hallway noise. I had no idea where I was. Then I heard the distant rumble of traffic and the hum of the air conditioner. I lay on my back, thinking about Angela and Johnny. I wondered what sense they'd made of my visit. Or of their own lives. And I thought about Theodore, the kid born with three strikes against him. He was born the same time as me, give or take a few days; he had every bit as much or as little right to be like me, eating steaks and drinking Scotch and slowly getting old and fat, instead of having his bones picked over by sewer rats in some drainage culvert. Why him and not me?

I turned it over in my mind for a while until I began to feel sleepy again. I rolled onto my side and put my hand next to my face on the pillow. I touched something smooth and warm that moved under my fingers. Hair. Long hair, flowing all over the pillow. Then I touched skin and smelled perfume.

"Hello," Lisa whispered.

"Oh."

"I didn't think you would ever wake up."

"How long have you been here?"

"Since right after you first went to sleep. I didn't have the nerve to come in when you were awake."

"I'm a little surprised. No, I'm a lot surprised."

She brushed my hand with her lips. "I never was very good at letting people know how I feel. Not ever. You least of all."

"I'm very glad you're here."

"I love you, David."

"I wasn't expecting that, either."

"I love you," she repeated. "And I'm an idiot. Because everything I've done has turned out backward. The closer I try to get, the more you push away."

"I couldn't figure out why this business with my parents was so important to you, and it was making me mad. I didn't trust you, I guess."

"I couldn't go on any longer without telling you."

My hand slid down her shoulder, over her breast, and paused on her belly. With one finger I traced patterns in and around her navel. "It's going to be a big change," I said.

She buried her face in my chest, but her words came through. "Up to now it's been safe."

"It's been safe 'cause we've been hiding from each other. Employer and employee."

"You were right about Mexico," she said.

"I wish you'd talked to me."

"It wouldn't have mattered. I wasn't ready."

"And you were right about something," I said. "About looking for my parents. I can't pretend it's not important."

"David?"

"Uh-huh?"

"Let's not talk anymore. I'm going to lose my nerve."

I touched her knee and slowly let my hand inch upward. I hadn't gone far when I felt a slick wetness on the inside of her thigh. "How long have you been—like this?"

"What time is it?"

I looked at the bedside clock. "A little after one."

"Mmm. About three months."

There was nothing to do but laugh at my own foolishness. I kissed her slowly on each eye and then started kissing everything else.

When I woke up it was morning. I wasn't sure exactly what time because the alarm clock had been displaced sometime during the night. The sheets were a tangled mess. Lisa and I were in each other's arms. She was still sleeping, her lips apart, snoring slightly. She was dreaming, twitching and making little noises. She sounded like she was enjoying herself, so I let her sleep. After a while I joined her. I had no idea exactly what the day would bring, but I was willing to trust that it would be good.

19

Lisa

Friday, 7:00 A.M.

I'D BEEN AWAKE almost till dawn, watching David sleep.
I was terrified that if I slept, it all would be snatched away. I
knew I didn't deserve it, not really. I'd made a horrible mistake
in Mexico, and the torture of working with David these last few
months and not being able to touch him wasn't nearly penance
enough for my stupidity. Stupid then and stupid right up to the
moment Ralph, God love him, set me straight. Just tell him, he'd
said. It was so simple it made me think that just maybe there
was grace in the world, after all. There was no other explanation.
I didn't deserve him, didn't deserve a second chance, and yet
here we were, sleeping side by side with the smell of him all
around me.

Anyone else would have been content to feel warm and
sleepy and well fucked. I was too busy worrying about the morning, how I would act, how he would act, whether he'd want me
again or if he wanted to be left alone. How was he going to
introduce me—as employee or friend or girlfriend? How would

we would handle the office? Would he treat me more like an equal or stop taking me seriously, or wouldn't it make any difference? Was it going to be all business nine to five? Was he seeing anybody else?

Finally, just as it was starting to get light, even I couldn't worry anymore, and I fell asleep.

When I opened my eyes, it was fully light. David and I were still in each other's arms. "Hello," I whispered. "How do you feel?"

"Like I've been run over by a truck," he said.

"That was wonderful."

"I missed you so much," he said.

I kissed him. "I'm glad."

Everything was different in the daylight; all the details were there, the scars on my hand and the tiny ingrown hair on the tip of his ear and the dark bite marks on my nipples. No possibility that this was a mistake or a dream.

"I really am here," I said. "It really happened."

"It's still happening. What if I made us some breakfast?" he asked.

"I've got a better idea," I said. "How if we fuck and then I make breakfast?"

Getting out of bed afterward was nearly impossible. Partly it was my fear that if I left him alone for even a second the spell would be broken; and partly it was David. Not that he did anything to keep me in bed. I think he was as hungry as I was. But his body was so full of interesting little places I liked to touch, the flat spot in the middle of his chest covered with hair, the ticklish area in the small of his back just above the crack of his ass, the mole on his left shoulder. I could have gone exploring all day and still left some of the best spots for later.

David made himself presentable enough to make a trip across the street to a convenience store while I padded around the suite's kitchen in his bathrobe, dreamily making an inventory of the pots and pans and dishes that came with the suite. The kitchen was equipped for making snacks or warming leftovers, not for real cooking. Just one small frying pan, one decent cutting knife, and not a spatula or even a kitchen spoon in sight.

David came back with the makings of a rough and ready breakfast—coffee, Spam, potatoes, cooking oil, and eggs—and I set to work, starting with a pot of coffee. I cubed the can of Spam and the potatoes, threw them into the frying pan with some oil, and threw in a good measure of the pepper and powdered garlic I found on the shelf. Each time I bent over to search a cabinet, a little of David would trickle down my leg, and I thought I was in heaven already. As the food smells filled the room, I finally began to relax. I was cooking for us, in our kitchen, in his bathrobe. We had Spam. Life was just about perfect.

I thought about David's apartment in Rosemont. It wasn't anything special, but it was roomy enough, and if we got rid of the ugly dining room table and changed the curtains . . . I forced myself to stop and pour myself some more coffee. We were here today, and the only thing certain to screw up tomorrow was to worry about it too much.

David came to the table straight from the shower, his hair still wet, with a towel around his middle and a T-shirt. The table was set with the most mismatched set of cups, dishes, and silverware I'd seen since college, and he didn't notice.

He helped me fill the plates and carry them to the table. When I sat down he saw me wince. "Sore?" he asked.

"I'll sit on some ice for a few minutes, when you're ready again."

"You don't have to do that."

"I wouldn't dream of saying no, David."

"All right."

"Ever."

He looked at me and gave my hand a squeeze. "Okay, then."

He chewed a mouthful of food and nodded his approval. "Things seem suddenly very simple."

"I made them complicated," I said. "Picking that fight in Mexico. I was afraid of getting too involved."

"No one's really afraid of that."

"Okay, so I was afraid of getting dumped after I *was* involved."

"What made you think I was going to dump you?"

"I have a news flash for you, David. I don't have the most self-confidence in the world."

"I don't know why," he said. "You're strong, and you're smart, and you're hell in bed. And I've missed you very, very much."

"When we were first together, I used to think, Philadelphia's a big city; how long is he going to hang around at the freak show?"

"I hope you're over that."

"I'm never going to get over it. All I can do is try to act as if I were over it."

"You're a woman now. What you were before doesn't matter. I was a little boy once. And before that, a baby. So what?"

"A month ago you said I shouldn't kid myself; that I shouldn't try to pretend I wasn't different."

"You're not different. You're special."

My breath caught in my throat. What could I have ever done to deserve him?

He touched the side of my face. "Unless you think of something really important, let's not talk about the past anymore. It doesn't matter to me at all, I've told you that every way I know how already. I don't think I'll be able to think of any more ways."

"I'm going to need a little time to believe in myself."

"You've got it."

I could feel my voice going. "Right now, I want you so badly I can't think straight."

"You weren't this way in January, and you hadn't been with anybody for years before that."

"Now I love you. Then it was just friction."

He checked his watch. "I've never gone to a funeral in a better mood."

"How much time till we have to leave?"

"Not enough."

"Damn."

20

David

Friday, Noon

THE MEMORIAL SERVICE, such as it was, took place in a grimy funeral home in West Hollywood with worn carpeting and a public address system that crackled. The crowd was small, no more than thirty. Lisa and I filed by the open casket. I'd only been to a couple open-casket funerals in my life—Conservative Jews have closed caskets, and the Orthodox don't even embalm.

I'd never met Aunt Rachel, so I couldn't judge the mortician's skill. She had pale skin, almost unlined despite her age. She was bigger than my mother, with a broad forehead, full cheekbones, and a straight nose. Her arms were hidden in a long-sleeved dress, but her hands were thin. If they'd curled from years of disuse, the skin gave no sign.

We sat on folding metal chairs and stared at the casket as if we expected something to happen. I saw Art across the aisle, and we nodded at each other. A few other cousins and second cousins were there, all with families. My uncle Ed had canceled at the last minute; heart trouble, apparently. A couple of very old ladies, too, were sitting by themselves. A large man in a bushy beard, casually dressed even by California standards, sat by himself in the rear row. We made contact, and he held my eyes until I looked away. I wondered what was going on behind his beard.

The appointed time for the service came and went; I suppose because the funeral director was hoping for a few latecomers to boost attendance.

I leaned over and whispered to Lisa, "I wonder if she knew anything, that time was passing."

"I remember things that happened when I was having surgery. The music the surgeon played. Somebody dropped something, and it clattered on the floor."

"When I was hit, in the war, I was out, but I can remember the medics talking about me."

She took my hand. "It's not scary. You're not anxious, not trying to do anything. You're just aware of sounds."

"I hope that's all it was."

She held my hand a little tighter.

The service was conducted by a rabbi young enough to be my son; evidently a young and hungry kid who did the circuit of funeral homes. He wore a dark suit with a trim, contemporary cut and black shoes with a gloss polish. I looked around; Art was in a sports coat, and the rest of the men were in shirtsleeves or light sweaters. Besides the rabbi, I was the only one in a suit and tie.

His performance was completely canned, of course; he hadn't known Aunt Rachel, and there was no one to tell him what she'd been like. But even though it was impersonal, it was recognizably Jewish—he even led the congregation in the Kaddish. I made a point of shaking his hand afterward and telling him he'd done a good job. He thanked me and discreetly passed me his business card.

I'd been to dozens of receptions after Jewish funerals in Chicago and on the East Coast. They were always at someone's home; the liquor flowed freely, and the tables groaned under the weight of delicatessen trays piled to overflowing with meats, rolls, and sweets. Always there were plates of hard-boiled eggs, cut lengthwise, to remind the mourners of the circularity of life. They were crowded, hot, noisy affairs, everyone in the family using the chance to catch up on gossip, brag or complain about their lives, gorge themselves, and get drunk. Usually there was someone from United Jewish Appeal, making a low-key but relentless pitch for more trees for Israel. The UJA knew to steer clear of me. At my aunt Sadie's funeral, right after the invasion of Lebanon, I drank too much Jack Daniel's and picked a fight about if all our money went for trees, where did all those tanks come from?

The reception was Californian; sleek, airy, and sterile. It took place in a modern reception hall, the kind I normally associate with weddings, big enough to hold five hundred comfortably. About twenty people were there, not even enough to stop the room from echoing to their footsteps. The sunlight flooded through the floor-to-ceiling windows, and I wished I'd brought along my sunglasses. Long tables were draped in white cloth, with a smattering of finger sandwiches. A cash bar in the corner. I steered Lisa in that direction.

The bar mostly served various types of fancy water, which was fine with Lisa. With a little prodding the bartender reluctantly produced bourbon for me. I ignored his glum disapproval and threw a five on the bar.

Lisa and I wandered down the tables of food; crackers, vegetables, cheese—and roast beef. Milk and meat together. What would my grandparents have thought?

A gruff male voice spoke from behind me. "You look like you're in culture shock. I'm a physician; I can help."

I turned around, and it was the man from the back row of the funeral—heavyset, at least seventy, with shoulder-length gray hair, wearing jeans and a dark sweater that did nothing to disguise his paunch. Thick wire-rimmed glasses and a smattering of Indian jewelry at his wrists and earlobes. His face was heavily scarred, puckered and smoothed in ways nature never intended. His nose was squat and angled to one side. All of the skin, except where it drew together, was shiny. Burns, very old. His beard was thick and curly and still held some streaks of black. Good for him he could raise such a thick beard; what was underneath probably wasn't pretty. "Dave Garrett." I stuck out my hand.

He gave me a strong grip from a callused hand. "Pleased to meet you, David. The treatment for culture shock is the same as for any other shock. Sit down, loosen your clothing— like that goddam tie, for instance—and drink plenty of liquids. What you've got there is a good start."

"I'd like you to meet Lisa Wilson, my assistant. Lisa, this is—" He moved forward, more quickly than I would have expected for a man his size and age, and shook Lisa's hand while he murmured a greeting. But he didn't look in her eyes; he started at her feet and moved slowly up her body all the way to the top of her head. It wasn't flirtatious or sexual; he kept his distance and just observed. She waited uncomfortably till he was done and met her eyes at last.

"I didn't catch your name," I said.

He shrugged. "You easterners, always caught up on protocol. Let's have a seat." We sat in plastic chairs that managed to be both flimsy and uncomfortable at the same time. Lisa tugged her skirt down and looked even more uncomfortable than the chair warranted. He leaned closer to me and put his elbows on his knees. "I'm Joel. You don't care much for LA, do you?"

"It's not my kind of place, but I'm trying to fit in."

"Is that why you have on the only suit and tie? Sure you're not being hostile?"

"And what if I am?"

"Not that you should give a shit, but I like you better for it."

I was about to reply when Lisa cut me off. "How do you happen to be here, Joel?"

He started up a broad smile that trailed off into something halfway sad. When he spoke his voice was flat. "I knew Rachel, before the coma."

She nodded sympathetically. "So why come now? All these years later?"

"Is that important?"

She pasted on a smile and brushed back her hair from her ear, a sure sign she was nervous. "I don't know yet," she said.

"Have I done something to upset you?" His tone was curious, not apologetic.

"Like not telling us who you are, and staring at me like that?"

He smiled again. "You've been in therapy, haven't you?"

Lisa took a sip of her water and didn't answer. When Joel realized the silence had gone on too long, he turned to me. "I hear you're her nephew, Barbara's son. You've come a long way."

"My mother couldn't come herself. She's on oxygen."

"COPD?"

"Excuse me?"

"I'm sorry," he said, and he really looked it. "I hate when people use jargon at me. It's very distancing. Chronic obstructive pulmonary disease."

"Emphysema is what they've always called it."

"Does she still smoke?"

"Only when she thinks I'm not going to catch her. She's cut way back."

He opened his mouth, but Lisa headed off his next question. "You seem to know a lot about the family," she said.

"I knew Barbara, too, back then."

Lisa leaned back in her chair, and a self-satisfied smile blossomed. "At least you thought you did."

"Good," he nodded. "Very good."

"There's only one psychiatrist named Joel of your age who'd have any business here, Dr. Weissberg."

He made a small, dismissive gesture. "I consider myself a radical therapist." He gestured at his clothes and beard. "As you can see. How long were you in therapy, Lisa?"

"Not long at all."

"So you come by your suspicions naturally?"

"Well, I was right to be suspicious, wasn't I?"

He made a shrug that suggested she was dodging his question. "I have a theory about that, I'll bore you with it later if you don't stop me first. I wanted to see David for myself. And I'll save you some time. I know you're here to look for your birth parents."

"Art told you," I said.

"I called him after I got your message. He was careful not to say what you were doing out here, or why you wanted to see me, but it wasn't hard to figure it out."

"Because you know that there's something to find."

"As far as whether she's your birth mother, I don't know, one way or the other." He paused. "She told you she was, didn't she, when you talked to her? How does that make you feel?"

"Like my worst fears are confirmed."

He shook his head. "That's not what I asked you."

"I feel—I don't know, sad. If you're right, she could have told me the truth."

"Sad, not angry?"

"There's nothing to be angry about."

He nodded slightly. "Are you sleeping well?"

"You know how travel throws you off."

"Your appetite good?"

"I don't like restaurant food much. Why do you want to know?"

"We can talk about that in a minute, David."

"You're not my father, are you?"

"I like a man who cuts through crap. No, I'm not. And I don't know who is, either."

Lisa asked, "So why are you so interested?"

"You *are* the suspicious one, aren't you?"

"It's my job."

"Or did you choose your line of work because you find it hard to trust people?"

She held his eyes. "An investigator shouldn't trust people too much."

"That's the second time you've evaded a question, but that's okay. It helps prove my theory, in a minor way."

"I'll bite," she said.

"An interesting choice of words, Lisa. Do you consider yourself an oral person?"

She gave him a thin smile. "What would you say, Doctor?"

"Was your therapist a Freudian?"

"I don't know his training—"

"So it wasn't a personal selection—you would know his background, that would have been your reason for selecting him; you were in a clinic, a hospital setting"—Lisa nodded slightly, but Joel didn't even slow down—"and you didn't stay with the program, which shows you have good sense; at least tell me you weren't exposed to one of those goddam Rogerians whose idea of therapy is to ask you how you feel about everything."

"It wasn't—"

"Good. So since you asked, let me tell you my theory."

Neither one of us said a word.

"Psychiatry got it wrong fifty years ago. 'Normality,' being 'well adjusted,' is a delusion. Freud understood that, but no one after him did. We're all the tiniest bit psychopathologic; the goal of therapy ought to be to help people use their neuroses constructively. Should the goal of psychotherapy be to produce patients who think that the business of life is to adjust themselves to the world? Old age should rage 'gainst close of day. And youth should kick some ass while there's time. Your fears and obsessions aren't anything to be ashamed of, or discarded. They're your best tools for making your life rewarding and interesting. Tell me, where does art come from?"

"Well, that's—"

"Fear of death, that's right! And where would we be if artists stopped worrying about their own mortality? Who would bother to create? And it's not just artists—it's all of us. Like me, for example—I've got a moderate-to-advanced case of histrionic personality disorder. Fortunately for me, I'm in a job that lets me give advice and feel self-important all day. And—"

"You have us in mind, not yourself," Lisa said.

"Damn, but it's good to meet somebody whose brains haven't been baked away by the sun. You're slightly paranoid, and David has depressive tendencies. Among other things, he's empathetic, and you're tough-minded. That makes you a good match."

"You seem to know a lot about us."

"Eric Berne, may he rest in peace, said that after a lifetime of experience, a thoroughly trained psychiatrist might be able to achieve the kind of insight into others that any six-year-old has intuitively." He shrugged. "I do my best."

She smiled slightly. "Maybe you wouldn't think I was all that distrustful if you knew more about me."

"I didn't say your suspicions and distrust were inappropriate; just that they were there. But you asked me a question—why did I come here? Partly nostalgia. I can feel self-pity as much as anyone else; the only difference is that I recognize it and try not to act on it inappropriately. Barbara is lost to me; Rachel was my last link to a happy time in my life. I was very happy, at times, with Barbara. The early years especially."

Lisa seemed lost within her own thoughts. "Did you know Rachel well?" I asked.

"She was a hard person not to know well, if you knew her at all. She was . . ." For the first time, he had to search for a word. "Vivid. Everything she did, she did full tilt. When she fell in love, she fell hard; when she decided to believe in a cause, she believed wholeheartedly. And very bright, and full of energy. Actually, thinking about Rachel was the beginning of the development of my view of psychology. Rachel was bipolar—what they used to call manic-depressive. But mild, not an out-of-control clinical case. When she was manic she could work for days at a time, compose poetry, stuff envelopes for Roosevelt's re-election campaign, study for school, and never need sleep. She never had violent episodes when she was manic. And although I certainly can't speak from personal experience, there's a bit of folk wisdom in the psychiatric community that there's nothing in the world like schtupping a bipolar in a manic phase." He shrugged. "And her depressions—achh, not so bad. Today, she'd get a little Prozac to help her over the rough spots, but she was never suicidal."

Maybe it was Lisa's presence, but I wasn't sure I wanted to trust him. "I never knew anything about her," I said.

"It's a sad story, but a familiar one. Rigid, perfectionist first-generation immigrant parents, child exposed to the values of a new country, lots of opportunity for conflict even if the child is completely centered. Add a touch of bipolar—"

I nodded. I knew this part. "So what happened at the end? The coma?"

"It was after Barbara and I were divorced. I only know what the treating psychiatrist told me. Sol Birnbaum; very distinguished man. She was going through a program of electroconvulsive therapy—"

"You mean, shocks?"

He looked uncomfortable. "The profession prefers 'electroconvulsive.' The patient doesn't get a shock like you would from a live wire. The doctor gives a muscle relaxer so that when the electrodes are applied the patient doesn't tense and break bones. Back then they used curare, with Prostigmin as the antidote. In the fifties they switched over to succinylcholine as the relaxer. After the shock and the convulsions they administer an antidote to the muscle relaxer. Rachel didn't respond to the antidote. Her breathing was interrupted long enough to cause brain damage."

"She was how old then?"

He thought. "Around twenty. She got the best care afterward, but there was nothing do be done. After a while they just put her in a convalescent home. A very good one—" He laughed without humor. "She lived nearly a normal life span, for all the good it did her."

"This therapy sounds dangerous."

"Actually, no." He looked around the room. "This is a peculiar occasion to say this, but it's actually very safe. The most common complication, which is still pretty rare, is a broken femur or humerus resulting from insufficient muscle relaxer."

"Do you do this stuff?"

"Years ago. In the sixties I stopped. It produced results, especially in bipolar cases. Even helped some schizophrenics when nothing else did. I stopped because no one understood *why* it worked. No one does, even now. It's like fiddling with controls on a machine when you're not sure what they do."

"Could Rachel have known anything about Barbara and me?"

"I doubt it. She was institutionalized a lot in the last three years before the coma. When were you born?"

"As far as I know, May of 1946."

"May of '46 . . . I got back from the war just before Christmas of '43, Barb and I divorced a year later, early '45, and she moved away. Rachel was hospitalized then. I had a little contact with the family after that, not with Barb's parents, but with her brothers and sisters. We got along fine. I was just back from my honeymoon with Sarah when I got the news about Rachel. So that would have been November of '45."

Lisa was way ahead of me. "Could Rachel be David's mother?"

He wasn't surprised by the question. "Nowadays, with all the pressure to release patients, the ones on the inside are too out of it to function sexually, for the most part. In the bad old days, with a lot of not too abnormal people locked up, more schtupping went on than anyone wants to admit—"

"Like with the manic-depressives?" she asked.

"Right. But a child?" He shook his head decisively. "Every clinic had a doctor on retainer, discreetly, for abortions. It was hushed up tight as a drum, especially if the family was paying privately for treatment. No, if she'd become pregnant in the institution, they would have dealt with it STAT to keep the family from finding out. Besides, whatever else you can say about Rachel's father, he always insisted on the best—she always had a private room, and she had very little contact with the other patients."

"Another theory shot to hell," I said. "Were you in contact with Barbara in early '46?"

"Not at all. I didn't even know she was back in town."

Lisa frowned. "I thought you said you stayed in touch with the family after the divorce."

"Barb's siblings, yes; but not her or her folks. Every couple of months I'd have dinner with one of her brothers. After I got married again, it gradually trailed off. But I don't recall any of them mentioning that she was in LA for months. I would have remembered—my second wife was very jealous." He corrected himself. "Insecure."

"About you and Barbara?" Lisa asked.

"About everything."

Lisa drummed the arm of her chair restlessly. "We know Barbara was here, probably staying with her parents. But the rest of the family didn't know she was here, or was afraid to say anything."

"If you accept the idea that she was trying to fool her husband, it all makes sense," he said. "If no one sees her, no one can deny that she was pregnant."

"Yeah," I said heavily.

Joel's manner turned quiet. "David? I know this must be hard for you."

"It's about what she did, not me."

"But it happened to you."

"That's like saying that basketball is about the ball."

He didn't smile. He took my hands in his. "Pay attention to me, David."

I was surprised to find him holding my hands; too surprised to pull away. "Okay."

"You don't have to feel this way," he said slowly.

"I think I do. What am I supposed to feel?"

"You should be upset; anyone would be. But you're depressed—"

"I'm not depressed."

"You're not sleeping, you don't concentrate, you don't eat, you're drinking too much, you don't have any energy; that's what depression is."

"Life's depressing."

"David, depression is anger turned inside. If you turn it out, you can get rid of it."

"There's nothing to be angry about."

"The woman who gave birth to you abandoned you. She was all you had in the world, and she walked away. You have to be angry."

"There's no reason to be angry. It wasn't anything personal. She did what she had to do."

He sighed. "Pretend you're angry."

"What?"

"Just humor me, okay? Pretend."

"Who am I supposed to be mad at?"

"Both of them; Barbara and your birth mother. Act as if you were mad."

"How do I act? Come on, this is silly." I started to get up, but he held my hands tightly. I sat down again.

"Close your eyes and pretend you're mad. Forget I'm here, but think about being mad and tell me why you're mad."

I shut my eyes. "What is this going to prove?"

"Just do it. Do it for me, please." He squeezed my hand.

"All right; I'll pretend I'm an irrational, selfish asshole. What would I say? I'd say, Damn it, Mom, I never did anything to you, and look what you did to me. Other kids got to grow up with their moms and dads, and you took that away from me. How's that?"

"Keep going."

"I'd say, I don't care if you had a hundred good reasons or just one bad one—I'm the one it happened to. Your reasons matter to you, but they don't to me. All I know is that I hurt."

"More."

"I have to wake up every day now and think about how you didn't love me enough to keep me, that you didn't give a shit about me when I needed you most."

"Keep going."

"Every other kid knows where he belongs and who's going to take care of him, but you ran off and left me alone. Why? Wasn't I good enough for you? Why didn't you love me? Why did you hate me so much that you threw me away?"

"Now Barbara."

"I'm mad. You cheated me out of my real mother, and you cheated me out of the truth my whole life. You said I was your child and that you loved me. I know you lied about the one, and how can I trust you that you're not lying about the other? You lied to everybody, including my father. You played us both for suckers, and neither one of us deserved it. You didn't give a shit about me—I was your insurance policy against Dad kicking you out. I wonder how many times you've laughed at both of us behind our backs."

"Again."

"I can't trust anything you tell me, you liar. I can't trust it when you tell me you love me. It's all a game to you, and you can always win because you make up the rules and no one else even knows there's a game."

"Hold onto that feeling. It's okay to feel rage. You've been betrayed. Let it come."

I thought about my words; no, I felt them. I felt my anger swelling up, I felt dizzy, even though I was sitting down. I wanted to hit, to strike out, to kick, to hurt . . . I don't know who. I wanted to scream. It boiled through me like a hot flood, sweeping away the walls and dams I'd built around how I thought about my mother. I realized how locked up, paralyzed, I'd been; and with the realization came release. The walls fell down. The darkness I hadn't even admitted was there dispersed and blew away. My breathing slowed, and I waited patiently.

"How do you feel now?"

I was at a loss for words. "Better than I've felt since this all started."

"Open your eyes."

I did.

"Are you all right?"

"I feel like a tornado's gone through my head."

"You had a lot bottled up."

"Thanks, Joel."

"You're welcome," he said, and let go of my hands.

I looked around. "I expected, somehow, the room would look different."

"Tired?"

"The opposite. I feel energized." I swallowed. "But yeah; tired, too."

"The Greeks called it catharsis. They understood the passions. Even the passion that leads to suicide, or murder."

"Do you think I was suicidal?"

"No, but you're prone to suicidal thoughts, and that's bad enough. It's wasted energy."

I took a breath. "I feel like I could climb a mountain, and I feel like I just did, all at the same time. It's—I'm up, and I'm exhausted."

"It takes a while to get your balance. You were using up a lot of effort keeping it all down."

"I guess so."

"Just keep in mind, David; you're very introspective, you're prone to intellectualizing, internalizing your feelings. This little exercise can help. Any time you need it, you can do it by yourself."

"Thanks, Joel. I'm in your debt."

He shrugged. "What we just did wasn't psychotherapy, David. If it was, it would have taken years and cost a lot of money. Its just a little mental thing you can do."

He looked at Lisa. "The two of you have a lot to look forward to together."

She stiffened. "What makes you think that?"

"Because a bright six-year-old could see it. Like I said before, you're a couple of neurotics, but you're well-matched ones. Let your neuroses work for you."

Lisa was ready to argue, but I took her hand and squeezed it. "Joel, I don't know how to thank you."

"Not to worry. And now, you should get to see the rest of the family. If you're all right, I have to go now." He stood up, and we shook hands. He leaned close to Lisa, whispered something in her ear, and went on his way. I watched him cross the room and go through the glass doors into the sunlight.

Lisa was white under her tan. Then she started to smile. Then she laughed, so hard that other people began to notice.

Finally she took my arm, and drew me into the chair next to her. Tears of laughter were running down her cheeks.

"What was that all about?" I asked.

"I thought I was so smart—you know what he just told me?"

"No."

She looked down at the red nail polish on her fingernails and began to giggle. "He said, he had a tip from one of his patients. Light pink or clear polish doesn't draw attention to the hands."

I put my hand around the back of her neck and kissed her. "You okay?"

"I'm fine."

"Really?"

She kissed me back convincingly. "Really."

"Let's make the rounds of the old ladies."

"Deal."

21

Lisa

Friday, 7:00 P.M.

DAVID TALKED TO every person in the hall, except for a few teenage second cousins who had sneaked out early to go to a video arcade across the street. I couldn't tell if he was being the dutiful son or the relentless investigator; I hoped for the former, because he got nowhere as the latter. Everyone clucked sympathetically about Barbara's health and about Aunt Rachel, but not a single new fact emerged.

David introduced me all around as his girlfriend. There were many noises of surprise and approval, and more than one tactless question about a wedding date. One elderly woman asked if I kept kosher, and I managed to put a hint of regret in my voice when I answered no.

Art was standing near the exit when he caught David's eye. "Got to run," he said. "I wanted to be sure we got to talk before you left."

"It was kind of a small funeral."

Art shrugged. "The family was never big, and it's been a

long time. Not many of that generation left." He put his hand on David's shoulder. "All the more important that you came."

"At least I accomplished that."

"That doesn't sound good."

"My search—I'm striking out, Art. I can't get a lead. And Lisa spent three days running down the birth records; there's nothing on paper, either."

Art looked at me. "If you're not going to be looking any more, would you have time for dinner tomorrow night?"

I smiled and hooked my arm around David's.

"Oh," he said. "Jeez—I—didn't—"

"It's okay. It's a very recent development," David said.

Art looked from one of us to the other. "Well, *mazel tov* to the both of you."

"Thanks."

Art looked anxious to change the subject, and I didn't blame him. "So it looks like Aunt Barbara covered her tracks pretty well," he said.

"I've got one witness who has a general impression she wasn't pregnant," David said. "But that's really all I've got."

"I wish I had a suggestion."

"I've been asking around, I might as well ask you. Any idea who the family doctor was back then?"

"I can sort of remember somebody, thin and dark. But the name? My parents moved out to the Valley when I was six, and they got a new doctor."

"One more blank."

"You know who would know, though, is Joel."

"I forgot to ask him."

"And he didn't volunteer it," I added.

"So?" David asked.

"So, maybe he didn't want you to know."

"We were busy talking about other things."

"Not all the time, David."

"No, not all the time." He put his hand on the one I had hooked to his arm.

Art was unavailable for dinner, which disappointed Dave but was fine with me. He needed rest more than he was willing to admit. When we said our good-byes, Art gave me a peck on the cheek. I took David back to the hotel in the afternoon, and we sat by the pool. Or rather, I worried about The Relationship, while he dozed in the sun.

It was after five when I nudged him gently awake with my foot. He stretched and gave me a lazy smile from behind his sunglasses. For the first time since I'd started this mess, he looked rested.

When I toweled off after my shower, I picked up his shirt from the floor. "Okay if I put this on?" I asked.

"There's clean ones in the drawer. That's the one I wore already."

"That's why. It has your scent."

He gave me a puzzled look. "Be my guest." The sleeves were so long I had to fold them back, and the split front didn't do a very good job of keeping me decent when I moved around, but being enveloped in his smell was wonderful. I started thinking of how to sneak it back to my own apartment.

I sat down at the table across from him and buttoned a single button. "What are you thinking?" he asked.

"Oh, nothing."

"You're *always* thinking, Lisa."

"Mmm. More of a feeling."

"Go on."

"That it's too good to be true," I said. "I'm worried. It's happening too fast."

"Lisa, we're not strangers and we're not a couple of kids. Everything is fine. Just stop thinking so much."

"So what are *you* thinking about?"

"About my parents."

"Do you want to talk about it?"

"I remember how I felt after Mexico. People talk about living for today, that it's the present that's important. That's crap. When a man and a woman are together, it's really in the future. What you have now is important because it's a part of what's coming. When we stopped seeing each other all I had were some mementos. They were just pieces of paper or whatever; they didn't tie into anything important anymore. Am I making any sense?"

"Yes." God, yes.

"Lisa, I don't know where this is going, and neither do you. But it's got some kind of a future, or you wouldn't have come back. And—I don't know how to say this—being connected on one end makes me want to connect on the other, with my past. Ever since my divorce I've been living in the present, and I don't want that anymore."

"All right." I hesitated and then decided to let it go. "And I'm sorry."

"You've got nothing to be sorry for."

"Until this week, until tonight, I never realized how important family is to you. The connections, the generations. I didn't know."

"So why are you sorry?"

It was too late not to say it. "No matter what happens, I can't give you that."

His voice was soft. "You really, really do think too damn much." Then he took my hand.

I was crying, but I found my voice. "It's a defense against being hurt."

"It's also a way of torturing yourself."

I ventured a small smile. "Under stress I fall back on the familiar."

"We're both bleeding from self-inflicted wounds," he said, and squeezed my hand. "Let's try to stop."

I put my hand lightly on his chest. "I don't think there are very many men like you. Do you have any idea how good you've made me feel about myself?"

"I'm glad," he said.

"And if I'd realized how insightful you become after getting laid, I'd have done something a long time ago."

"Thank you, I guess."

I turned serious, which isn't hard for me. "We've wasted a lot of time."

"Let's not waste any more."

I gave David the grand tour, visiting many familiar locations, some new ones, and affording him some unexpected vistas. Afterward I lay with my head on his chest, watching the light glint off the hairs as they moved to his breathing. Somehow I still had his shirt on. The shirt and I reeked of sex.

He was stroking my hair and looking at the ceiling. "Penny for your thoughts," I said.

"Mmm. Just wondering who I am."

"A blank slate is a scary thing."

"I'm not scared."

"You're angry. And the drinking didn't help."

"What does?"

"Time. A day, a week, a month."

"I was angry," he admitted.

"I'm sure she had lots of reasons for not telling you."

"If she lied about that, what else did she lie about? How can I believe anything she ever said?"

"I thought you said it didn't matter,"

"Exactly who my birth mother is doesn't matter. That was a long time ago. I talk to my mother every week. Every time she doesn't tell me, is a new lie."

"Your birth mother, I wonder what she's like?"

"I have no idea," he said slowly.

"You have some kind of mental picture, don't you? Doesn't

some face come to mind? Try imagining her when she was young."

"She was probably dark, and probably not short."

"That's just deduction. I mean, don't you see a face? Don't you—*feel* anything?"

"All I get is sort of a brunette version of Donna Reed."

"So, what do you want to do tomorrow?"

"Keep looking."

"This isn't just to get me off your back, is it?"

"You said something the other day; I was mad at you, but I remembered it anyway." He took hold of my hand; the way he looked at me took me nearly over the edge. "Maybe I remembered it *because* I was mad. You said even if I didn't want to meet her now, what if I change my mind later, and she's gone then? That was a good question."

"You want to keep looking even after all this?" I asked.

"What's happened doesn't change the reasons for looking."

"David, you're the bravest person I've ever met."

"Just obsessed."

"Want to get dressed and get some dinner?" I asked.

"Let's get room service." He ran his finger down my cheek. "I like the way you're dressed right now."

22

David

Saturday, 7:00 A.M.

THE TELEPHONE RANG. And rang and rang.

It stopped for a minute and began ringing again. Lisa looked at the phone with unconcealed annoyance. "Doesn't sound like they're going to give up, does it?"

"I might as well answer it."

"I guess." She brushed her hair away from her face and sat up. "You just smeared a gob of K-Y Jelly into your hair," I said.

Her attention was focused on untying my wrists. "That's the least interesting place I have it," she said, and she was right.

She released me and handed me the phone. "Hello?" I said. I don't know if I sounded very professional, but fortunately it was a terrible connection.

"David?" It was an unfamiliar voice, a woman's.

"Yes," I said over the static. "This is Dave Garrett."

"This is Sophie Sckloff, your mother's neighbor from across the hall. We met during the blizzard; you carried in my groceries for me. You were such a nice boy."

"I remember," I said, lying. I motioned for Lisa to pick up the extension on the table near the window. As she walked over, I saw she was wearing a tiny pair of red bikini panties that were more lace than cloth. I wondered when she'd put them on, exactly. "It was no trouble, Mrs. Sckloff."

"I'm calling for your mother, David. Now, don't get excited, it's not such a big megillah, but she went into the hospital last night."

This was her second admission of the year, and this was only June. "What happened?"

"She called me last night, said she didn't think her oxygen was working right; so I came over. It was working fine, but she said she still couldn't get any air. She took her medicine and used her puffer but it didn't help, so we called Dr. Mashwami, and he said to call the ambulance."

"Go on."

"I went in with her, in the ambulance, all the lights on and everything. At the hospital they put her on a heart monitor, and they increased her oxygen, and they're giving her an IV. They want to keep her for a couple of days yet. I'm going to go in this morning as soon as visiting hours start."

"I appreciate that very much, Mrs. Sckloff."

"It's no trouble. She'd do the same for me. And don't worry; I'm taking care of Stan."

"Did she ask me to come home?"

"No, she just asked me to call and tell you. She said to say hello."

"Please say hello for me, and tell her I'll be home soon."

"Do you know when?"

"No," I said. "Not yet." I got her off the phone as quickly as I could and called Dr. Mashwami's office. When I gave my name and said I was calling from California, they put me right through.

Physicians hate wasting time even more than lawyers do, so I plunged right ahead. "Doctor, this is Dave Garrett, Barbara's son, and I was wondering if you could tell me her status."

"Oh yes, Mr. Garrett." His voice had the gentle rhythm of India, where the words ran together and each sentence was a song. "Sorry to say your mother has compromised pulmonary function, low blood gases, but good cardiac responses—very good now. I saw her this morning already, and her blood gases improve a little. She is conscious."

"Just how sick is she?"

"I think this will not be her last hospitalization."

I knew he meant it as good news, but it wasn't easy to accept it that way. "What caused this episode?"

"Could be summer allergies with her hayfever; could be stress; could be no reason, just time for it to happen. We manage as best we can."

"I'm here in Los Angeles on business. Should I come home?"

"There is other family here?"

"No, I'm her only child." It was quite a day; I hadn't had breakfast, and I'd already lied twice.

"Good for her not to be alone, if possible. Emotions are important in calming breathing, yes."

"Thank you, Doctor," I said, and hung up.

Lisa was sitting in a chair by the desk phone. "Well," I said. "You heard what I heard."

"I'm glad you called the doctor."

"Sophie wasn't very specific."

"No, I mean—"

"You mean?"

"David, I'm sorry your mother's sick, but if she had just called herself and said she was a little short of breath—"

"You would assume it was phony."

"She knows we're close to something, David, and she wants to keep you from finding it."

"She sent me here in the first place."

"Rachel was dying, and your mother couldn't go. She didn't have much choice."

"I wouldn't have come on my own. I never knew Aunt Rachel."

"But she knew you were thinking of coming anyway; and if you found out later that there was a funeral out here, a good excuse to be in Los Angeles, and she didn't tell you, then you'd be even more suspicious. And mad, too."

"So I would have been mad. So? I think she wants me to look."

"I think she thinks she's got the secret so well buried you'll never get to the bottom of it, anyway."

"Joel was right; you are the suspicious one."

She shrugged; she was getting better at it. "It goes with the job."

"And with me?" I asked. She raised her eyebrows, waiting. "Because I trust people too easily?" I added.

"Good jobs are hard to find."

"So is good help."

She stretched slowly, knowing I was watching. "So what now, boss?"

"As much as I'd like to continue where we left off, why don't you call the airlines, and I'll get a shower?"

She fished the yellow pages out of the drawer. "We can probably get out by eleven if we're not too fussy about the connections," she said. "But we probably won't get there before visiting hours are over."

"So look for something at the end of the day, early evening."

"You want to keep looking?"

"We've blown four days and three grand already, and we've got nothing to show for it. One more day isn't going to cost a thing."

"You're sure you want to go on?" she asked.

"This is a switch."

"David, I've been watching this, the last ten days. . . . I've seen it eat at you. I'm sorry I ever started this. I thought I could pick up the phone and find out that Ozzie and Harriet are your birth parents, and we'd all sit around and drink lemonade. I didn't realize what this would be like." She swallowed. "I didn't realize what this would *feel* like."

"I'm not afraid, Lisa."

"Maybe you ought to be."

"For the couple of hours I thought I was Ted Hertel, I was. Can the truth be any worse?"

"I hope not."

I forced a smile. "Me, too."

By the time I finished my shower, we were booked on the six o'clock that afternoon.

Lisa came back from her shower as I finished dressing. I looked out between the curtains; the smog was especially bad today. "I won't be sorry to leave this behind."

She came up behind me and put her arms around my chest. Water droplets soaked through my shirt, and I didn't care. "It hasn't been a good town for you," she murmured.

"It gave me my start," I said. "Somehow."

"We'll get to the bottom of this someday. We cleared away a lot of bad information. Saxon can try following up."

"I'd be embarrassed to give a friend such a dead end. Where's he supposed to look?"

She came around in front of me, and we kissed. "We have today left. What do you want to do?"

"Let's see if Joel can have breakfast. I was so tied up in myself, I really didn't interview him."

"You're being too hard on yourself."

"Interviewing isn't just asking questions. It's about letting the person talk and listening to what they say."

"You think he's holding out?"

"Do you?" I asked.

"He could have volunteered who the family doctor was."

"If people volunteered things, being a detective would be easy," I said.

She gave me a smile that was almost maternal in its pride. "Start checking out, and I'll call," she said.

Two hours later the three of us were sitting at a Mexican sidewalk café, finishing a breakfast of chorizo and huevos rancheros and drinking strong Mexican coffee. We were an odd table. I was wearing a suit and tie, defiantly East Coast to the end. Somewhere along the way Lisa had bought a peasant dress that was pure California; a full, flowing red-and-yellow-flowered skirt and a white lacy top with puffy short sleeves and a collar scooped so low that our waiter gave us the best service of any table in the restaurant. Joel was wearing a sweatshirt and jeans again—I suspected that they were exactly the same ones he'd worn to the reception. In the sunlight his scars looked worse, glossy and red.

He put down his coffee cup. "So tell me how you're feeling, David."

"It seemed so clear, when I was back in Philadelphia. I mean, your mother is in California—go find her. You just do it. Why? Like I said, it seemed—" I stopped myself. "Life has a way of surprising you."

"Are you afraid that if your mother turns out to be a mess, you'll think less of yourself?"

"It's not a fear; I know I would."

"You're smart, David. You've accomplished a lot. That all comes from somewhere. You won't be disappointed when you find out, trust me."

"You really can't know."

"I know you, at least a little, and the rest is a pretty safe bet."

"I hope you're right." I played with my cup. I'd been fishing, but he hadn't bitten. It was time to be more direct. "I'd like to talk about you for a minute, if that's okay."

"My favorite subject."

"What happened to you and Barbara?"

He nodded slowly. "I was on an escort carrier in the Pacific. I was just an ensign, the communications officer. There was a fire." The word hung in the air. "The navy brought me back to Los Angeles and did all they could for me." He gestured briefly at his face. "Now, this would be considered a lousy result. Back then, I was the glamour boy of the burn ward. I really was. They didn't have all the techniques they have today, split thickness grafts and compression bandaging." He pursed his lips and didn't speak for a minute. "Some of the men in that ward . . . didn't ever go home."

"They died in surgery?"

"They killed themselves when the hospital tried to send them home. That's what made me decide to go to medical school and become a psychiatrist. They were so angry about what had happened to them, and there was nothing for them to do with their anger except turn it inside. The racists, the idiots, blamed it on the Japs and got along fine, thank you. The ones who wondered what it all meant, why them—some of them didn't make it. And that was the germ of it, right there." He looked me in the eye. "No one ever said survival was pretty."

"What happened when you were released?"

"Barb was already gone. She'd seen me. It was a very bad time for both of us." He drank some coffee. "We got over it, in our own ways."

"I'm surprised to hear you talk about it so calmly."

He regarded me for a moment. "You look like you're old enough to know the truth. I sent her away. Told her to clear out before I was released."

"Oh."

"It was a bad decision, and I accept responsibility for it. It was based a lot on my own bad self-image; and I underestimated her, too. I took away her freedom of choice. She was angry with me for that, and after a while I became angry at me, too."

"Were you angry at her parents?"

He started to say something and stopped. "No." It was the first one-word response I'd heard.

"How did the two of you get along?"

He considered his answer. "Fine, fine."

Lisa and I looked at each other, equally puzzled. But there was nothing to do but press on. "It must have been hard, being alone."

"I had to go back to the hospital every couple weeks for scar revisions. Not much to do in between. It gave me time to think. When you're in one of the so-called learned professions, you break your neck for years learning all the subtleties of your craft, and then when you're out in practice you never have a minute to stop and think." He paused. "Stop. And. Think. It hardly ever happens. I got to do my thinking before I ever started medical school. Anyway, that's when I started working on my theories. Took fifteen years to germinate, but that's where it all began. Lots of talks with Mark Levin; he was good to bounce things off."

"Mark Levin?"

He seemed surprised I didn't recognize the name. "My doctor. Family practitioner. Made house calls, too. Came out every week at the end of the day, stayed and talked and got half drunk with me."

"Nice to get treatment like that."

"People did a lot for servicemen back then. And he was young, just starting out; he wanted to build a practice."

"How did you meet him?"

"Barb went to him first. The regular family doctor went off to the war. He went down on the *Liscombe Bay*."

I made eye contact with Lisa. "Do you know if Levin was her doctor after her divorce?"

"Sure. By then he treated the whole Potok family."

"When did he die?"

"I don't know that he did. He moved out to Pasadena ten years ago when he retired; hell, he must have been seventy then. We lost touch after that, little by little." He tugged on an earring. "We didn't always agree about everything, but we always respected each other."

"So he might still be alive, in Pasadena?"

"So? Even if he's alive, and remembers, anything he would know would be confidential."

"You saw him over the years after 1946. Did he ever let anything slip about where Barbara got her baby?"

"It never came up. We talked about medicine mostly. We left the past alone, Barbara and Rachel both."

"Any reason we shouldn't try to contact him?"

Joel looked puzzled. "Except that he can't discuss anything that's doctor-patient privileged, no. So what would be the point?"

"We'll worry about that one." I looked at my watch. "Joel, I want to thank you again. I wish I'd met you a long time ago."

I was ready to go, but Lisa interrupted. "Joel, you saw Barbara after the divorce, didn't you?"

"From time to time. There was anger, but we'd been together a long time. We had a lot going for us, in some ways."

"When you saw her the last time, how was it left between you?"

"That it was time for both of us to move forward. I was halfway through medical school, and she wanted to start a new life away from LA."

"Did you stay in touch with her over the years?"

He shook his head. "We knew how to get in touch with each other if we ever needed to, but we never did."

"Never?"

"We were both married; she lived on the opposite coast."

"Thanks," she said. We stood up. "No long good-byes," he said, "but the feeling is mutual." I got a handshake, and Lisa got a hug.

"If I find anything out, I'll be in touch."

"Be in touch anyway, David."

We found a pay phone in a Holiday Inn across the street. The desk clerk had a Pasadena white pages, and there was our man, complete with address.

As I waited for the operator to clear my credit card, I ran my hand down Lisa's forearm. It was warm from the sun.

"Don't start something you can't finish," she said.

I thought about it and decided to stop. "How about that with Barbara's parents?" I asked.

"If Art was right, Joel would have every reason to resent them. Why not let it out?"

"What was going on back there, you and Joel?" I asked.

"You didn't catch it?"

"I guess not," I admitted.

"He made a slip."

"So you think he's hiding the ball?"

"He said they were still seeing each other up till he was halfway through medical school. If he was being treated through 1944, the earliest he could possibly have started medical school would have been the fall of '45. Even if he somehow started in '44, he was still in contact with Barbara when you were conceived. Maybe even when you were born."

"He said she was moving away the last time he saw her. When she moved, she met the man who would be her second husband."

"David, getting halfway through medical school is a milestone. There are boards to take, it's a major step. He knows when that was. He's not confused."

"Maybe he meant 'partway,' that he'd finished his first year."

"He said what he said, David. Don't let him off the hook because you like him."

"So why wouldn't he just tell me?"

"That he was screwing your mother while she was married to another man? He doesn't know how you'd take it, what kind of relationship you had with your father. And I think he's a decent enough man to feel ashamed of it."

"He completely denied he could be my father."

"Yeah, practically the first words out of his mouth. Didn't that seem a little forced to you?"

"So that means Barbara was pregnant in 1946 after all. What about the guy who mowed the lawn?"

"I have shocking possibilities for you to consider, David. People make mistakes. Or they lie."

Before I could retort, the line began to ring. An answering machine picked up. "Hi there, pals; you've reached Mark and Judy, and we'd love to talk to you. Now, don't hang up, just listen—" The message stopped, and a cheery male voice said, "Hello?"

"Dr. Levin?"

"You've got him. How're you doing?"

"Just fine, thanks, and you?"

"Never better. Retired, no work, no hassles—"

"Doctor, my—"

"Call me Mark; everybody does."

"All right, Mark. I'm Dave. Have a minute?"

"A minute? I've got all day."

"I got your name through Joel Weissberg. Remember him?"

"Joel? Sure I do. Haven't seen him in five, six years. He still meshuga?"

I laughed. "He said you might say something like that."

"He's a real mensch, Joel is. I should give him a call. He still have that earring?"

"Sure does. We just had breakfast together."

"What can I do for you, David?"

"Well, Joel said you were the family doctor for the Potoks for a long time—you remember them?"

"Sure, sure. Myron was a hell of a guy."

"Well, it's not the kind of thing I want to get into on the phone, but I've got some news I'd like to pass along, if you could just give me a few minutes."

His manner deflated. "Bad news, huh? People give good news on the phone, bad in person."

"Bad."

"Barbara?"

"No."

He sighed. "Then it must be Rachel."

He didn't phrase it as a question, and I didn't answer. If I was going to interview him at all, it was going to be face to face. "All right, Dave—what did you say your name was?"

"Garrett."

"When do you want to come? Tomorrow?"

"Would this afternoon be all right? I'm headed back to Philadelphia tonight."

"Then it'll have to be this afternoon. I'll have Judy make us some sandwiches."

"I'm traveling with a friend, if that's no trouble."

"Bring him along."

"It's a her."

"Even better." He gave me directions, and I said we'd see him at one.

23

David

Saturday, 1:00 P.M.

MARK AND JUDY Levin lived in a large rancher on a tiny lot just north of the city. I parked in the driveway behind a new Cadillac with a vanity plate that spelled SOTRIC. I lingered, trying to figure it out, while Lisa headed up the walk and rang the bell.

Dr. Levin answered as soon as she rang. I was still on the walk, to one side of the door, when I heard him say hello and saw a deeply tanned forearm reach out and shake her hand. Lisa said she was pleased to meet him and turned to me.

Mark Levin was wearing the kind of outfit that proclaims its wearer is retired; loud golf clothes and white shoes. He even had on a golf cap. He was broad in the belly and face, with the hairiest forearms I've ever seen. I stuck out my hand, and his eyes shifted from Lisa's chest to my face.

He was smiling when our eyes met, but after a moment of puzzlement his expression went dead blank. His hand stopped in midair, six inches from mine. For a long moment he just stared at me. His mouth hung open, revealing a row of gold-filled teeth. Underneath his tan, his face was pale. His Adam's apple moved, and he wet his lips. "What did you say your name was?"

"Garrett. Dave Garrett. From Philadelphia."

"Garrett," he said slowly.

"Yes. We spoke this morning." I glanced over at Lisa, but she was staring at Levin, too.

"Doctor," I asked. "Are you all right?"

That mobilized him. He swallowed, shut his lips, and said, "No, I don't think so."

"Let's sit down," I said. "You'll feel better."

He shook his head. "You have to go."

"Doctor, we just got here."

"Go now, please."

"If you're not well, we can call someone, run you to your doctor's . . ." I looked at Lisa; this time we made eye contact, but she didn't understand what was going on, either. "Doctor," I said, "if there's—"

"I don't want any trouble." He backed away and began to close the door. I put my foot in it.

"Doctor, we drove all the way out here because you invited us. I'd—"

"There's nothing to tell you."

Lisa put her hand on my arm, but I ignored her. "You already told me, Doctor; it's too late now."

"I—"

"You know who I am, don't you?"

"You're Barbara's son, aren't you? Barbara Potok's son."

"That's what I used to think."

"What are you doing here?"

"I'm here to find my parents."

"Where's Barbara?"

"In Philadelphia."

"What did she tell you?"

"She fed me a line of BS," I said simply.

"And your father?"

"Barbara's husband is dead."

He looked from one of us to the other. "I've got nothing to say."

"You had a general practice, years ago, Doctor. And when you had a female patient in trouble, you did abortions, didn't you?"

"Abortions weren't legal then. You ought to know that."

"And in '45 a young woman came to you. She asked you to give her baby a good home, didn't she?"

"I can't discuss what happened with patients."

"You knew how much Barbara wanted a baby."

He was still for a moment. Then, very slightly, he nodded.

It was my turn to be still. The search was over, and the proof was in front of my eyes. "So why wasn't there an adoption?"

"Barbara didn't want her husband to know. She was afraid he wouldn't want an adopted child. It had to be one of his own."

"So who was my mother?"

"You got it figured out, David. Some young girl, not a regular patient, somebody who was referred to me. I didn't see her after. I can't remember after all this time."

"Was she referred for an abortion?"

"Maybe she was, and maybe I told her she was too far along. It was long ago. There were a lot of girls like that, back then. The war was just over, the boys were home, things like that happened."

"And the father?"

"I wouldn't have asked. All I can remember is that she was young, and she wasn't married."

"You have office records?"

"If a doctor was seeing a woman for an abortion, he wouldn't keep records. He'd deal in cash and make sure there was no trace she'd ever been there."

"But what about the prenatal care? The birth?"

"No records. There was no insurance back then. You only kept the records you needed, and only the ones that didn't get you in trouble."

"You're sure there's no record?"

"When I sold my practice, I destroyed everything but the last ten years. Even if there ever was a file, it's long gone now."

"Isn't there—"

Levin looked down at my foot in the door. "I've said all I'm going to say."

"I—"

"This is your last warning, David. Go."

"You still—"

Levin turned his face away. "Judy!" he shouted. "Dial 911!"

We left.

24

David

Saturday, 1:30 P.M.

I DROVE TO the nearest intersection and parked behind the stop sign, in the shade of a palm tree. Lisa put her hand on my arm. "Are you okay?"

"I feel like—I don't know, that I'm falling. My stomach is up somewhere in my chest."

"You want to go back and try to talk to him some more?"

"He only said what he did 'cause we caught him off balance. We show up again, we'll find out what color cars the Pasadena police use."

"And you're not even licensed out here."

"It's one thing to reason things out; it's something else to meet somebody who looks you in the eye who knows for sure."

"Something's wrong here," she said.

"No shit."

"Do you think he really can't remember the name?" she asked.

"I've forgotten half the names of the clients I had last

year. If she never came back to him again, why should he remember?"

"It bothers me that Joel sent you here," she said.

"Only after we interviewed him a second time."

"They wanted to make it just hard enough that you wouldn't be suspicious."

"If this is 'just hard enough,' I'd hate for them to make it tough. And who's 'they,' anyway?"

She played with the tip of her braid. "Levin recognized you right away. You must look just like one of your birth parents."

"So?"

"We don't know what Joel looked like before the fire, but Levin does. And this business about Barbara's parents. If they disliked each other, why is Joel so quiet? And if he liked them, how did the rumor get started? To throw people off the track?"

"Joel and Barbara were separated, divorced—"

"David, when I was a lawyer I did my share of divorce cases. The clients complain about how horrible their spouse is, how they never pay child support, how much they detest them, how much they want to hurry up and be divorced—and there's a study that shows that in half the cases when the father visits the mother to see the kids, they still get it on."

"You told me that part already."

"So would it be so bad if Barbara was your mother after all, and Joel was your dad? It's kind of romantic actually."

"It doesn't matter how nice it would be if it wasn't true."

"Since you're not going to know anyway, why not fantasize about Joel and Barbara?"

"Being Hispanic was kind of nice."

She took my hand. "David, you know that it doesn't really matter."

"Isn't that what I said back in Philadelphia?"

"It matters; of course it matters. But it doesn't affect how I feel about you."

I raised her hand and kissed each one of her fingertips. "Or how I feel about you."

Her eyes were dark and wide. I saw pride and surrender, hunger and fulfillment, fear and hope. I was awed that I could matter that much to anyone.

I leaned across the seat awkwardly, and we kissed. Lisa was right, and she was wrong. If who I was didn't matter to her, then it didn't matter at all.

The car was rocked by the passing of another car, close and fast. I looked up and saw the rear of Levin's Cadillac, with its vanity plate. "Just the time for an interruption," I said.

"He's going somewhere in a big hurry."

"Let him," I said.

"You taught me not to believe in coincidences."

Right as usual. I started the engine and trailed him from half a block. He drove through a commercial district, then onto a side street, and through a development that looked like it dated from the thirties. I was about to wonder out loud where he was going when he slowed and turned sharply into a driveway. As we drove by I saw a stone gateway with a discreet sign, BLOOMBERG CONVALESCENT CENTER.

I made a U-turn in the nearest driveway, counted to ten to give him a lead, and followed him inside.

Once past the stone gateposts, we were on the grounds of a palace. As far as we could see stretched manicured lawns, groves of carefully tended shade trees, and immaculate graveled paths. Up ahead, on a gentle hill, was a complex of low white adobe buildings with red tile roofs. As we got closer we saw that the buildings were arranged in a loose quadrangle, with one large building making up two of the four sides. People were in the courtyard, reading, talking, or just sunning themselves. Most were old; the only young person I saw had no legs below the knees. Everyone wore casual summer clothes. No bathrobes or pajamas for these folks.

Levin's car was nowhere in sight. I parked in the visitors, section of the lot and went looking for the administration office. Inside, it smelled of palm trees and oranges. Our feet echoed on the red tile floors. The white stucco walls were bare except for a few tasteful landscapes of local scenes. The only hint of the purpose of the building was a heavy-duty railing at hand height, and even that was made of grainy dark wood, not metal.

We passed by a door with a polished brass plate marked CHAPEL, and I was surprised to see a Gothic stained glass window with a Star of David. I thought about the name and realized that for all its Spanish architecture, this was a Jewish nursing home.

We turned a corner and found ourselves at the main office, a large open area separated from the hallway by only a low counter, desks in the front, near the counter, and computers and other office equipment in the rear. I puzzled about the arrangement for a second until I realized it was designed to make access easier for the patients. Even someone in a wheelchair could deal with the staff face to face. I had a brief memory of a woman in a wheelchair I'd known once. It seemed a very long time ago.

A young blond woman in a white dress, not a uniform, looked up from her typing. "Yes, I'm Beth. How can I help you?"

"You've got a nice place here."

She smiled. "Thank you. We're very proud of it."

"How long have you been here?"

"About a year."

"I mean, the building."

She giggled. The idea that words could have more than one meaning was evidently a novelty to her. "Oh, the building. Gee, we first opened back in the twenties, I think. Before the Great Depression." She made it sound like a geological feature.

"What kind of a place is this?"

She liked that question better. She knew how to answer it. "Well, it's a purely private facility." She looked at me before she went on. "We're only open to members of the Jewish faith in the Los Angeles Valley area. We provide all levels of care, from personal living assistance to complete custodial care."

I hated the euphemisms, but I'd heard them often enough to know what she meant. "Is Dr. Mark Levin on staff here? We're looking for him."

"Our full-time physician is Dr. Rakosky. Hold on a moment." She typed something into her computer. "No, there's no Dr. Levin on staff. Sorry."

"He may just have staff privileges."

She typed some more. "No, he doesn't. Sorry."

"He told me he was coming down here, and I was hoping to run into him." Not bad, I thought; working two lies into a single sentence.

"Sir?" said a voice from the rear of the office.

I looked up and saw an older woman, stout and dark-haired, standing by the copier. "Sir, are you looking for a Dr. Levin?"

"That's right."

She put down her papers and came up to the counter. "Sorry, but you just missed him. He was here for a moment, and then he left."

"Darn," I said. "I was hoping to catch up with him. I have to catch a plane back to Philadelphia this afternoon."

"Looks like this isn't anybody's day."

"How do you mean?"

"Dr. Levin had a wasted trip, too."

"Oh?"

"We couldn't help him, either."

"Some days are like that," I said. I looked her over; like the blond, she wore a white dress, not a uniform. Middle fifties. No name tag, but she carried a leather-covered notebook and a gold pen. Someone with a little authority; at least more than the blond. "I forgot to introduce myself. I'm Dave Garrett, and this is my friend Lisa Wilson."

"Linda Timberlake." We shook hands; her fingers were

stained with ink. "MSW. I'm deputy administrator. So you're looking for Dr. Levin?"

"I was at his house, hoping to see him, and they told me he was here." By "they," I meant my two eyes, but I didn't think it was necessary to be that specific.

"I hadn't seen him in years," she said. "I almost didn't recognize him."

"He told me he closed down his practice years ago." Telling the truth was a welcome change.

She smiled. "Some of the retired physicians are here more than the practicing ones. 'Just checking in on Mrs. Steinman,' they'll say. They can't give it up."

"Like the horse that stops at the old delivery stops."

She smiled again and nodded. "More true than you would know."

"So, what was Dr. Levin stopping in for?"

"The old transfer logs."

"What are those?"

"If a resident is discharged, that's that. But if a resident has to go to another facility temporarily, we keep a log. They're still a resident here, even if they're somewhere else for a few days, so we want to keep careful track."

"Of course. When you say someone goes to another facility, that would be for an operation, or inpatient testing, things like that?"

"Or home visits. Anything that involves physically leaving the facility for at least overnight that isn't a discharge."

"How old were the records he was looking for?"

"He asked about 1946 in particular."

The room seemed to get warmer quickly. To buy a half second, I nodded and shrugged and mainly tried to act casual. "Sounds like you don't have them."

"Lord, not that far back. We keep ten years' worth, and that's plenty."

"I guess that depends."

"Sir?"

"Was a Rachel Potok a patient here?"

"Are you family?"

"She was my aunt."

"She was our longest-term resident. I want you to know, sir, she was very comfortable here."

"I'm sure she was."

"It was—she missed so much."

"Almost everything. She was, what, twenty when she came here? Was she ever conscious at all?"

"I'm not involved with resident care, but I've been here twenty-four years, and I never heard anyone mention any activity."

"Could I see her chart, please?"

"I'm sorry, sir. I can't do that without permission."

"Well, I *am* her nephew. Except for my mother, her sister, I'm her closest living relative."

She hesitated, and glanced at the blond. Before she even looked back at me, I knew I'd screwed up. I should have talked to her outside the hearing of her coemployee. "I'm sorry, sir, but I can't let you do that."

"I was hoping I could have a look—"

"We can't allow it without the permission of the attending doctor."

"I'll bite—who's that?"

"Sol Birnbaum."

"And where do I find him?"

Without hesitation, she said, "You can reach him at the department of psychiatry, UCLA Medical School."

"Do you know him?"

"Oh, no. I've never met him personally, but we're very honored that he would associate with our facility. Most doctors of his stature don't want anything to do with care facilities. They just want to teach and do research."

"So he's on staff?"

"And on the board of trustees. He served a term as chairman a few years ago."

"What did you mean by 'his stature?' "

"Dr. Birnbaum founded the UCLA neuropsych department. He was president of the state psychiatry association, he's examined murder defendants all over the country in insanity cases, he started a clinical MSW program at Albert Einstein in New York—I'm sorry, some of this may not mean anything to you, but in mental health circles, he's pretty famous."

"Sounds like he has trouble holding a job. So tell me, how do I find UCLA?"

Five minutes later I was looking for freeway signs while Lisa struggled with the road map of Los Angeles. "What's your guess?" she asked.

"About why Levin would be interested in the '46 transfer records?" I said. "He wanted to destroy them; whether he's trying to protect himself or somebody else, I don't know. Here's the freeway; east or west?"

"Hold on . . . west. I think. No, what you want is 110 south. It goes out of the way to the west but then it kind of doubles back."

"How much longer till the plane?" I slowed and turned onto the ramp. For once, traffic was light. I stayed in the right lane and tried to keep up. It was easy to concentrate on the case; there was nothing to look at except billboards and concrete flood control channels. "So what do you think happened in 1946?"

"I think they pulled a switcheroo," said Lisa.

"I'm all ears."

"Barbara had her eyes on that baby. She was waiting for it to be born, and she wanted it born healthy, safely, and with no paperwork."

"And she had a doctor and the rest of her family behind her," I added.

"What if they moved your aunt Rachel out for a few days, put her in some other place or just took her home, and brought in the woman who was about to give birth under Rachel's name? After the birth they discharge your birth mother, bring Aunt Rachel back, and there's no record that your birth mother was ever hospitalized anywhere."

"They said they provided all levels of care," I said. "But would it be worth all that trouble?"

"Barbara didn't mind trouble. And the only way to make the whole thing work was to ensure that there was never any paperwork."

"But . . . to take out a comatose woman, bring in a healthy woman about to give birth, saying it was the same name, you'd need—"

"—the cooperation of the doctor and the family and the woman and the facility. And you had it."

"Huh."

"Yeah," she said.

"How much farther to UCLA?"

25

David

Saturday, 3:00 P.M.

AFTER A FEW days in Los Angeles you become used to the
scale, but the UCLA campus was still an overwhelming place.
The buildings were too large, the quadrangles too vast, the walk-
ways too wide. Even the plants seemed impossibly large. Summer school evidently hadn't started yet, because we only saw a
few students, all of them tanned and ridiculously healthy. The
emptiness made the place seem even larger.

After a couple of wrong turns we were directed to the Behavioral Medicine Complex, a twelve-story precast concrete
edifice the size of a city block. We presented identification to a
security guard and were directed to the ninth floor.

The corridors were wide and well lighted, and each door
bore signs that were barely English: "Neurobiology," "MKG
Analysis," and "Behavioral Phasing—No Admittance." Even
with the air conditioning, the place smelled of disinfectant. Lisa
wrinkled her nose and looked at me.

"I wonder," I said, "if the basement in this place is full

of jars labeled 'normal brain' and 'criminal brain'?"

"Probably."

"I thought you might say that."

We found a door bristling with the names of doctors and professors; near the bottom was "Sol Birnbaum, Professor Emeritus." Inside we found ourselves in a small security area, facing another door with an intercom.

"A lot of security for an office building," I said.

"Maybe it's those criminal brains in the basement."

I pressed the button. "Yes?" a female voice answered.

"My name is Dave Garrett, and I'd like to see Professor Birnbaum, please."

"Do you have an appointment?"

I hate when people ask questions they already know the answer to. "No, I don't."

"Doctor Birnbaum doesn't see anyone without an appointment."

"This is a personal matter."

"Personal?" Even over the intercom she sounded surprised.

"It's a family matter."

"I don't believe he's ever mentioned any family."

I sighed. Talking into the metal grill was getting on my nerves. "A long time ago he treated an aunt of mine who just died. We'd like to get his permission to look at her records."

"You ought to submit that request in writing."

I counted to five. "I live in Philadelphia, and I have a plane to catch in two hours. Do you think he can spare five minutes?"

"I'm sorry, but—"

"Look, can I just come in and discuss this with you face to face?"

"Well—"

"Two minutes; and if you don't think I should see him I'll get on the plane and have the lawyers handle it."

I don't know if she disliked the intercom as much as I did, or if the L word made a difference; but the latch buzzed, and we went through the door.

Beyond it was a plush reception area, with lights so dim I bumped into Lisa when she stopped suddenly.

A middle-aged woman turned up the reading light at her desk. Her hair was fresh from the bottle, she was showing too much cleavage, and her wrists and fingers sparkled with jewelry. I tried to get close enough to see if she'd had a face-lift but Lisa was already in front of me, for the same reason.

"Thanks for letting us in," I said. "This is my assistant, Lisa Wilson." I started my sales pitch, but she wasn't listening. She was just staring at me, her mouth hanging a little open. Then she closed her lips.

"The doctor isn't in today, but let me try his home." She picked up the phone and spoke in Spanish in a low tone. Then she hung up and wrote down an address. "He'll be expecting you. It's just on the edge of campus."

Lisa and I exchanged looks; mine was puzzled. Hers wasn't. "Well, thanks very much," I stammered.

"No problem, sir."

I nodded, still trying to understand the change in her attitude. "Have you worked for him long?"

"Ever since his retirement. He's emeritus now; the university gives him an office and support staff, but he doesn't have any teaching or research responsibilities." She looked around the room. "You'll have to pardon the lighting, but Dr. Birnbaum has a vision problem. He really can't see very much anymore, and the light hurts his eyes."

"That's too bad," I said.

"I guess doctors get as sick as anyone else. That's why he retired."

I looked at the slip of paper with Birnbaum's address. "Guess I'll pay the doctor a quick visit."

"I'm sure he'll be glad to see you," she said cheerfully as we headed for the door.

SOL BIRNBAUM, FOR all his prestige, lived simply in a neat but unremarkable garden apartment on the edge of campus. It was an older building, within sight of the Behavioral Medicine Complex. If he was as much a workaholic as he seemed, he would have picked it, many years ago, for exactly that reason.

Lisa was reading my mind. "I bet he's the kind of guy who slept in the lab till they kicked him out."

"Looks like he did the next best thing."

The bell was answered by a plump Filipino woman in white with short black hair. "Yes?" she asked tentatively. It didn't sound as if Birnbaum got many visitors at home.

"I'm David Garrett, and this is Lisa Wilson. We were just at the medical school. The secretary called."

"Oh, yes. Come in and he see you now."

She led us into a dimly lit, immaculate, unused living room to the back of the apartment and knocked at a closed door. "You go in here. This is his office at home," she said, and disappeared.

I put my hand on the knob. "I wonder what we did to get this kind of treatment," I said.

"It's nothing you did."

"Huh?"

"Go in, David. Go ahead."

The office was huge; it must have been designed as the master bedroom. Like the rest of the apartment, it was barely illuminated. Dimly I saw the outlines of diplomas and certificates covering all the walls. Thick curtains were drawn across the windows, and the only light was a tiny gooseneck reading lamp on the desk with a magnifying attachment. The light was on, and all I could see was an outline seated behind the desk.

"Hello, Doctor Birnbaum. I'm David Garrett, and this is Lisa

Wilson. If we could have just a couple of minutes, Doctor, it won't take long."

"What would this be about?" His voice was thin, barely above a whisper.

"I'm the nephew of a former patient of yours, someone from a long time ago."

"I can't discuss cases, young man; you ought to know that."

"She's dead now. And I wasn't really here to discuss her treatment."

"What was your name again?"

"David Garrett."

"And this relative of yours? Who was that?"

"Rachel Potok."

He paused for a moment. "You two, sit down, please."

He swiveled his chair away from us, fiddling with something on his credenza, while Lisa and I made ourselves comfortable in two of the leather wing chairs in front of his desk. He finished shuffling his papers, turned back to us, and turned down the wattage on the desk light.

My heart stopped beating; I'm sure of it. Two, three, four beats—I don't know how many. The first syllable of a word came from one of us, but what word, or whether it was from Lisa or from me, I can't say. I stared at him, and then my fingers went to my own face.

I was looking at my father. The hair was gray, and thinner; but he had balded the same way my own hair was going. His eyes were fixed straight ahead, but otherwise ours were the same. Same nose, same mouth, same cheekbones and skin and ears and lips.

"Well, young man, what can I do for you?"

I couldn't possibly speak. Lisa bought me some time. "Doctor, I'm Lisa Wilson. We understand you treated Rachel Potok."

"That's right. I was her attending. They called me."

"We came to town for the funeral."

"Such a shame. So long ago. She missed so much."

"I understand you were her doctor at her last therapy session," Lisa said.

He sighed. "Well, there's no secret about that."

"The family would like a better idea of what happened, exactly. The funeral has brought some of the family together who don't see each other much, and they have some questions."

"After all this time?"

"Well, David here is from Philadelphia. He was never even aware of his aunt Rachel before last week. I know it's a long time ago, but anything you can remember—"

He looked down at the desk, his face full of sadness. "Oh, it's clear in my mind," he whispered. "Like it was yesterday."

Lisa pressed on. "I understand it was an anesthesia accident."

"Yes."

"I thought that these treatments were safe."

"Safe." He let the word hang in the air. "Safe," he repeated. "We take medicine for granted. There's a measurable mortality rate on almost any medical procedure. Appendectomies. Tonsillectomies. Every once in a while someone will die from taking some perfectly innocuous medication. People don't want to be reminded of the risks, but they're there."

"What happened, exactly?"

"It was such a long time ago—"

"You said you remembered, Doctor."

"If I didn't, it would be easier."

"So what happened?"

"She was on the last session of a six-session protocol, with sessions three days apart. Previously she'd had a series of six and shown good improvement, for a while. No medical problems at all. She was strapped to the chair, the nurse administered the curare intravenously, and her respiration stopped. That told us she was in deep muscle relaxation, and the electroshock was administered. No problem there. Immediately after, the nurse gave the antidote, Prostigmin, but she didn't respond. I ordered another injection, but after a minute there was no response. I ordered a third; again, nothing. I declared a medical emergency. The hospital had a medical clinic on premises, and we rushed her there. They gave her a fourth dose of Prostigmin, and she finally responded to that one. But by then it was too late to prevent massive brain damage from hypoxia."

I found my voice at last. "What happened next, Doctor?"

"I wasn't involved in that phase of her care. It was a medical and rehabilitative problem. Almost immediately after, within the next two weeks, I was called up for duty in Korea."

"How well did you know her?"

"I treated her on an outpatient basis when she was fifteen. It must have been about a year later when she had her first hospitalization. She was one of those revolving-door patients; in and out, in and out. She was on at least her fifth admission when . . . it happened. She was twenty then."

"Did she need to be hospitalized?"

"The time period we're discussing is 1940 to 1945. The pharmacopoeia of mood-altering drugs we have now—lithium, Valium, Prozac, Thorazine—none of them existed then. There were no halfway houses, no community-based treatment centers. Then, the mentally ill were either locked up or left to their own devices . . . and there were social factors."

"Her parents disapproved of her behavior."

"She was still a minor, and they were responsible for her welfare."

"It sounds like you've given this case a great deal of thought."

"Psychiatry doesn't often involve a medical catastrophe, thank God."

"Do you have any theories why the first three shots of Prostigmin didn't work?"

"I don't really have much background in biochemistry or pharmacology; I'm afraid I can't answer that."

"Where did it come from?"

"Well, the hospital provided it, in fifty-milliliter dosage bottles."

"How big is that?"

"Oh, about two ounces."

"The kind where you stick the needle through the lid and draw out what you need?"

"That's right."

"The shot she got at the emergency room, that was from a different bottle?"

"The nurse was in charge of the medication. It was my job to set dosages and monitor the effects."

"But as far as you know, the bottle that the first three doses came from stayed in the treatment room?"

"It was analyzed and found to be within normal limits."

"A very impressive recitation, Doctor. But you've had forty-five years to practice it."

"I don't—"

"What color is Prostigmin?"

"Clear."

"Like water, Doctor?"

He didn't answer.

"Did you switch a real bottle of Prostigmin for your water bottle in the excitement on the way to the clinic, or did you do it later?"

"Why would I do that?"

"To cover up that you'd switched water, or something like that, for Prostigmin in the first place."

"Why would I want to deliberately injure one of my patients, especially one so young, with so much promise?"

"Because she was pregnant with your baby, she wouldn't agree to a quiet abortion, she was going to tell her family, and your career was on the edge of the tidy bowl."

"It's easy to throw wild allegations around, Mr. Garrett. I'm afraid I don't have the luxury of all the time in the world to listen anymore."

"I bet you really weren't trying to kill her, or leave her in a coma. I bet all you wanted was for the stress to cause a miscarriage. That would have solved all your problems."

"You're going to have to leave now."

"Who paid for Rachel's care all these years?"

"Well, I assume—"

"She never earned a nickel in her life, and yet she was a private patient in one of the nicest nursing homes in the county for more than forty years. Who could have afforded that?"

"I have nothing more to say."

"Then I'll talk. And I'll say that if we subpoena the financial records from the nursing home, we'll find that you've been paying the bills all these years."

"I think I ought to be talking to my attorney."

"We're not the police, Doctor. I'm just looking for the truth." He didn't answer. "You've wanted to tell someone all these years, haven't you? Get it off your chest. I know already. It isn't going to make it worse."

"That's what you think."

"You want to tell, and we want to listen. You've never told anyone, have you?"

"I'm not saying anything more. What happened after her accident, I don't know—"

"Doctor, please cut the crap."

"It was an honest mistake—"

"Is that why you ran away as fast as you could?"

"My unit was called up—the war—"

I stood up and pounded my fist on his desk so hard that the framed pictures rattled. "—in Korea didn't start till June of 1950, and you're a goddam liar!"

No one said anything. Then I took a ragged breath and sat

down. "You told her father it was an accident, that you'd take responsibility for her bills. Malpractice suits were almost unheard of back then. You said you'd take care of it privately, no publicity. He was so ashamed of having a daughter who was in a mental hospital he jumped at it. He never thought about whether there was something more to what happened."

He waved his hand at me impatiently, as if swatting away a fly. "This is just talk. Talk. Now go."

"Not just talk. There's proof."

"Proof? Proof of what?"

"There was a baby. Your baby."

"No!"

"Try again."

"There couldn't be . . . he . . . no, there couldn't be."

"There was a baby. A boy."

"There wasn't."

"When Rachel came to term, Levin moved her from the nursing home. A couple of days later he took her back."

"He wouldn't do that."

"He spent this afternoon at the nursing home trying to get his hands on the transfer papers."

"He did?"

"He didn't get them. Call him and ask him."

He looked at the telephone and then down at the top of his desk. He took a deep breath and let it out, along with fifty years of silence. "The parents never knew about that part. When Rachel was discharged from rehab, to the nursing home, I made arrangements to have it aborted."

"And you'd left in the meantime."

"Yes."

"You asked Mark Levin to take care of it."

He turned his face away. "I'm not going to involve anyone else in this."

"Then deny it was Levin."

He was silent.

There it was, the entire design. Aunt Barbara; Rachel, my mother. Dr. Birnbaum, my father.

"Doctor, before that last therapy session—she was a minor, and in an institution, and maybe you could have even sold one of your buddies on the idea she was mentally incompetent—why didn't you just arrange for an abortion?"

"She didn't want one."

"Doing it against her wishes would have involved the family."

"I never intended it to happen."

"But you took the risk anyway. No, that's not right; you made her take the risk, and she never had a choice."

I looked at him; old, scared, and feeble. "You have any family, Doctor?" I asked.

"My wife died some years ago."

"Children?"

He shook his head. "She was in the camps. Starvation, maltreatment . . . We wanted a child, badly, but it never happened."

"Rachel was as close as you got."

It was a long time before he answered. "I've thought of that, from time to time."

"As often as you thought about Rachel?"

He didn't respond to the barb. When I stood up to go, I saw that his left hand was trembling. He looked ten years older than when we'd come in.

"The child," he asked. "What happened? Where is he?"

I turned back to him with one hand on the doorknob. "Dead."

26

David

Saturday, 10:00 P.M.

OUTSIDE IT WAS night, and the cabin lights had been turned off. I had the window seat, looking down into the absolute blackness of the midwestern countryside. The moon was down, and the only lights were the stars and the green light that marked the wingtip.

I turned to Lisa and patted our hands with my free hand. "It would have been the perfect crime," I said, "if Levin hadn't messed up."

"It was never meant to be what it turned out to be."

"I wonder why Birnbaum didn't just give her a shot to cause an abortion."

"If there was such a thing in 1945. And even if there was, she would have known what he'd done. The way he planned it, he could tell her afterward it was an accident."

"I wonder why Levin didn't do the abortion."

She rubbed my hand. "I'm glad he didn't."

"Me, too. I wonder if he thought he was doing a good deed,

salvaging something from the mess, or if he was just being greedy. And I wonder what my family knew—my grandparents, I mean."

"They sure knew Rachel was pregnant; they visited her all the time. But they always thought she was wild. They had no reason to connect it to Birnbaum. Only Levin did, and he had no reason to tell. It worked out fine for everybody but Rachel."

"Birnbaum must have paid half his income for forty-five years."

"For what he took from Rachel, it's still not fair."

"No, but that makes it a little less unfair. That's all you get, sometimes."

"It scares me to think how close you came to not being here, David."

I thought about the fragility of this tiny shell of aluminum and plastic, suspended in the frigid darkness six miles up in the sky. And I thought about all the mishaps that could scatter this machine over a square mile of the hard Midwestern earth below in the space of a heartbeat. But maybe, just maybe, if all went well, the thousands of gears and valves and levers would work properly, the other planes would miss us, the landing lights would come on and the gear would snap down and the flaps would deploy; and the pilot would glide the thousands of tons of speeding metal to that exact invisible point in the night, and no other, that would let the wheels kiss the earth ever so gently and bring us safely to the terminal . . .

I said nothing.

"I called my mother," she said after a while. "From the airport. I told her about us."

"What did she say?"

"She was a little surprised."

"You two never talked about me before?"

"She knew we went to Mexico together and that I went to work for you after we broke up. That's all."

"She must have been more than a little surprised."

"Well, she'd seen your picture."

"Picture?"

She squeezed my hand. "When we were up at my cabin in the coal country I took your picture. Just a snapshot near the woodpile. I keep it in a frame next to my bed."

"When I was in your room I didn't see it."

"I turned it facedown before I passed out."

"Afraid I'd see it?"

She nodded. "I shouldn't have been. I should have let it sit out for you to see and taken you to bed that night once I was feeling better." She closed her eyes. "Having tea with you in the middle of the night . . ." She started to say something else and stopped, blushing.

"So what does your mom think?" I asked.

"She's afraid I'll get hurt."

My fingers traced a pattern on the back of her hand, the one with the red crisscrossed scars. "It's a burden, being the first real boyfriend of a gorgeous woman who's almost forty."

"I'm only thirty-seven."

"You're not eighteen."

She squeezed my hand again. "Believe me, I know."

"She thinks you're riding for a fall?"

"Mom's a pessimist. I'm trying not to be."

I kissed her, right there with the beverage cart on one side and a pasty-faced businessman with a laptop on the other. This is what love ought to be about, I thought. A little island of quiet and sanity that the two of you create, a little bubble that holds together no matter what is going on outside.

"David, please promise me something more? I know I'm strong-willed, and I've spent my entire adult life on my own. I don't have a lot of experience being part of a relationship. I can't change that, and I'm not going to apologize for it. But when I screw up, please promise you'll say something and not just walk away?"

"If you'll do the same for me."

"Deal," she said.

"This has been on your mind, hasn't it?"

"Since we first woke up together."

All the things that were going on silently behind those brown eyes. "I wonder if I'll ever understand you," I said.

"You understand me just fine, when you pay attention."

I thought about kissing her, and I realized she was thinking about it, too.

"Penny for your thoughts," Lisa whispered in the darkness.

"Thinking about Rachel and Birnbaum."

"How it was between them?"

"We'll never know. If he told me she was trying to use him as a ticket out of the hospital, I wouldn't know whether to believe him or not."

"He's used up his chances."

She nodded. "In lots of ways."

"My mother—Barbara—was right all along. It was a mistake to do this."

"But you know the truth now—you cut through fifty years of lies, and you found out."

"And now I know my mother was a nut, and my father was a murderer."

"You only got the good things from them, David; her fire, his discipline; their intelligence. What happened to them, what they did with their gifts, doesn't change who you are."

"That mental exercise that Joel showed me . . . I owe him a thank-you letter."

"So," she said. "We know you *weren't* born May 12, and we don't know when it really happened. Going to keep looking to find out your real birth date?"

"I couldn't care less."

"Are you going to stick with May 12?"

"No. That's her lie, not mine."

"We could pick a week in May and celebrate every night, like Chanukkah." She mispronounced it, with a hard *C*.

"Hanukkah," I said.

"I'll get the hang of it." The moment she said it, we both knew we were going too fast.

She patted my hand and changed the subject. "What are you going to tell Barbara?"

"I don't know."

"She knew you were going, the questions you were going—"

"I know."

"You're going to have to decide pretty soon."

"When I see her, I'll know what to say." I kissed her lightly on the tip of her nose. "I'm glad you were part of this. It was important to me."

She put her head on my shoulder. "I wouldn't have missed it for anything."

27

Lisa

Sunday, 1:00 A.M.

IT WAS RAINING hard when we reached the hospital; a
steamy, warm eastern rain laced with a gusty wind from the
northeast that sneaked under our umbrellas and plastered our
hair to our heads. David shook out his umbrella in the lobby.
He needed a shave, his clothes were a sodden mess, and his
eyes were bloodshot. "How do you feel?" I asked.

"More people have asked me that question in the past ten
days than in the whole rest of my life."

"Want a cup of coffee before we go up?" I asked.

"At this hour I'm sure she's asleep. All I want to do is look
in on her."

We took the elevator to her floor. Except for a couple of
nurses at the station, there was no one else in sight. I thought
they would stop us, but no one looked up.

We found a closed door with her name on it. He eased it
open, and we saw that the light was on. We shared a puzzled
glance, and then we stepped inside.

It was a single room, small and functional. Mrs. Garrett was propped up in bed in a fuzzy pink robe, her face turned to the door. A nasal tube was in place, and an IV tube dripped a clear fluid into her elbow. "David, you shouldn't have come so late." The voice was weak, but clear.

He sat in the chair next to the bed. "You shouldn't be up, Mom. You have to save your strength."

"I talked to your cousin Art. He told me you were leaving."

"Mom, you shouldn't have waited up."

"I should be able to go home in a few days, maybe."

"I haven't seen the doctors yet."

"No hurry. They'll lie to you like they lie to me."

"Mom, I want you to meet Lisa, my girlfriend."

Her eyes turned to me, and I saw no surprise at all. I guess she understood us better than we understood ourselves. "Nice to meet you, Lisa."

"Sorry it has to be like this. We'll get you home soon."

"I hope so."

"How are you feeling, Mrs. Garrett?"

"Not so bad, I just can't get any air." Her eyes moved back to David. "So how was everything?"

"There aren't many of the old-timers left, Mom. We had dinner with Art one night; we had a good time. They had a service at a funeral home, a reception after." He shrugged; if I hadn't been there, I think he would have added "goyish" to his description. "The old neighborhood is all Mexican now. None of the old people are left."

"Mexican?"

"Things have changed. The old synagogue is gone; they moved to a new one out near Brentwood."

"It was so nice there, after the war—"

"The Mexicans I met were very nice; but it's different." David took hold of her hand. "It's late. You have to rest. We'll come back in the morning and talk more, Mom."

She wasn't ready to let him go. "David?"

"Yes, Mom?"

"You said you were going to see what you could find out about your birth certificate."

"All that stuff was a long time ago, Mom. It's all gone."

"So what did you learn?"

"I learned I love you very much." He kissed her on the cheek. "Now get some sleep."

"Good night, David."

In the hall, I put my hand on David's arm. "You surprised me, in there," I said.

"You surprise me. You're crying." He brushed the tears off my cheeks.

"I'm very—I don't know what; I'm just—I'm proud of you, and I love you, and . . ." I trailed off.

"Would it suit you to come home with me?"

"I can't think of anything that would suit me better."